I0545510

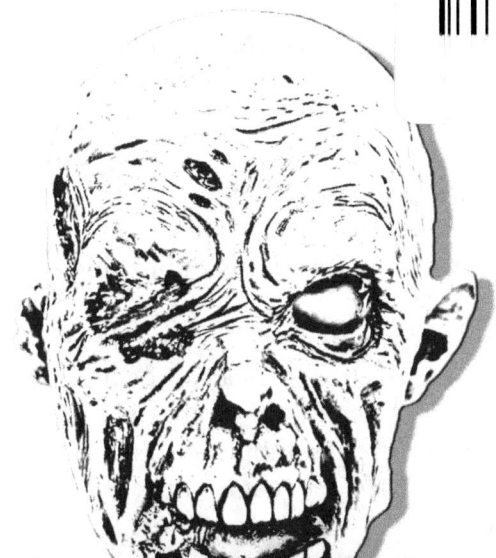

RICKY FLEET

HELLSPAWN DOMINION

HELLSPAWN SERIES - BOOK 5

BRICK, NEW JERSEY

2017

HELLSPAWN: DOMINION – Book Five in the Hellspawn Series
©2017 Ricky Fleet
First Edition
Edited by Christina Hargis Smith
Cover art by Jeffrey Kosh Graphics
Published by Optimus Maximus Publishing, LLC

ISBN-10: 1-944732-35-7
ISBN-13: 978-944732-35-6

DEDICATED TO

The fifth book in the Hellspawn series is dedicated to all my amazing Hellspawnians out there. To my friends and readers and the Fleetie's Sweeties. My incredible beta reading team who do a sterling job of picking up mistakes. I couldn't do this without you.

And finally, to Lisa Ashdown. A great friend who pushes my work wherever she can and took time out of her busy schedule to set up my fan page. Her caring heart is an inspiration to us all and I'm proud to have her on my team.

HELLSPAWN

DOMINION

BOOK FIVE IN THE HELLSPAWN SERIES

A Novel by
Ricky Fleet

OPTIMUS MAXIMUS PUBLISHING
Brick, New Jersey
2017

CHAPTER 1

"Good morning, sleepyhead," Matt said, smiling from across the room as Clarissa opened her eyes.

Still partly asleep, she panicked and frantically tried to scoot her way up the bed, drawing the duvet around herself protectively. Rubbing at her face, the fog of unconsciousness receded and she relaxed a little. Her eyes still bore the legacy of her ill treatment, red rimmed and haunted. Matt approached cautiously and, after asking for permission with an expressive nod, laid a tray across her lap. Two slices of toast were softened by the melted butter and a bowl held dry cereal.

"We only have long life carton milk," Matt apologised with a shrug and held out a small jug for her to sample.

With a scrunching of her nose she declined and picked up one of the pieces of bread. Gnawing at a corner like a rabbit, her face lit up at the forgotten taste and she couldn't resist taking a proper bite. Matt was overjoyed to see a small grin of satisfaction appear.

"Good?"

"Mmmhmm," she nodded.

Sipping from a cup of black tea, he sat down and watched her eat. Feeling the familiar swell of pain blossom inside his heart, he looked away before she could misconstrue the agonised pout.

RICKY FLEET

He had not been fast enough. Putting the unfinished breakfast down, she regarded him with concern, "Are you ok?"

Taking a shaky breath, he turned and smiled, "I'm fine, sweetheart. Finish up your breakfast."

"Mr Hay, why are you doing this?" she asked quietly, yearning for, and dreading, the answer in equal measure.

He thought how best to reply. How much should he reveal to this young girl when he had never explained his life before the apocalypse? Not even Craig knew anything other than he was hard, brutal, and unflinchingly loyal. Taking a deep swig of the tea to buy him a few seconds, the liquid burned painfully as it flowed down his throat. Her eyes were wide and fearful at the extended pause, and this hurt more than the scalding brew.

"I have children of my own back in Scotland," he began, quietly.

"I'm sorry. I hope they're ok."

A wan smile spread across his lips as he replied, "I hope so too. My home was very close to an obsolete cold war bunker in Crail. My wife would've collected the boys and then headed there, I'm certain."

It was the truth, but it didn't take into account human behaviour of any other survivors. Scots were a hardy people who still valued cooperation and neighbourliness. He prayed this was still the case even after the dead dragged themselves from the grave.

"What's a cold war? Is Crail a place?" she asked innocently.

"It's a small village on the east coast, about two miles from our house. A cold war is one that doesn't have great battles, thank goodness. Powerful countries that could wipe out the world with the press of a single button do a lot of their fighting via espionage and other means, otherwise no one wins."

"Do you think that's what happened with the bad things at the walls? Someone pressed a button?"

Matt frowned. It was a very good question and he did not have an adequate answer.

"I don't know, sweetheart," he pondered. "If it was a biological disease then maybe, except the things outside are definitely not suffering from a virus. This outbreak is something else."

"Like radiation or space aliens?"

Matt laughed at the idea of hovering spaceships raising the long dead. "It's as good a theory as any I've heard. You're probably right."

Beaming at the praise, she took another bite of the toast. Between chewing she broached the question again. "I still don't understand why you're helping me. There are other kids in here that deserve it as well."

"Sadly, I can't rescue all of you. I've made sure that the younger ones are off limits and it will stay that way. I'm going to do what I can to stop the others being hurt, but it will take time. We all owe a debt to your father and his ingenuity in building the tunnels. Allowing us to get at the food in local shops and homes is the only reason we're still able to survive."

Her gratitude was written on her soft features at the mention of her beloved parent, then faded and was replaced by wrenching fear again. Dawn had broken and she would be leaving for work duties shortly.

"Mr Keeping will be coming to visit me in the wash house today. When he gets me alone he will be telling me everything he did to mummy last night. Then he does awful things..." She broke down into uncontrollable sobs and Matt rushed over. Holding her tight, he was shocked at her frail form. It was all skin and bone and he felt a pang of anxiety about how his own children would be faring without a constant food supply. That was if they weren't

5

wandering the hills and glens, groaning as their bodies slowly decayed in the unforgiving highland weather.

Shaking the awful image from his mind, he gingerly touched his bandaged arm and took her tiny hand. His huge, calloused paw dwarfed the frail girl's own.

"Mr Keeping is gone. He won't ever hurt you or your mother again."

She searched his eyes for any falsehood, before asking naively, "Where did he go?"

"I killed him," Matt confessed. Prepared for her to cower away, he was astonished when she held him tightly in an embrace.

"Is that where all your cuts came from?"

"He was a strong and dangerous man, but the prison is safer with him gone."

"I'm sorry that you got hurt standing up for me," she whispered, squeezing his hand.

"This?" Matt pointed at the bandages, "It's nothing. I've hurt myself worse while shaving."

She giggled and pushed at him playfully, "Why is someone so lovely in a place like this?"

There was no judgement in the question, it was simply the inquisitive nature of youth. He decided to tell the whole, unvarnished truth.

"When I was younger, I mixed with some very bad people. I met my wife as an angry twenty-year-old and she took me away from the life of crime I was involved in. My wife had our first son, but during the second pregnancy it was discovered she had cancer."

"I'm so sorry."

"Thank you, sweetheart," he said, stroking her hair. "We tried to get treatment for her but it was a rare form of the disease and the UK was lagging way behind the treatments available in the USA. There was no way a trainee mechanic could afford the fees, until a job offer was put my way. It was an armoured car robbery with an inside man. I was desperate for any solution and did a deal with the devil."

"What do you mean? A man was inside the armoured car?"

"In a manner of speaking, yes. The man whose job it was to count and organise the money worked for my previous employer; he was an old acquaintance who stole cars with me back in the day before he got a steady job. It was a guaranteed quarter million pounds for me, with the rest going to the silent partners who organised it."

"And you got caught?" Clarissa asked.

"Yes and no," Matt replied, "I spent a lot of time watching the depot, making sure I was seen a couple of times before it went down. One of the conditions was that I would hand myself in and take the blame so the police didn't look too closely into the background of the job. It had to look like a single gunman who took his chance."

"So, what happened with your wife?" Clarissa interrupted, eager for good news.

"We got her the treatment under an assumed name and she made a full recovery. I could only stay with her for a few days before I had to fly home and take the rap which broke my heart. Her family stayed with her while I went to trial and got the maximum sentence because I wouldn't tell them where the money was. I made a deal with my old contacts that ensured Hazel, my wife, received a small income every year from the remaining two million pounds which had been in the truck."

Grinning from ear to ear, she couldn't hide her joy that his wife had been healed. "You're like Robin Hood… kind of."

"Not really. I robbed from the rich to give to myself and other bad men."

"But you did good things with it! That's what matters."

"The police and courts didn't see it that way," Matt chuckled.

7

"Then they're idiots," she declared. "I'd have let you off with a warning. Helping your family should be an ex... exit..."

"Extenuating?"

She clapped her hands, "Yeah, that's it! Extenuating circumstance! I heard it on a police show I watched before the monsters came; a judge let a lady go free after she stabbed her boyfriend. He had been hurting her for a long time..." Her voice trailed off as she recognised the similarity to her own existence.

Matt lifted her face and met her gaze. "Let's hope one day, when all of this is over, that you get the chance to be a great judge. Just like the one on the TV," he replied with a smile, easing her out of his arms. "Finish your breakfast before it gets too cold."

Resuming her feast, Matt brought his chair over. Sitting down, he looked at her gravely, "I need you to listen carefully, Clarissa. No one can know what we've talked about in here, or the fact that you haven't been mistreated. You must always look like you're afraid of me."

"I can do that." She nodded firmly, grasping the full gravity of the situation.

"Only you and I, and your parents can know what's going on. Until I can think of a better solution, this is how it has to be."

"I understand," Clarissa replied, tears welling in her eyes and bottom lip quivering.

"It's ok, sweetheart. Everything's going to be ok." Matt tried to soothe her until she broke out into a massive grin.

"How was that? It was my *I'm upset face*," she giggled at his confusion.

"I don't know about a judge, but you'd make a really good actress," Matt replied, shaking his head in wonder.

CHAPTER 2

"Y ou know the layout of the farm far better than I do," Carpenter called out to Max and Angela from the Warthog, "Where do you want me?"

"The house is sealed up tight," Angela replied, pointing at the building which came into view. "This way!"

She ran off up the path, beckoning the drivers to follow. Every window on the ground floor had been removed and bricked up, with only a small hole left in the centre. The broken glass and frames were stacked against an outbuilding, scraps of flesh still hanging on the fragments.

"You had some trouble here?" Eldridge shouted, nodding at the debris.

"The first few days were a bit rough," Max admitted, "We can talk about it over a vodka when we're safe."

One entrance remained unblocked except for a thick wrought iron gate which had been fixed to the outer wall. Taking out a set of keys, Angela removed the heavy-duty padlock as Max directed the vehicles.

"If you park against the brickwork either side of the front door we can build a barricade around you."

Eldridge relayed the message across the radio and the APCs manoeuvred as close to the building as possible. With the sides of the vehicles parallel to the walls, it provided a much smaller target for the undead to surround them. Cutting the engines, the soldiers disembarked and gathered around their sergeant. Rushing from the dark home, Max tossed a set of keys underarm to her sister. Three red setter dogs followed excitedly, jumping at the newcomers and trying to lick their faces.

"Rohan, Ash, Jasper, get back inside!" Angela shouted, bustling the frenetic hounds back inside the home.

"I love dogs," said Harkiss.

"We know," Carpenter replied, "We've seen your previous girlfriends."

Before another argument could ensue, Holbeck spoke up, "How can we help?"

"You can't right now," Max replied.

"We don't have time to show you how the bale loaders work," Angela added by way of explanation.

"We're used to humping heavy loads," Dougal boasted.

"Moving some hay will be a piece of cake," Harkiss added.

"Our six by five round bales weigh around a tonne each. Feel free to carry as many as you can," Angela said with a grin.

"A tonne? Well, I didn't think they'd be quite so heavy," Harkiss mumbled.

"It wouldn't be a very good barricade if the big bad wolf could blow it down, would it?"

"I guess not," Harkiss conceded.

"Leave the poor boy alone," Max admonished. "If you can get a few pairs of hands, you can topple and roll them. Time is of the essence."

"We could use some protection too. You've made enough noise to wake the dead." The others groaned at Angela's pun. Leaning their shotguns against the wall, the sisters hurried away towards the huge barn.

"Langham and Dougal, you're on watch. Harkiss, Walker, Petermann, Carpenter, help with the bales.

Eldridge, on me," Holbeck ordered and the troops complied in a frenzy of activity.

***

Marching back to the marshland boundary, Holbeck radioed back to base. "Hawkeye, this is Early Bird. Give me an update, over."

"Sir, you've got a shit storm coming. I've conducted a circular sweep and the undead are growing in number. I can only assume it was the noise. Over," Morrow replied.

"Estimate on numbers? Over."

"Around two thousand. The largest concentration are the ones following from Witterings and Almodington. Small pockets are approaching from the north and south as well. They've got you boxed in, suggest you fall back. Over."

"Negative. We have a defensible position which we are fortifying now. Is there any possibility of cover from the gunners? Over."

As the soldiers reached the embankment, they waited patiently for a reply. In the distance, the zombies made their way haphazardly across the uneven terrain. Looking through the binoculars, Eldridge had to stifle a chuckle as a heavy-set male corpse reached a particularly boggy section of ground and sunk through the surface. Within seconds, his whole body and finally the head had disappeared, leaving only a pair of hands. The fingers flexed, seeming to wave at the soldier. The grin died, replaced by a grimace as she thought of the cadaver slowly liquefying, forever submerged in the quagmire.

"What do you see?" Holbeck asked.

"We may have made a mistake in using the guns and explosives, sir."

"It doesn't make any difference," he replied with a shrug, "If it wasn't today, it would've been tomorrow when

11

we hit the entertainment complex. Every monster we can kill is one less we need to worry about in the future."

"Fair point."

The radio crackled to life, "Early Bird, this is Captain Hayward. The undead are too widely spread so I've decided the use of our remaining artillery assets is a waste of resources. Over."

"Shit!" hissed Eldridge.

"I'd have made the same call," Holbeck admitted. Pressing the transmit button, he replied, "Received, sir. We'll do what's needed. Over."

"Please don't misunderstand. We're going to use them to mask the coming firefight, instead. If you give us a minutes warning, we'll fire periodically on all local towns to draw the attention away from you. We can't do anything about those already inbound, but hopefully we can cut off their reinforcements. Good luck to you all. Over," Hayward finished.

"Clever bastard," Holbeck muttered to Eldridge, smiling with admiration. "Thank you, sir. Over and out," he said, ending the transmission.

"Orders, Sarge?"

"I have a couple of tricks up my sleeve," Holbeck replied with a wink. "Let's see how the others are getting on."

Glancing through the binoculars one last time, Eldridge could see the massive horde was gaining ground. Her stomach fluttered in apprehension; this was different to the island barracks, with no fast-flowing river or high fences to keep them safe. They would literally be face to face with the festering dead in the coming battle. Turning, she jogged after her superior.

***

12

Langham and Dougal skirted the massive barn and positioned themselves to give a full field of vision. The two farmhouses were protected on three sides by the marshland, with only a bottleneck to reach the buildings themselves. Spreading out in an arc from the access road to the north was the farmable land. Wheat was abundant as far as the eye could see, providing perfect concealment for the approaching dead.

"I thought they harvested in the summer? You know, make hay while the sun shines?" Dougal called out.

"Beats me, just keep your eyes open. I can't be there to save your ass all the time," Langham shouted back.

"It's winter wheat!" Maxine shouted from the barn, "We plant in the autumn and harvest in the spring."

Angela peered around the corner, "I don't think we are going to be able to make it this year with what I've got planned."

The two soldiers exchanged a confused look at the statement before returning their attention to the approach road. Dougal checked his magazine, before switching the safety off. The sounds of machinery vibrated into life through the corrugated steel cladding as the two fearsome farmers went about their business. Unable to see any clear and present danger, he started to kick at the loose stones on the ground. It would not detract from his awareness, but he hated the inactivity of guard duty. Fidgeting and an excess of energy had led to a couple of reprimands during his early soldiering career. A short sharp whistle caught his attention and he turned to see Langham pointing at the fields.

"We've got company," she called out.

A shambling group of zombies pushed their way through the tall crops. The wheat had been unforgiving as they had forced their way through, with slashed skin and sharp stems embedded deeply in their flesh. Ten had become twenty and Langham raced over to a bare sycamore tree.

"What the fuck are you doing?"

"Climbing a tree," Langham replied, sarcastically, "What does it look like, you tit?"

Lost for words, Dougal ignored her and banged on the steel barn. Harkiss came running, sweat pouring from his exertion in moving the heavy bales.

"We've got incoming," Dougal explained, "If we can't hold them off I'll whistle twice."

"We'll come running, brother," Harkiss declared and went back to work.

"Are you going to come down or am I doing this on my own?" Dougal barked up at Langham.

"Don't piss your pants." Her eyes were rapt on the fields, watching for any movement. The parting of the crops was a sure sign of an approaching zombie and she nodded almost imperceptibly with each discovery. Satisfied with her findings, she jumped down from branch to branch before landing lithely on the ground. "I count about fifty-five, with twenty heading towards us on the road."

"Let's close the gate, it'll buy us some time," Dougal offered.

As he swung it closed and slid the bolt home, Langham took a stray piece of timber and wedged it against the metal. With a few solid kicks, the lower end embedded in the ground, providing more stability.

"Shall we fix bayonets?" Langham asked with a sly grin.

"Are you shitting me? You want to get all stabby with a hundred zombies?"

"It's about seventy-five. Don't exaggerate," she mocked light heartedly.

"Fuck it, why not. It's not like they're clever enough to dodge, is it?"

Removing them from their equipment, they twisted the blades to lock them in place. Sliding the scabbards off, they grinned at each other.

"It's like being back at basic training at Catterick," said Langham.

"I never thought we'd ever get to actually use them," Dougal replied.

"I bet you've got a shit war face," she teased.

"RAAAARRGGHHHHHH!" Dougal screamed as fiercely as he could.

Langham doubled over with laughter, "I've pulled scarier faces while having a shit."

"Oh yeah? Let's see yours then!"

"RAAAAARGGGGGGGGGGGHHHHHHHH!" she screamed, twisting her face into a mask of rage.

"That's a bloody good war face," he grudgingly conceded.

"Playtime's over," Langham muttered, face set in a scowl.

Metal rattled as the first body hit the gate, quickly followed by the others. The combination of the wooden brace and bolt were solid enough to ensure their safety for a short while. Caught in a cross wind, the stench of their assailants washed over the soldiers. Stomachs churning from the vile fragrances, the sights were even worse and threatened to rob them of strength. Each of the cadavers was in an advanced state of decay. Blackened stumps of teeth gnashing in mouths without lips. Eyes that were little more than mushy, dribbling orbs of jelly. One of the zombies was pressed hard into the top railing and, with a pop, his distended stomach burst, showering the ground with entrails and gore.

Raising the rifles by the handguard and stock, the training kicked in. With short, sharp thrusts, the soldiers stabbed at the surging mass of rotten flesh. With each scream of hatred, the fear was banished until the muscle memory took over. The razor-sharp blades sank through eye sockets and foreheads like a hot knife through butter. A growing pile of bodies was causing the latecomers to flail out of range of the bayonets. With a quick nod, they twisted them free and laid them on the ground to be cleaned later. *Corporal would have been proud,* Dougal thought, remembering the instructor who had at first yelled how useless he was, before showing him the errors he was making.

"You need to up your game," Langham mocked, "I've already killed eighteen to your thirteen."

"You had time to count? I was just trying to stay away from their mouths and hands. I don't know if a scratch is fatal, but I don't want to take the chance."

"Pussy!" Langham grinned, shouldering her rifle and firing single shots into the undead.

***

"Watch out!" Angela called.

As she swung the tractor through the entrance, Harkiss marvelled at the long black bale spear attached to the machine.

"You could do some real damage with that thing," he gloated, cupping his genitals. "I should know."

"Yours is the size of a toothpick," Carpenter replied. "The only damage you could do is popping balloons."

"Oy! It's not the size that matters but how you use it. I've never had any complaints."

"Only because the women had fallen asleep before you finished."

"Yeah? And? It makes it easier for a Romeo like me to slip away." Harkiss puffed his chest out.

"If you ever tried that shit with me I'd kick your ass," Carpenter remarked.

Harkiss was lost for words. There was no mistaking the subtle invitation in the warning or the way her gaze lingered for a second longer than necessary. Staring at her pretty face and dark hair pulled back in a tight bun, he found his mouth drying out. They had always shared some good natured and flirty banter, but never had he imagined she was interested. *She's out of my league,* he decided, shaking his head at the absurdity. In his peripheral vision, she turned to stare at him and the heat spread to his cheeks. She gently bumped her rump against his hip; a promise of what may be.

"Stand back!" Angela yelled, expertly inserting the steel rod through the closest bale.

"Oh my," Carpenter sighed.

Harkiss's glowing red cheeks grew a deeper shade of scarlet at the suggestive tone in her voice and he was glad when the fiery twin dropped it at their feet. Standing side by side, the soldiers started the laborious task of turning and guiding it through the wide opening. In spite of the day's chill, after fifty feet they were all sweating profusely. By the time it had rolled to the farmhouse, they were aching and gasping for breath.

"Look at the state of you! Call yourselves soldiers?" Holbeck ranted, unable to hide the grin as Max guided a trailer around the corner loaded with twelve bales.

"They're... heavy... as..." Petermann tried to gasp a reply, but his superior dismissed the protests.

"I thought you were meant to be fit and strong?" Max shouted from the driver's seat.

"Step back and let the experts work," Angela added as she trundled past.

Picking up their solitary bale, she moved it into position and dropped it close to the Warthog. With a final nudge, it sat snugly against the armour. Repeating the process all the way around the two vehicles, the sisters headed off to collect another load.

"I've got a nice surprise for those undead bastards if I have a couple of volunteers?" Holbeck asked, sliding a wooden box from the back of the APC.

Laying it gently to the floor, he pried the lid off and carefully removed four individual containers. M18 Claymore was imprinted on the side of each box and the soldiers whistled their appreciation.

"We're going to try and funnel the bastards between the trees at the rear of the property. If we can get a decent concentration of zombies then we blow the things. If not, we leave them and reclaim them after the fighting's done and use them later," Holbeck explained.

Carpenter mused for a moment before speaking, "Why don't we mount them on the top of the embankments?"

"What would that achieve? The explosion would disperse the bearings over open ground instead of into a group," Eldridge replied.

"Not if we play it right. What do these things crave more than anything else?" Carpenter posed.

"Us," Harkiss answered.

"Exactly! We need some fresh bait." Her eyes stared at Harkiss until he held his hands up.

"No, no, no. Fuck right off! I'm a fighter, not a distraction."

"You're certainly a distraction," Carpenter agreed, teasing him even more, much to the amusement of the others, "But we'd all need to be fighting as well."

"I don't follow," Holbeck admitted.

Carpenter scored a rough line on the ground with the toe of her boot representing the southerly curvature of the piece of land they were on. Kneeling down, she drew four arrows pointing west.

"We have the biggest threat coming from that direction. I suggest two man teams, armed with blunt weapons at each Claymore; lengths of wood should do. When they reach us, they've got to fight their way up the slope before we're in any real danger. Using our sticks, we keep them contained for as long as possible until the numbers reach critical mass and we have to fall back. Then… boom!"

"Good thinking, Corporal," Holbeck clapped her on the back, "That'll be our first line. From there we fall back by the numbers taking out as many as we can before we reach the APCs."

Controlled gunshots rang out from the farm entrance, breaking into their planning. "Walker, on me!" Eldridge cried, racing towards the disturbance.

Max and Angela were on their way back with the second load of tightly compacted hay. The fortification was taking shape and would provide some much-needed cover. Bales were laid two deep against each other on the ground tight to the Warthogs, with a third placed on top of the outer row. Ten-foot-tall and weighing thousands of pounds, it made for a solid barricade to fight the coming horde.

Eldridge came jogging back, "They've got it under control. I've left Walker to support."

Holbeck nodded and gathered the mines. Waving at the two vehicles, the sisters leaned out to hear his shouts, "We're setting up a welcoming party to the west."

"Do what you have to." Max stuck her thumb up. "If anything shows up we can just run it over."

Angela made a squelching noise for dramatic effect and picked up the next bale. Holbeck and the soldiers skirted the farm building and made for the piles of discarded windows and assorted rubbish. Laid amongst the junk were offcuts of fence posts in varying lengths.

"We use the long ones to jab them back down and the short pieces like bats to clout them with," Carpenter explained.

Picking up a selection, the group carried their loot to the edge of the property and dispersed them along the perimeter. They spent a few minutes picking the best sites for each device.

"Do you remember how to use them?" Holbeck queried.

Everyone nodded. Claymores were one of the most dangerous pieces of equipment they could set up and a healthy dose of caution had been drilled into them by the instructors. Reserved mostly for special forces, the regular soldiers had not laid eyes on them since the open fields of their training. Laying down, they peered through the peep sight and positioned each charge at an angle which would ensure as many head injuries as possible. Being especially careful, they inserted the blasting caps.

"Sarge, are we using tripwires?" Petermann asked.

"No. We're going to spool out the wire as far as it'll reach towards the house. We'll use the triggers once we've all fallen back to a safe zone."

Four lines of cable were quickly unwound and laid behind the brick outbuilding. The detonators were left unplugged to minimise the chances of a deadly mishap. From across the field, the guttural moans were getting louder.

"Let's get prepared," Holbeck growled, turning from the approaching horde, "I want all boxes of fifty-cal on the roof in easy reach. Because of the angle of fire, they'll be our second line, and finally the hay and APCs themselves."

"What about the grenades, sir?" asked Petermann.

"We only use them when the dead are thick at the walls," Holbeck stated, "I don't know what the density of the hay will do to slow the fragments. At least with meat in the way it will disperse some of the blast."

As the troops reached the front of the farmhouse, Angela was dropping the final bale into place. The wall was tight to the brickwork and surrounded the vehicles totally on all sides.

"All done!"

"Great work, ma'am," Holbeck said, banging a fist against the curved fortification. "Everyone, put your weapons down and shoulder charge the wall with me."

With a roar, the row of soldiers hit the barricade as one and it didn't move an inch. Satisfied, he nodded.

"What's the matter, don't you trust our building skills?" Max called out.

"Just being thorough, no offense intended."

"We'll get these stowed away and be right back," Angela added, turning the tractor around.

"There's a set of stepladders around that corner." Maxine pointed to the far side of the farmhouse then followed her sister out of sight.

***

"Not too shabby," Langham sighed, switching the safety back on.

The unmoving corpses lolled against the steel gate and with a twang, the bolt sheared off, dropping them into a gory, green pile.

"I'm not cleaning that up," Walker declared.

"I vote Harkiss," Dougal added.

"Agreed," Langham chuckled, "We'll tell him the good news if we survive the afternoon."

"Are you nervous?" Walker asked them both.

"A bit," admitted Dougal, "But at least we don't have IED's or insurgents with suicide vests trying to blow us up."

"It's the smell that does it for me," Langham said, pinching her nose.

A deeper rumble sprung into life inside the barn, piquing their interest. As they left the fallen zombies, Angela emerged from the darkness. Grinning like a madwoman, she steered the combine harvester towards the farmhouse.

21

"What the hell?" Walker asked, jogging to catch up.

Holbeck's head peered over the wall and he broke out into a grin of his own. Stopping the huge thresher machine, Angela and Max climbed out of the cab.

"Mavis should be good for a single pass before her blades seize up," Max explained.

"Mavis?"

"Our trusty harvester." Angela slapped the solid yellow body.

"I think we've got our second line of defence." Holbeck nodded appreciatively.

"Huh?" Max frowned.

"We've set up mines at the perimeter. Once we have detonated them, we're going to fall back to the fortification. If you ladies wouldn't mind shredding the first undead who follow, I'd appreciate it."

"Of course," Angela confirmed as she hopped down into the space between the rear of the APCs.

Everything was prepared and it was just a matter of time until contact. Petermann was on sentry and would fire a single shot to signal the horde was five minutes away. Opening her front door, Angela released the excited hounds. The innocent bounding immediately cut through a palpable layer of tension which had been growing. She winked to her sister who was perched at the top of the steps, and Max smiled back. Making a fuss of the three dogs was a calming distraction and the soldiers scratched, stroked, and coddled for all they were worth. A whistle from inside the house called them back and Angela emerged with a tray of shot glasses. Tucked under her arm was a bottle of Russian Standard vodka and she placed the tray down before filling each small container with the clear liquor.

"Sarge?" Eldridge asked, seeking permission.

Looking at the eager faces of his troops was enough and he nodded. "You warriors deserve it. I'm proud as hell to stand by your side," he declared, tipping the glass back and swallowing with a hiss. "That includes you too." He indicated the brave twins.

"You'll have me blushing," Angela said, waving a hand to cool her face.

"I'll take a shot to Petermann," Walker offered, jumping the barrels like a rabbit without spilling a drop.

"We should all get ready," Eldridge said, placing her glass down, "It won't be long now."

The dogs were locked away and Max requested a grenade to use just in case they were overwhelmed and had to fall back to the house. It would suffice to blow out a sealed window and give the beloved pets a chance at freedom should the worst happen.

Pouring a second shot, Max toasted, "To the best sister in the world. Don't die or I'll kick your ass."

"To the second-best sister in the world… love ya."

With a steely resolve, she and Max loaded their pockets with shotgun cartridges and followed the soldiers.

"Thanks for the drink. I needed a bit of Dutch courage." Petermann smiled, the fruity, wheat flavour still fresh on his tongue.

"After this we'll have a proper drink," Max replied with a firm nod.

"Sergeant, we'll run between you all and pick off any little blighters who try and flank you," Angela explained, snapping the double-barrelled shotgun closed.

"We're in your debt." Holbeck nodded and lifted the radio. "Hawkeye, this is Early Bird. We're ready for that distraction now, over."

"Received. Happy hunting, soldiers. Hawkeye out."

In the distance, the first fiery eruptions rose into the air followed by the shockwave and crack of detonation. At each mine, the troops started to yell and scream obscenities at the shambling hordes. Unable to ignore the inhuman cravings, the undead raised their arms and gurgled in excitement at the imminent meal. Strings of black drool, disturbed by the first movements in their lungs for weeks dribbled from their mouths.

"It's working!" Eldridge shouted down the line, seeing the lumps of timber jabbing away at the growing mass of flesh.

Tempted by the red headed twins, a lone female zombie started to clamber up the bank. Leaning in to the recoil, Max's gun spat its lethal shot at point blank range, blowing the head apart. Decapitated, the body rolled back down to join its shattered skull and brain matter.

Walker and Petermann were stabbing at their growing crowd. The blunt ends of the fence posts crushed faces and skulls, but with each new zombie they were losing ground. They had to drop the extended lances and use the bats as the zombies were forced forward by the crush of bodies at their rear.

"We're struggling here!" Walker shouted, swinging the wood into the temple of a male zombie. Like a startled rat, the man's filthy black toupee jumped into the air and landed on the sticky face of another. Unable to see, the monster tripped up and rolled back to the bottom of the bank, knocking down zombies like a bowling ball.

"Did you see that?" Petermann asked, laughing nervously. It was a pointless question considering Walker had been stood by his side during the spectacle.

"Move!" Max barked and knocked him sideways. Unloading both barrels, the zombie which had been close to grabbing him went cartwheeling off into the crowd.

"Can you hold for another minute?" Holbeck yelled from further down, "We're nearly at full saturation here and I want to kill as many as possible with the claymores."

"Do your thing!" Angela called back, then turned to the soldiers. "We'll hold them back with the shotguns if you can watch our backs?"

Petermann and Walker nodded, dropping the timber and picking up their rifles. The wide spread of the cartridges worked better than the rifle ammunition and as each new crop of unwary dead neared the top, the sisters would blow them to pieces. The awkward angle of the falling bodies was buying them precious seconds, and with a final wolf whistle, the four teams broke for the brick outhouse. Ducking behind the solid cover, the designated people picked up their clacker and connected the waiting wire.

Looking at Holbeck, they nodded to each number as he counted down, "Five, four, three, two, one, *now!*"

The curved mines exploded in unison, sending thousands of steel bearings into the horde. Peppered with the expertly angled shrapnel, anything within fifty feet fell dead to the floor leaking emerald blood from dozens of holes in their heads. Further out from the kill zone, the zombies were shredded, skin tearing away as they were hammered to the ground. Ricochets twanged from the brick shelter and after a further count of three, the group broke cover and raced for the compacted straw fortress. Eldridge risked a glance at the destruction before following. Small, smoking craters were all that remained of the explosives. The conical swathes cut through the masses of undead were quickly filling in with the slower arrivals.

"Eldridge, move your ass!" screamed Holbeck and she quickly followed the others.

Angela was poised in the idling combine, the blades spinning slowly. She was loving the action and could barely contain herself.

"Harkiss, Eldridge, on the HMGs. Everyone else get behind the wall," Holbeck ordered, "You too, ma'am."

"Hell no." Max was resolute and reloaded her shotgun.

Holbeck could see there was no point arguing. "Ok, we'll cover your sister together."

"How long do you want me to hold back before setting out?" Angela shouted to them.

"Don't be a hero. You know the capabilities of the machine better than I do, so you judge how many it will take down," Holbeck replied.

Peering down the side of the farmhouse, he could see the wave of dead flow over the top of the banks a quarter mile away. Waving his arms, the sergeant wanted to ensure they came on in a straight line making an easy target for the machine to grind them to paste. He could feel the adrenaline building as the procession snaked forward. Angela let the airbrake off with a hiss and started forward. Putting all power to the blades, they spun in an ever-increasing blur.

"Follow me," Holbeck said. Raising their weapons, they quickly accompanied the grumbling machine and the priceless sibling cargo.

Unaware of their impending doom, the metal hit the outstretched arms of the zombies. Shearing them off cleanly, the thresher swiftly dragged the rest of the body in. The effect was as spectacular as it was disgusting. A torrent of gore rose like a geyser, pulled on the upward rotation of the blade and coating the cab. Chunks of meat splashed down around their feet and they dodged as much as they could. Small groups were being minced without problem but the larger force had arrived and was fast approaching.

"She needs to get clear!" Max called over the noise, fearing her sister would be surrounded if she made it much deeper into the horde that it was now beginning to spread out.

"Take left, I've got right. Pick off any that she misses!"

Hitting the first large group of dead precipitated a rending shriek as some unseen mechanism inside the blades sheared off, stilling the rotation instantly. Without slowing, Angela climbed out and jumped down into Holbeck's arms.

"That was great, you got at least fifty of them."

"I was hoping for more," she said with disappointment. "The accelerator is wedged too so it should keep rolling over them."

The powerful machine pushed on, knocking the zombies aside or dragging them under the huge wheels. Small groups were beginning to appear from all angles of the farm, threatening to cut them off from the other soldiers.

"I'll cover you," Holbeck shouted, picking off the fastest moving targets as the sisters backed away.

"That's pretty gross," Angela muttered, hurrying past the trail of twitching viscera spread all over the ground.

Chattering gunfire from the assault rifles warned of contact at the wall and Holbeck cautiously looked around the corner. A massive group had arrived from the west, taking them by surprise and they were in full battle mode. The restrictive angle on the turret was working against them and Harkiss was firing short bursts into any target that presented itself.

"There they are!" yelled Eldridge, "Come on!"

Walker and Petermann were poised at the top of the eastern wall having already removed the ladder. Maxine reached them first and, after slipping the strap of her shotgun around her shoulders, they pulled her up without difficulty.

"Now you!" Holbeck pushed Angela forward, seeing the monsters flooding around the corner of the stacked bales.

Petermann and Walker clasped hands with her and pulled. Holbeck was kicking out at the creatures which were swiftly surrounding them, but two of the corpses managed to fasten onto the frantically kicking legs. Slinging the rifle, he withdrew his tactical knife and, like lightning, drove it into the base of each skull before the rotten teeth could find flesh. With a final, triumphant yell, the two soldiers dragged her over.

"Sarge, step back and we'll clear a path!" Petermann shouted.

Holbeck was forced further away from the wall and could hear the rapid approach of those from the rear hemming him in. Shaking his head slowly, he gave his order. "I'll try and find cover, now do what you were trained to do!"

"Find somewhere safe and sit tight," Walker called, tossing two magazines of ammunition, "We'll find you."

Seeing the path to the barn was cut off, Holbeck was forced back towards the route they had just fled. Using his superior agility, he ducked under the reaching arms and was gone out of sight.

It was a blow to the group, but they weren't prone to panic; if anyone could survive it was their hard-as-nails sergeant. More detonations and shockwaves were washing over the area from the artillery strikes on the surrounding villages.

Eldridge prayed it was working as she lifted her radio. "Hawkeye, this is Early Bird. Status report, over."

"This is Hawkeye. Drone imagery shows the distraction is working and some of the dead are peeling away to investigate. The main bulk of the force will be with you in under ten minutes. After that it's just stragglers. Over."

"Received. Over and out."

"Fuck this!" Harkiss barked, slamming his fist into the turret shield.

"What?"

"I can't get an angle on them. Do you want me to remove the gun?" Harkiss replied in frustration. The rest of the team were picking away at the growing crowd but the power of the HMG would be a godsend.

"How long?"

"Two or three minutes including getting the tripod fitted."

"Do it!" Eldridge was facing the same issue but her limited experience with the mounting kits made it pointless to attempt the removal. With the greater number coming from her side, it was possible to get four or five kills to every monster that Harkiss destroyed.

Like a bursting dam the real swarm arrived, pouring around the building and slamming into the makeshift barricade. Through sheer weight of numbers, the top layer of bales near Eldridge was pushed back a few inches.

"We need to hold them back. Walker, Dougal, stay by Harkiss, everyone else on me!" Eldridge shouted, jumping out of the turret.

Max and Angela had miraculously replaced their double-barrelled shotguns with pump action varieties, but there was no time to ask how. The flaring barrels tore through the closest threats and the destroyed bodies fell into the throng to be mashed underfoot. At point blank range, the slugs punched clean through, blowing out the back of the skulls which embedded in those behind. As soon as one fell, two more took its place and the crushed bodies were giving each new wave extra height to get at the soldiers.

"Remember the barracks!" Eldridge shouted, "Take out those at the back!"

Ignoring the imploring arms which were steadily rising, they opened fire on those to the rear. Heads snapped back as the undead brains were destroyed. Harkiss had retrieved the HMG and pulled the charging handle. Adding the impressive firepower to the fight, he let off short, devastating bursts. The frantically raking claws of the front line were shredding the bales, inch by inch. Each layer peeled away like an onion, diminishing the overall weight of the barricade.

"Shit!" Angela complained.

"It was a good idea, but we should fall back inside the house while we can," Eldridge ordered.

"Only take the rifle ammo. We can pick them off through the windows," Langham added.

Max opened the door and pushed the agitated dogs back inside. Dougal and Langham hopped down, forming a human chain to slide the boxes through the doorway.

"How secure are the windows?" Eldridge asked, feeling another shift in the wall.

"Rock solid. We tied them in properly to the surrounding walls," she confirmed.

"Grenade!"

Eldridge couldn't make out who shouted the warning in time to stop them. As the small ball arced before falling at the feet of the crowd, they all ducked instinctively. The dull crump acted like a stone dropped in water, pushing the undead away like ripples and driving them against the straw which finally collapsed under the assault.

"Get inside!" Eldridge screamed, stamping down on an arm which shot out and clutched her ankle. The bone crumbled and the floppy limb withdrew, but was instantly replaced by many more as she backpedalled furiously.

"Get off me!" Walker shrieked.

The crazed soldier beat wildly at the hands that were dragging him inexorably towards the snapping jaws. Petermann tried desperately to pull him back, yelling his fury. One man against a horde was an impossible fight and he was left with no choice but to let go or follow him into death. Walker's guttural cry of agony was cut off as the undead closed over their meal and fed.

"Quickly!" Angela shouted as the last of the defenders ducked inside.

The steel gate was pulled shut and through the solid bars, she snapped the padlock back through the loop of the bolt. As the lower bales gave way to the creatures, Max slammed the door.

"It'll hold," Angela affirmed as the first dull thuds carried through from outside.

"Just like the fucking hay bales would?" shouted Petermann. Grief boiled over and he started to punch the wall, bloodying knuckles to vent the rage which was, he understood, unfairly aimed at the sisters.

The three dogs encircled their mistresses and started to growl, but a few soothing words calmed the beasts before they could attack. Ceasing the barrage of blows, he slowly turned to them and the apology was written in the tear streaked face. No words were needed and they nodded in commiseration.

Everyone was in a daze except for Eldridge who was calculating the next move. Pressing transmit, she spoke into the radio, "Hawkeye, this is Early Bird. Ceasefire. Walker is gone and Holbeck's status is unknown. We are safe in the farmhouse and will update you when we have secured the area. Over."

As the last concussive waves shook the home, gradually falling into silence, their commanding officer came back. "You have my condolences, private. We knew the mission was going to be tough, but you can take heart in knowing their sacrifice was for something much bigger. Compose yourselves, remember your training and we'll be standing by for further instruction. Over."

"Thank you, sir. Over and out."

"We're sorry about your friends," Max said, looking from face to face, "We got them killed."

"It's not your fault," Eldridge replied. "The bales were an excellent idea, we've just never seen them in a frenzy like that. Nobody could've foreseen they would tear through so quickly."

"Beth's right. We had a river separating us on the barracks," Harkiss added.

Eldridge's face darkened as the memory came back, "Who threw the fucking grenade anyway?"

"Walker," Petermann sighed, "He could see they were about to break through and wanted to buy us time. It turns out he was the Big Bad Wolf who blew the whole house down."

"Oh…"

"It's going to be dark soon," Angela said to break the tension, "Let's rustle up some food for you and we can see about getting out of here in one piece."

Apart from the groans of the dead, the house fell silent.

CHAPTER 3

"It's crazy to think people used to live like this," Braiden said, staring at the decorative finish of their plush bedroom. His own was covered in mould and peeling wallpaper.

The incessant snoring of certain, older survivors had driven them to distraction and Kurt reluctantly agreed to let them sleep away from the main group. The rule was that the door was to remain locked at all times even though it was only a forty foot walk from the Baron's Hall.

"Now it's our home," Sam replied.

"You really kicked ass on the wall, like one of those knights you were always writing about."

"Couldn't have done it without you by my side." Sam put a hand in the air and Braiden did the same while making a clapping noise. The 'air five' was just easier when they were both warm and snug.

Braiden looked over at his brother on the other four poster bed with a mixture of pride and guilt. Even though his adopted sibling bore no malice about it, the schoolyard bullying would haunt him until his dying day. What had once been an unhealthy, vindictive jealousy had grown into a fierce loyalty and love. He would spend the rest of his life repaying Sam's, no, *his*, family back for their faith.

"I woke up in the night and forgot Paige and granddad were gone," Braiden sighed, then went back to studying the plasterwork, a lump forming in his throat.

Sam felt the boy's pain and tried to distract him. "I had a dream about us all having a medieval feast. Granddad was gnawing on a joint of meat and barking orders at Mr Vincent."

Laughing in spite of the painful memory, Braiden replied, "I don't think he would've let Mr Vincent back into the castle like dad did."

"Maybe it would've been better," Sam said cautiously, judging the response of his brother.

"He made the right call. It would've ruined the atmosphere in the castle if everyone thought dad was a psycho killer."

Sam gawped at the hot-headed teen. "You were going to kill Winston yesterday and feed him to the zombies."

"That's different."

"How?"

"Winston was with *them*," Braiden spat, his face darkening.

"Yeah, and now he's with *us*. You trust Mrs Blume, don't you?"

Braiden gave it some thought before letting out a huff. "I guess so."

"She was right about a certain young hell raiser." Sam pointed both fingers and prodded them towards Braiden dramatically.

"Ok, ok! I'll take her word for it but I'm still going to keep a close eye on him."

Sam climbed out of bed and stretched. After weeks of slumming it and sleeping on whatever they could find, the soft mattress was difficult to adjust to. Knotted muscles protested with a vehemence Sam thought reserved only for the elderly.

34

Braiden groaned his own discomfort and their eyes met. "Floor tonight?"

"You read my mind," Sam grumbled, "I don't think I can sleep in that bed again, it's way too soft."

"We'll put something together later."

Sam wiped at the icy moisture on the window and paused. "It looks like you can keep an eye on him easier than you thought."

"Huh?"

Sam nodded towards the glass so Braiden approached and squinted through the water streaks. The teenager was out in the main courtyard, breath fogging in the chill. He would jog for a few seconds before clutching his sides and bending over. Watching his brother from the corner of his eye, Sam was surprised when instead of mocking laughter, Braiden nodded.

***

Pain. Such unbearable pain. Winston was in a state of abject torment. Each intake of breath was like inhaling acid. Unseen creatures gnawed at his flank, desperate to tear free through the burning stitch in his side. A dull throb had turned into an incapacitating spasm in the small of his back.

Why are you doing this to yourself? He thought miserably. It wasn't as if he would ever win any beauty contests with the stretch marks and sagging belly. Perhaps it was time to accept that he was just not cut out to be slim or fit. Running over short distances had kept him alive so far and maybe that was all he needed. Brute strength was also a boon and far less painful to maintain.

Stopping dead, he kneaded his sides, trying to massage some of the pain away, but it was deep and unheeding. His mouth was so dry he couldn't even muster enough saliva to spit or swallow. Moving his tongue around, it felt like a gummy, alien slug. The unresponsive sublingual glands seemed to have dried up like a starved well and he finally called it a day. Or eight minutes of hell according to his watch.

Crunching gravel broke through his misery and he whirled around to see it was only Braiden and Sam. His survival mechanism was still on high alert even within the safe confines of the castle walls. He was grateful that the fierce burning in his cheeks from the exercise prevented a fresh bout of embarrassment from blazing to life. Lowering his head, he started to walk away, angling himself around them to avoid a confrontation with Braiden. They ignored the manoeuvre and intercepted him but he was too exhausted to even offer a witty remark.

"Here." Braiden held out a bottle of water and Winston stared at him in disbelief.

"Take sips," Sam added, "Don't guzzle it or you'll feel worse."

Braiden pushed the bottle forcefully towards him with a nod. It was obvious from the narrowing of his eyes that it would be a while until he was accepted by the teenager. Mustering up his most disarming smile which appeared instead as a lopsided, gasping gurn, Winston accepted the gift.

"Come up to the top of the castle grounds with us. Gravel is too uneven and your ankles won't be strong enough yet," Sam explained.

Winston looked longingly at the arched doorway which then led to his sofa and the warm fires of the sleeping area. With a monumental battle of wills, he turned away from the promise of comfort and followed the younger boys.

"This is going to be awful for you," Sam said, looking at the portly teen, "You know that, right?"

The water had softened his parched mouth enough to speak and Winston nodded. "I know. But I need to get fit."

"We'll ask Jonesy and DB for some better advice later, but for now we'll just do circuits of the upper bailey. I guess it's about half a mile give or take."

"Half a mile?" Winston blurted, his face changing from flushed to pale at the thought.

"Don't worry," Sam said with a reassuring smile, "One of us will stay with you the whole time and we'll take it slow and steady. Ok?"

"You don't have to do this."

"Yes, we do," Braiden muttered, "It's a good idea."

"You'll have to forgive my garrulous brother for rabbiting on too much," Sam quipped, playfully pushing the scowling youth to try and banish some of the tension.

"It's ok," Winston replied. He would take it slowly, proving himself and earning the trust of the survivors.

"Ok, this will do," Sam pointed to an empty flowerbed with a low stone wall enclosing the barren soil.

"Did you stretch?" Braiden asked.

"Umm..."

"I thought not. Touch your toes," Braiden continued.

"Funny," Winston muttered. It had been a favourite taunt of his father to ask how long it had been since he had seen the wiggling digits.

"It wasn't meant as a joke," Braiden declared, "It doesn't matter if you can't touch them yet, it's more about the movement to stretch out the hamstrings."

"Oh," Winston sighed. The shape of his body was an inescapable impediment to the task, but even halfway down he could feel the twinge of muscles pulling.

"Now your thighs," Braiden said and the three boys went through a complete warm up routine.

Sam was keeping out of the discussion, content to let Braiden take charge as it meant he was finally talking properly to the newcomer without a knife in hand. Moment by moment, some of the mistrust ebbed away as the tearaway offered pointers and support.

"Most of the cramps have gone now. Thanks," Winston grinned.

"Let's get going," Braiden mumbled in reply, re-erecting some of the barriers.

"We'll walk the first circuit and see if there are any holes or obstacles to avoid," said Sam.

"After that I'll run around while Sam paces with you. Once I've lapped you, I'll stay with you until he does the same. How does that sound?" Braiden asked and the two boys agreed.

Winston was dreading the coming ordeal but also, deep down, knew it was for the best. Beneath the understandable hostility shown towards him, there was an undercurrent of kindness. They hoped against all hope that he would prove to be as genuine as he claimed. It was not an opportunity he was prepared to waste. The blood started to flow with each pace and the well-tended grounds were as perfect as Sam and Braiden had assumed.

Reaching the starting point, Braiden had a few final words of encouragement for Winston, "This isn't going to be much easier for us, we haven't run properly in months. See you later, bitches!" With a raised middle finger, he started to jog away, pumping his arms and increasing his stride as he gained confidence.

Winston looked at Sam with nervous anticipation. "Ready?"

"Yup, you?"

"No," Winston groaned and started to run.

Winston tried to match the long paces of Braiden until Sam eased him back. "Slow it down a bit, he used to be on the athletics team. Neither of us could keep up with him."

Unable to answer through the rapid constriction of his chest, Winston nodded.

"Try and take deeper breaths and time them to your feet. I take one breath over two steps and let it out over the next two steps," Sam said, watching the boy as he struggled to fill his strained lungs.

Slowing down a little, Winston focused on each footfall. Left, right, breathe in, left, right, exhale. He managed about a quarter of the distance before it became too much. Raising a hand in surrender he started to slow, but Sam grabbed him by the arm and pulled.

"Not yet, give me another twenty feet!"

Winston felt the familiar self-doubt, but before it could grind him down and win, he took another step. Then another, and another. Nearly forty feet had been covered in a sweaty blur before he slowed to a walk.

"Brilliant, mate. Well done," Sam praised, "Now, don't stop walking, even if you think you can't go another step and take long, deep breaths. We'll give it thirty seconds and then we do a little more."

"Kill... me... now!" Winston croaked.

"That's the spirit!" Sam laughed, his own breathing nearly back to normal.

"Slackers!" Braiden shouted from their rear as he approached. Stretching out an arm to mimic a relay pass, he reached them and Sam took the invisible baton and jogged away.

"It's like being back in training," Braiden exclaimed, taking deep breaths of his own in time with Winston.

"How are... you not... dead?"

"In a month, you'll be keeping up with me," Braiden grinned without a hint of sarcasm. The combination of exercise and subsequent endorphins had put him in a great mood.

"I doubt I'll survive... the morning."

"Bollocks! Can't you hear? Your breathing is already slowing down."

Winston was surprised to find that Braiden was right. His body's resistance to the exercise was being replaced by the same energised feeling which flowed through his companion.

"The mistake you made was trying to run flat out straight away." Braiden patted him on the back, "We need to build your stamina gradually. Let's go."

In place of the earlier groan was a determined nod and the two boys started to jog again.

"Mind if we join you?" yelled Holly from the flowerbed they had used to stretch.

Accompanying her were most of the fellow students as far as Braiden could tell. Three more came hurrying from the lower keep to make it the whole class. Winston was flagging again and was horrified at the thought of reaching them as a red, sweaty, gasping mess. Braiden refused to let him slow and urged him on.

"Nearly there!"

The rest of the youngsters could see the pain contorting his face and shouted their own encouragement. Winston stumbled to a halt and everyone congratulated him on pushing through. As one, the whole group started to walk in time while he regained his composure.

"You got this," Braiden said confidently as Sam reached them, before sprinting away to show off to the girls.

"Why are you out here?" Sam asked everyone, taking a sip from the water bottle.

"What's rule number one of the zombie apocalypse?" Holly inquired with a raised eyebrow. "Cardio." Everyone burst out laughing at the joke. The movie from which she had stolen the phrase made light of the true horror, but it brought back fond memories of Columbus and Tallahassee's zombie killing exploits.

What had started as a freezing, agonising, lonely endeavour had grown into something else entirely. Winston looked around the happy faces walking alongside and felt an inner glow which had eluded him for his whole life. It was belonging.

CHAPTER 4

Shifting his weight to account for a spreading cramp in his thigh, Pesci laid the scoped rifle down and decided to take the opportunity to relieve himself. Rising into a kneeling position within the concealment of the bushes, he uncapped the bottle and held his breath lest a waft of the stale urine assail his senses. The freezing temperatures were keeping the vile fermentation of his bodily fluids to a minimum and he was grateful for that. Placing the bottle out of reach, he nibbled sparingly on a dry cracker and sipped from his water bottle before fluffing the thick blankets on the ground.

The silence was only broken by the occasional moan of nearby zombies as they bumbled along, driven by whatever unfathomable instinct was animating them. Pesci hadn't really given it any thought, much like his whole life up to this point. He avoided them because they were dangerous, but that was a peripheral concern to the main mission. Craig had asked him to survey the castle and any surviving occupants, and for the last two days he had lain in the thicket, oblivious to all else, even the cold. His ability to get a job done was legendary, or so he had been told by criminal acquaintances and fellow prisoners. Their praise had never filled him with any pride; he normally just nodded and ignored it.

All through his younger years, his parents had been filled with a growing hopelessness as they tried to unravel his bizarre behaviour. Thirteen years had been their limit and the day that the social workers arrived to remove him was forever etched in his memory. For eight months, he had sat in the room of his new home and analysed every aspect of the event. The anxious, tear streaked creases of his mother's cheek as she sobbed. The stoic frown of his father which couldn't hide the well of unshed sadness which threatened to spill from his dark lashes. The cruel grip of his collector on the flesh of his upper arm and the way the fingers dug painfully into his left triceps muscle as he was led to the waiting vehicle.

Attempts had been made to get him to go to school from the children's home, but his mind simply wouldn't allow it. Although they shepherded him to and from classes, he was unresponsive. Food had been consumed and perfunctory cleaning undertaken when they had urged him, but every time he would return to the scene in his mind. He harboured no animosity towards his birth parents, they were just two people he had lived with for a while. Love was an emotion he had never experienced, a concept as alien as the stars he could see in the night sky. Had he been fortunate enough to be born twenty years later, he would have been diagnosed as being on the autistic spectrum. His personality would have been better understood as being victim to hyperfocus and obsession.

It was these traits which made him such an efficient burglar and 'psycho' as people labelled him when he had reached adulthood. He would sit patiently for days on end to note the habits, and comings and goings of their marks. Where others would get restless and fidget, Pesci, or Harry as he had been christened, would be in his element. The same compulsion took him when he felt slighted. Instead of dealing rationally with the insult, he would not rest until the person was either laid in a coma or the grave. There was no satisfaction, just a mechanism in his mind that then closed that episode and moved on. It was thus a murder that got him sentenced to eighteen years in prison and under the protective wing of Craig.

Finishing his stretching routine, he lowered himself back to the blanket insulated ground. When he was settled, he re-covered himself with the thermal sleeping bags which Mike had arrived with. Luckily, they were black and blended in well with the dark shadows of the old fox run which he had found. He placed his cheek on the stock of the Remington Model 700 bolt action rifle and stared back through the scope. By his reckoning, the guard on the wall would be changing in about forty minutes. This gave the sentry a four-hour window to patrol their section of battlement or tower. Pesci found himself watching each new guard and wondering why they had to be so careless. Like clockwork, the first thirty minutes would be spent carefully scanning the horizon for movement. They would gradually lose interest and take out a hidden book or magazine, or disappear for ten minutes and fetch more firewood for their dying brazier. The last three hours would then be spent giving a cursory glance over the wall at random intervals. Anyone wanting to approach stealthily would be able to wear neon lights with a huge flashing arrow pointing down at them and still go undetected. Now and again a survivor would appear who wasn't cut from the same cloth. They had the look of people who had seen too much, who knew what evil lay outside the high walls. And not just the rotting kind either.

Looking at the note pad on the dead leaves and twigs, scribbled notes had been written by one of the other inmates. It took Pesci a while to understand each word, but he wasn't totally illiterate. He had already ticked off the two soldiers who were detailed on the paper. They had been easy to spot in their combat fatigues. Sam and Braiden had question marks by their names as he had seen several teenagers which could match the descriptions. One name had been underlined and circled to display its importance; Kurt. Craig had left him in no doubt that if he was to bring confirmation of only one person, it was to be him. Reasons weren't sought as they were moot; he had his mission and that filled his whole psyche.

If Pesci had arrived a day earlier, he would have witnessed the man leading the clean-up operation and subsequent incineration of the zombie corpses at the eastern wall. As it was, the only glimpse had been during the manic arrival of the crane and the fat kid. The belching, snorting machine had crashed through the undergrowth twenty feet from where he lay. He had watched with bemusement as the vehicle had been driven at the wall and the dripping, crumbling entourage had surrounded it. A protracted discussion ended with the driver being dragged up and over the stone parapet where he was then bound and removed. A period of extreme watchfulness slowly ebbed away over the following day until the slovenly observation had taken its place once again.

A shout came over the field and he could see his target gesticulating and berating the man who he was replacing. The argument was brief and with a bowed head, the individual stomped away in shame. Kurt turned the book over in his hands as if he hadn't seen anything like it before. With an angry shake of his head, he tossed it into the fire which devoured it gratefully. Pesci was under strict instructions not to shoot anyone, especially Kurt, so he removed his finger from the trigger guard just in case. Better to be safe than sorry. The thin black crosshair centred on his face, and for a split second it appeared Kurt was looking directly at him. Slowly capping the lens with his hand, Pesci blinked a couple of times until his closed eye had adjusted and watched carefully. Fearing a stray flash of the reflected glass, he exhaled slowly when Kurt moved away from him onto other sights. Nothing about his

45

body language spoke of tension or recognition and Pesci relaxed a little. His watch displayed 1.17PM and he had all the information required to fulfil Craig's brief. Carefully folding the bedding, he placed it all inside his backpack. All evidence that he had been sheltered in the bushes was taken even though the chances of someone human coming to look were infinitesimally small.

An excited rasp caught his attention from a nearby corpse who had noticed the clandestine retreat. Pesci moved deeper into the foliage as the zombie ducked through the animal forged tunnel. With one eye on any available break in the branches, he watched Kurt move away to the north out of sight before acting. Teeth gnashed in eager anticipation of the meal until the knife found its way through the eye socket and into the brain. Clutching the creature's worn leather belt, he pulled the carcass out of sight into the darkness. With a final check of the walls, Pesci broke through the rear of the hedgerow and dodged expertly between cars, staying out of sight. He would be back at the prison, eating a warm meal within six hours. Craig was going to be thrilled that his enemies yet lived. Pesci didn't feel much one way or another.

CHAPTER 5

A frigid wind had taken hold, whistling between the tower's battlements. Kurt was unaware of the icy embrace which tousled his greasy, lank hair. Personal hygiene had been the first victim to the paralysing grief which had settled in his heart since the funeral. Staring at the dark patches on his hands, he picked at the filthy fingernails which hadn't seen soap since the canal boat. Mixed with the dried gore of their enemies was a mottled brown crust. Memories flooded back of John's death and Kurt paused. The flecks of dirt blowing away in the breeze had once been the life blood of his father. Falling to his knees, he tried to pick up the specks but the wind thwarted his efforts until they merged with the more commonplace detritus of the tower.

"What the hell are you doing?" he asked himself, and a mournful wail from the zombies below was the only reply. The rational side of his mind understood it was a facet of the grieving process; a peculiar refusal to let go of the last vestiges of his parent. *Pull yourself together, people are relying on you,* he thought, shaking his head. Footfalls from the staircase caught his attention and he stood up, leaning against the wall to look down at their foe once more.

"Hey, Kurt. How're you holding up?" Denise asked, emerging from the shadowy archway.

"Honestly? I think I'm losing my marbles," he sighed.

"With everything you've suffered, I'm not surprised," she said, taking his cold hand and squeezing. "You've been subjected to weeks of terror, never relaxing, never knowing if you would live to see the following day. Most people would've cracked long before getting here."

"It was hell out there," he admitted with a shudder.

"I can't even begin to imagine. It was bad enough when Patricia and I fought our way inside the castle, and that was only a mile during the first hour of the outbreak."

Kurt snorted and Denise looked at him with a puzzled expression. "Do you know what's even more bizarre? In some small part, I miss being out there. I felt… alive. Now I just feel drained. How crazy is that?"'"

"It's not crazy at all. Now that you're safe, your body isn't sure what to do with itself. It misses the rush."

"You make it sound like I'm a danger junkie," he chuckled wearily.

"An unwilling one, perhaps," she continued, "Being a beat cop back in the States I can relate to the feeling. On the streets you're always on edge, waiting for the next call, knowing you are a constant target. When I retired, I found it hard to adjust. Adrenaline is a tough habit to break."

"I'm not sure I want to break the habit." Kurt shrugged, "It's how I've kept my family safe."

"I understand, but you can't maintain it. You'll burn out and be good to no one."

"What's your advice then?"

"Enjoy the fruits of your labour; You and your family are safe."

"Until the food runs out, we get attacked by the prison, or the zombies overwhelm us," he replied scornfully.

"Can you do anything about it right now?" Denise asked, trying to get him to see sense.

"Well … no, not really. It doesn't stop me worrying, though," Kurt huffed.

"You need to share the load and let others take some responsibility. We all have a stake in this world."

"Do you think I don't know that!" he fired back, anger flaring, "My dad took responsibility and look where that got him! What about Maura and Greg?"

Denise reached up and took his grimy face in her hands. "They all fought and died for their friends and loved ones. None of it is your fault."

"I should've seen the zombie." Kurt's voice broke and Denise pulled him into her arms. "If I'd been standing closer I could've saved him."

They stood there for a while; Denise cooing and stroking Kurt's matted hair as he took the first tentative step on the long road to acceptance. Coming from a highly dangerous occupation, she had lost friends along the way and knew all too well the feeling of responsibility, however unwarranted. When the time was right, Kurt took a deep, composing breath and broke contact. With a nod and a smile, he wiped at his tear streaked cheeks and returned to the vigil on the wall without saying a word. Denise wanted to ask if he would be ok, if he would rather be alone with his thoughts. Although only knowing him for a couple of days, she was certain Kurt was a man who would not hesitate to say if that was the case.

Moving to stand alongside him, she stared out at the dead town. A place of incredible heritage and architecture was now a dark, foreboding maze for the unnatural creatures of hell to wander. They were stood upon the tower of the western barbican; the fortification which housed the huge portcullis which now kept them safe. Below lay the public courtyard where she and Patricia had fought to buy time for the survivors to reach the castle. The undead stood shoulder to shoulder in the confines and stretched out through the archway and over the wooden drawbridge to the grounds beyond.

"I've been thinking," Kurt said, "We need to start hardening the rest of the group."

Denise nodded in agreement. Their insulation from the true horror of the events was dangerous for everyone and she waited for his plan.

"I know they'll be up in arms if we send them against a small horde of these creatures. I've been looking in the maintenance rooms and there's enough pipework and equipment for me to rig up a sprinkler system along this wall. With the temperatures constantly below freezing, the zombies will be rendered popsicles and the weaker members can kill them in relative safety."

"You know they'll still piss and moan," Denise cautioned.

"I've no doubt. Can I count on your support?"

"Always," she replied without hesitation, "This godawful situation isn't going away, and the only way to win will be through blood."

"I'm glad you see it that way too. My dad used to say there were two kinds of people, sheep and wolves."

"Which was fine in the old world," Denise continued, "But now the sheep will get eaten. Literally."

"I'm going to find the castle's maintenance engineer and get this system constructed. Would you mind letting everyone know that there's going to be a meeting later? We can tell them the good news."

"Of course, sweetie." Denise smiled and made to leave.

"Thank you."

Turning, it was clear he was referring to the emotional support and not the errand. With a wink, she left him to take measurements on the stonework.

***

"This takes me back to my apprentice days." Kurt grinned, glad for the distraction of good, honest, manual labour.

"I can't believe they hadn't thrown it away," replied Bob, the castle repairman, pointing at the object.

In Kurt's hands was an old, hand driven drill; an archaic tool which had decades ago been replaced by electric powered versions. The length of copper pipework stretched around the twenty feet of battlement, peppered with tiny holes. Clipped tightly to each merlon, the tube would cover the whole expanse of the entrance courtyard if Kurt's calculations were correct.

"How high do you want the cistern?" Bob asked from the ladder.

Laying the drill down, Kurt flexed his aching fingers to get rid of some of the cramping pain. Bob chuckled at his discomfort and held the bracket high on the keep wall, waiting for Kurt to give him the nod on where to fix it.

"Give me a break, I haven't done any real work for weeks," Kurt laughed, indicating a position close to a higher window in the castle. "There should be just fine, the higher the better to give us more pressure and it means we can fill it safely by pouring water out of the window without climbing the ladder each time."

"Good plan."

Kurt cleaned and soldered the pipework into position while Bob used the drill and bolted the brackets into the stone. Giving them a hefty tug, they were sturdy and would do the job. Swapping places, Bob reached up and offered the makeshift tank to Kurt. It was an old water butt which had been taken from the gardens and adapted with a bottom outlet for its new purpose. Balancing it on the iron struts, Kurt took the final length of copper which Bob passed up and pushed it into the connector. Using a pair of wrenches, he tightened the nut and the contraption was complete. It would not win any plumbing beauty contests, that was certain, but it would serve its purpose.

51

"Do you want to insulate the pipes to stop them freezing?"

Kurt looked along the copper and thought about it. "It's only the vertical drop of pipe that I haven't drilled so there's not much point, mate. The lagging will just get in the way of the sprinkler holes."

"Fair point."

"Besides, the water won't be in there for long. I'll relocate a brazier just in case, and if we have any issues we can use the burning logs to defrost them."

"What about using hot water? That'll keep them flowing well."

"Hot water can actually freeze faster than cold water in some circumstances, so we'd be in even worse trouble," Kurt replied.

"Fuck off!" Bob scoffed, articulate in his rebuke.

"I'm deadly serious!" Kurt laughed. "It's known as the Mpemba effect. The molecules in hot water sit further apart as the hydrogen bonds stretch which has been observed to speed up the freezing process over that of cold water."

Bob scowled at the younger man, unsure if he was the victim of an elaborate ruse. Seeing no subterfuge in his eyes, the maintenance man coughed and spat on the floor. "Well you learn a new thing every day, don't you?"

"Indeed, you do, Bob. Shall we give it a try?"

"Why not? I've got no date lined up tonight."

"A fine figure of a man like yourself? That surprises me," Kurt chuckled and climbed the ladder with the bucket of water.

"Careful you don't fall. I may have to make a move on your wife if you end up crippled."

"She's all yours, mate. The way I smell at the moment, I'm sure she'll swap us without me needing to fall and break my neck," Kurt replied with a grin.

Tipping the liquid into the high set vessel, both men watched and waited. With a gurgling rush, the water filled the horizontal tube and a fine spray arced out of a hundred holes. Pouring forth from so many tiny outlets, the bucketful was gone in under ten seconds. Kurt and Bob peered over the walls and watched the misty rain soak the cadavers below.

"I'd say you nailed it," Bob stated, glancing around.

Kurt stared hard until he was satisfied. "It looks like it," he said, pointing, "There are only a couple of dry patches from what I can see."

Amongst the milling dead, the men could see the bare courtyard floor. Where the water had hit, the zombies had a sheen of moisture and the stone itself was a darker shade of grey. Very little was untouched by the ingenious sprinkler system.

"I think you may need more water, though."

"You think?" Kurt replied, sarcastically.

"I'd offer to help hump it up all the stairs, but my old war wound from 'Nam means my knee is gimpy," Bob sighed, tapping at his perfectly good leg.

"I didn't realise we were ever in Vietnam," Kurt grinned.

"Did I say that? I meant Dagenham. I fell over a railing after getting pissed on a stag weekend."

"I'll get the kids to do it."

"Now you're talking! Those young'uns need to earn their crust and keep us old farts in the luxury I plan to become accustomed to."

"You're in the right place for luxury, Bob," Kurt chuckled.

Bob waved disdainfully, "This place is a slum, but it'll have to do until I can get to Buckingham Palace and take my rightful place on the throne."

"Sorry, your Majesty," Kurt curtsied like a maiden and both men burst out laughing.

"Let's go and tell the kids the good news."

53

CHAPTER 6

"What's the plan now that we're trapped?" Petermann asked, picking despondently at the vegetable soup.

The past few hours had been spent silently mourning their brothers in arms. Eldridge had been crippled by despair after the loss of Walker and Holbeck, but with each passing moment the old fire returned. "We continue the mission, it's what they would've wanted."

"Can we take on this bunch of motherless bastards as well as the ones at the entertainment complex?"

"You bet your ass we can," Dougal boasted.

"We won't have the ammunition left to take both groups on directly, so we'll have to get inventive at the holiday park," Eldridge replied.

"A lot of the trailers will have LPG cylinders for heating and cooking," offered Max.

"You could do some barbecuing of your own," Angela added.

"Before any of that we'll need to clear the farm." Eldridge turned to the twins, "I assume the holes were left to act as gun slits for you to fire from without being in danger?"

Angela nodded. "We found it easier to just stab the fuckers in the end though. The gunshots were far too loud in the confines of the downstairs rooms and the dogs would go nuts."

"From the upper floor, you should be fine as long as you have ear plugs. We can jab their eyes out while you shoot them from an elevated position. I'll pop the pups into the cellar so they don't get in the way," Max continued.

Angela offered round a handful of walking sticks with the ends sharpened into vicious points.

"You aren't old enough for one of these," Harkiss muttered, touching the tip and wincing as a spot of blood rose from the broken skin.

"Hell no! But I used to make them for the locals when I was bored, and now most of the locals want to eat us. Ungrateful bastards!"

"You just can't trust anyone these days," Harkiss sighed.

"Let's get the weapons and ammo upstairs," Eldridge ordered, "We can then judge the best way of handling the threat."

The troops hastily finished their meals and handed back the bowls with grateful nods. Carrying the drab, metallic boxes, they spread out into each bedroom and divided the ammunition evenly. A sea of undead waited below, pressed tightly against the outer walls and APCs. Opening a window, the wet gurgling was unbearable at such a proximity.

"Close it for now," Eldridge said to Harkiss.

"I thought we were going to wipe them out?"

"It's getting too dark. We'll get some rest and fight them at first light when they are sluggish. That way, we can take our time and kill one for each shot. It'll conserve the last of the ammo."

Harkiss shrugged and eyed the king size bed in the corner. "Dibs?"

"What are you, five?"

"Mentally? Maybe," Harkiss replied. Walking to the stairs, he called out, "Ange, Max, can I call dibs on this bed in the back room?"

A chuckle preceded the answer from Max. "That's my sister's bed. I'm sure she won't mind sharing."

Eyes widening, his mouth opened and closed like a goldfish as he thought of a suitable reply. Time stretched out and before he could say anything, another voice called out from below. "Is that a yes or no? I warn you, I snore like an old man. Even the dogs can't put up with it."

"Erm... I think the sofa will be fine. Thanks anyway."

Neither sister could hide their amusement as they peered up the staircase. "You're far too easy to wind up," Angela teased.

"We'll take the sofas, you can take the beds. It's going to be a busy day tomorrow and I think you should be fully rested," explained Max.

"If you feel me get into bed with you, don't be afraid." Angela winked at the young soldier. "I sleepwalk sometimes."

Aghast, he glanced at Eldridge who was grinning from ear to ear. "Is she serious? Can I climb out and sleep on the roof of the Warthog?"

"Pussy."

CHAPTER 7

"Ok, settle down, everyone!" Denise shouted.

"Listen to what the man has to say, goddammit!" Patricia emphasized.

The swell of argument in the room slowly diminished but arms were folded and mouths set in tight lines of dissent. *It is like dealing with a room of petulant fucking children*, Kurt thought wearily. Over the past couple of days, the castle survivors had split into two factions. On one side were the young and the brave who knew the reality of their new existence. On the other were the whiners and malcontents. When guard duty rolled around they invariably treated it with contempt and any request to do extra work was refused. Jasmine was central to this insurrection. She had surrounded herself with a small clique of nodding sycophants who hid their laziness beneath a façade of anti-authoritarianism. Much to Kurt's eternal relief, the greater number were on his side in the argument which was raging.

"I don't know how many more times I have to say it," Kurt sighed, frustration growing with each passing moment. "You won't be in any danger. The system I have created will ensure they are frozen solid while you destroy them."

"Then why do you even need us?" Jasmine countered with a smarmy grin. "You're the fearsome zombie killers."

"Yeah," piped up another belligerent voice from a no mark, "You've already killed thousands, what's a few more?"

Kurt glared at the man and after a few seconds his cheeks flushed and he looked away. Anyone lacking the bravery to form an independent thought without hiding behind the skirt of their ringleader was unworthy of a response.

"It's about preparing you for the future," DB said.

"The only way to survive is to fight," Jonesy added.

"Really? We seem to have done pretty well so far."

"And when the food runs out?" Kurt demanded.

"It's not going to though, is it? You know as well as I do that you wouldn't leave these people to starve." Jasmine waved a condescending hand at the other group.

"And you think that after we risk our lives, you will get a share of the food we bring back?"

"Of course," she replied arrogantly.

Though far from being Debbie, some of the same character traits were evident and Kurt felt the hairs rise on the back of his neck. Taking a step forward, he felt a warm hand reach out and take his own, gently pulling him back.

Sarah smiled and said, "Sit down, sweetheart."

Denise, Jodi, Patricia, Christina, and Gloria joined her and faced the dozen rebels. Sarah continued as the spokeswoman. "We figured this would be your response, so we've come up with a plan. This place is plenty big enough for both of our groups and after the meeting we'll help you move into another area, or into the bedrooms themselves. You will be given a quarter of the weapons, but only swords, axes and bows, not the guns. The food will be split into similar shares and to prevent any misunderstanding, we will lock ours away somewhere cold and safe, and you will do likewise."

Jasmine scowled; she had been fully prepared for a shouting match and threats. "And the wood for the fires?"

"A quarter," Patricia confirmed.

"We don't want to do any more guard duty either. It's bloody freezing out there!" chimed in another lady.

"Fine," Gloria agreed, "But you get a smaller share of the wood to keep the braziers alight for the rest of us."

They commenced a small huddle and quickly agreed.

"And when you bring food back, we get a quarter of that too, right?" Jasmine asked.

"I'm afraid that's where our deal ends." Denise shook her head slowly. "You'll be responsible for sourcing your own food, as will we. Our groups will be completely independent of one another."

Angry mumbles broke out and one of the group whispered about finding the hidden stash and simply helping themselves to the spoils of war as and when they needed it. No padlock could stand up to the battle axes adorning the armoury walls, mentioned the earlier wastrel.

"My husband is a good man. You may think his kindness makes him weak, but you'd be forgetting we stand behind him. All of us." At that, the boys, Peter, and the soldiers stood up too.

"Is that meant to scare us?"

"Yes, it is. And you're right, Kurt would never let these people starve. But a bunch of scheming, would be thieves, who want to live off the hard work of others? That's a different story."

"You can't stop us," Jasmine replied, emboldened by her lackeys.

Gloria coughed politely. "If any of you come near our food with the intent to steal, I will shoot you myself. That will be my only warning." Coming from the articulately spoken lady it was hard to ignore and the dissenters looked at each other with uncertainty.

"It's good to see everyone getting along so well," snorted Mr Vincent sarcastically from his dark corner.

Sadly, Kurt had to agree with the disdainful outburst.

59

CHAPTER 8

"Winston, please come and take a seat," Christina said, beckoning him inside.

Gloria waved at the doctor and gently closed the door as her charge entered.

The visitor's first aid room had been converted into a small doctor's surgery. Christina was scribbling notes about Phillip, an older resident with a heart condition. His treatment was limited by the scarcity of available beta blockers, so she chewed on the pen in contemplation as the young man seated himself.

"Are you ok, Dr Hargis?"

Closing the pad, she turned to him and smiled. "Yes, I'm fine. Just trying to figure out how to treat fifty people with barely enough supplies for ten."

"I don't know if it helps, but I passed a medical supply facility on the outskirts of Ford on my way here. A truck had crashed into the side of the building and I could see all manner of bandages and stuff on the shelves."

"Interesting. You'll have to show us exactly where it is."

"I'd be happy to. Do you think there would be medicine inside as well?"

"As far as I know, the supply depots also delivered drugs as needed. Did you happen to see any refrigeration units as you passed?"

"I'm afraid not. I had a few friends on my tail who wanted to nibble on my fine figure."

Christina chuckled. "Yes, they have a habit of being a bit bitey."

"What are they, Doctor?" Winston asked.

"Zombies. The living dead. Walking corpses."

"I know that!" Winston said with a grin. "I meant did you have any knowledge of what's causing it. I'm digging the attention from the female zombies, don't get me wrong. It's just they smell a little bit funky for my normal, high standards."

"I have been trying to unravel the mystery ever since the first day. There is no physiological explanation for their reanimation, but I noticed a slight aberration in the brain stem when I dissected them at the hospital. It's as if they're a car which has been sat rusting for many months. Whatever happened that morning was the spark which jumpstarted their engine."

"How does that explain how something which has been rotting can get up and walk?"

"It doesn't. Nothing about this whole mess has any basis in scientific fact."

"What about science fiction?"

"You may be closer to the mark than you think. If I was a betting woman, I'd suggest a supernatural cause."

"I remember Gloria talking about a pulse of energy from that facility in Europe."

"The Large Hadron Collider?"

"That's the one! I'm guessing the eggheads really messed up."

"A worldwide apocalypse would be better summed up as a complete fuck up."

Winston burst out laughing. "I like you, Doc."

"And I like you. Now, how can I help you today?"

Taking off his coat, Winston rolled up the sleeve of his sweater, revealing the dark bruising on his arm. Luckily the skin was unbroken, but the purple and yellow injury covered most of the forearm.

"Ouch," Christina remarked, turning the limb over and checking all around.

"I said a bit more than ouch."

"I should imagine you did. How on earth did this happen? If I didn't know better, the shape seems to be that of a bite."

"It turns out the zombies aren't the only thing that wants to eat me," Winston replied, lowering his head in shame.

"What happened? If you feel like telling me, that is."

"I was in the scrapyard to the south where I borrowed the crane and I had a feeling I wasn't alone. I thought it may have been a zombie lurking, but it was a starving guard dog. It attacked me and I couldn't reason with it."

"Oh, honey," Christina whispered, clutching his hand.

"I had to get it off me or I'd be dead right now. All I had was my axe…"

"You did what you had to do. No one can blame you for that."

"I can still hear the squeal as I cut it. The poor thing only wanted to survive."

"This world is a Godawful place now, but kind people like yourself are a light in the darkness. Never forget that," she replied earnestly.

"Do you think it's broken?" Winston asked, changing the subject.

"Without an x-ray, I can't say. From your range of movement, I would say it's unlikely. Hairline fractures are a possibility based on the level of deep tissue bruising."

"What do you suggest I do with it? You don't have the equipment to put a cast on it, do you?"

"I'm afraid not."

"I could always knock up something with an old sock and some papier mâché," Winston suggested.

"I'd rather you didn't. The best thing you can do is rest and let it heal; I'll give you a bottle of liquid morphine for the pain. You can take ten millilitres every four hours."

"Is it good stuff?"

"The best," Christina chuckled. "Try not to get addicted or I'll have to put you in the castle's rehab facility."

"You've set up a rehab facility?" Winston marvelled.

"Yes, it's called the dungeon!"

"I can't believe I fell for that."

Standing, Christina moved over to a store cupboard. "Put this on as well. It'll hurt, but keep the swelling down a little."

Stretching the elasticated dressing in her hands, Winston slid his arm into the sleeve.

"Shit!" Winston hissed as it started to tighten painfully.

"I told you it would smart a bit. Get some of the morphine inside you and you'll feel right as rain. Well, high as a kite, anyway."

"Thank you, Doc. I'll let Kurt know of the supplies."

"You're welcome. I'll check on you in a few days, young man."

CHAPTER 9

ey, handsome," Angela said to the moist, peeling face which snapped at her from the break in the brick sealed window. The creature snarled and bounced its head against the solid barricade, leaving scraps of flesh on the coarse surface.

"Just kill it," Max admonished, ramming the walking stick spear through another eye socket from her own position.

"I was just seeing if they could respond to human interaction," she replied, stabbing it and pulling the weapon out of its brain with a sickly pop.

"It's not worked before, why would it now?"

"I don't know. It was a fool's hope I guess."

Max paused and regarded her sister with love. "Your hope kept us alive and look at us now. We've been rescued by the army when we thought everyone else was gone except for us and the pups."

"Technically, they've brought most of the undead on the south coast with them. At the moment, we're the ones doing the rescuing," she replied, impaling another monster through the forehead.

"That's true, but you have to give them credit for trying."

"Do you really think we'll be safe on their island barracks?"

"God knows. But I'd sooner have a couple of hundred guns on my side than none. It feels good to know that we may be able to fight back after all that's happened."

"Revenge is going to be sweet," Angela agreed. "They can fuck right off if they think I'm doing all the physical training, though. I'll go as far as a light jog and riding a few miles on a bike."

"You can't outrun the dead anyway. If what Private Eldridge said is true, the biggest fight will be on the Portsmouth bridge. No running needed when we will be holding a position against the zombies."

"And if they overrun us?"

"I think the water may be a bit nippy for a swim."

"I'll make sure to bring a couple of rubber rings so we can float away in comfort."

"You're the best," Max replied.

"I've always said so. It's good you've finally admitted it."

***

"Does everyone have their earplugs in?" Eldridge shouted from the rear bedroom.

Lacking the specialised combat plugs which were stowed in the Warthogs, they had to make do with the cheap, foam versions. Her words reached their ears, muffled and obscured, but they all called back affirmative. It would be disastrous for them to go into battle at the holiday camp deafened by the confined gunfire. Below, their enemy waited. Slowed by the overnight frost, their normal exuberance was dulled.

"It's like shooting fish in a barrel," Harkiss called out.

"We're the ones in the barrel, you pillock," Carpenter shouted back.

"Ok, that was a shit analogy. Cut me some slack!"

"Knock it off and fire at will!" Eldridge yelled.

65

From every corner of the old house, death was dealt. The probing tips of the sharpened stakes erupted from the lower apertures, piercing flesh and bone before withdrawing. Muzzle flashes lit up the gloomy bedrooms above like a flickering strobe. At the outer edge of the horde, bullets scalped the undead. Skulls disintegrated and faces imploded under the barrage, coating the farm with a growing skin of green ichor. After an hour, layers of the dead fanned out from the building. Their arms, once raised for a promise of meat, stretched out above their heads, looking akin to a final plea for absolution from a God that had long ago forsaken them.

"Ceasefire!" she yelled. Hearing the gunfire continue, she was about to reprimand the soldier who was ignoring the order, until Harkiss located the source.

"It's coming from outside!"

Eldridge pulled her ear plugs out and couldn't hide the elation at the stuttering reports.

"It has to be the sarge! Quickly, sweep the front yard around the APCs while I get the twins to open the door."

Petermann and Langham resumed the assault, picking off the final cadavers who milled amongst the slain. In minutes, the inner door was opened and the remaining soldiers were ready to move out. With the way clear, Angela unlocked the gate and forced her weight against it to clear the rotten bodies. With each push, more vile liquids erupted from the pustules and decaying skin. Unperturbed, the dogs pushed forward, eager to sniff the putrid leavings. Rohan managed to sneak between her legs and the lolling tongue almost made contact with the dripping gore.

"No! Bad dogs!" Max snapped, pushing them away.

"Are we clear?" Eldridge called up the stairs.

"Clear!" came the reply. "Go and get him, we'll cover you from the windows."

Sweeping their rifles over the bodies, they remained wary for any movement. Any that still twitched were shot in the head at point blank range, just to be certain. Controlled gunfire rang out from the south of the farm and they followed the sharp cracks like a beacon. Hopping over bodies like rabbits, they raced for the source. Surrounding a mighty oak tree were a couple of hundred zombies. One by one they fell as Holbeck unloaded his remaining bullets into the crowd.

"Sarge, hold on!" Harkiss shouted.

Placing fingers in her mouth, Eldridge let loose a piercing whistle. Most of the shuffling corpses turned and advanced, with only a few determined stragglers fruitlessly reaching for the sergeant on his perch. Forming a line, the soldiers switched their rifles to fully automatic and opened fire. The undead stood little chance against the onslaught and fell in a tangled heap, holed and sundered by the hot lead. Overcome with excitement, they surged forward and destroyed the remaining cadavers at the tree.

Holbeck stared down, a smile forming on his lips. "Get the kettle on. I need a brew."

***

"Wait until the guys back on base hear about this!" Dougal declared, topping up the mug of his sergeant.

"They'll sing songs of our battles against the undead!" Harkiss added.

"This isn't The Lord of the Rings; all we'll get are report forms to fill in," Eldridge replied.

"True. But we've got to make sure we have a proper send off for Walker. He died a hero."

"You can count on it," said Holbeck.

"Sarge, I hate to ask, but how did you make it through the night out there?"

Eldridge chuckled. "Death fears the sarge, you know that."

"He paid me a visit, that's for sure. We came to an arrangement, though."

"What arrangement?" asked Harkiss.

"I offered to send all the dead back to him. He wasn't happy about being cheated out of what's rightfully his."

"We'll help you keep that promise, Sarge."

"I know you will," Holbeck replied. "I'm so proud of you all and how you handled yourselves. It happened like this…"

***

Holbeck slapped aside a pair of grasping arms and kicked another zombie in the chest, sending it reeling. Gunfire continued chattering from his troops and he was filled with pride at their stoicism. From every angle, the undead were converging and his avenues for escape were diminishing by the second. Crushing a face with the butt of his rifle, he considered the brick storage building for a split second. Between the approaching bodies he could see clear evidence of rot in the door and frame which would collapse under any kind of sustained assault. This only left the stranded combine harvester or the open marshland beyond and if he should become trapped in the quagmire he would swiftly be torn apart.

"Fuck it!"

The unmistakable trail of shredded green gore would have guided him if he had been unable to see the top of the yellow machine and the belching exhaust pipe. After dropping awkwardly from the embankment, the huge wheels spun uselessly. Hopping between wet patches, the zombies were slipping and stumbling over their blended fallen. It gave Holbeck small windows to dodge the hundreds of corpses which had been slower to arrive. Among the walkers were the shredded forms of those who had absorbed the non-fatal claymore shrapnel. Limping or crawling, peppered with gaping holes like swiss cheese, they posed the bigger danger. Their madly thrashing bodies could easily trip him as he jumped over and there would be no time to regain his feet before being swamped.

"Damn!"

The zombies standing in between himself and the stranded vehicle had closed in, forming an impenetrable barrier of decay. Glancing over his shoulder, the access to the outbuilding was also sealed off. Backing up against one of the wide oak trees which circled the properties to provide a wind break, he took a deep breath. The only available route left was the marshland and he instantly dismissed the idea, choosing to make a last stand instead. He needed freedom of movement, so quickly shouldered the rifle, unholstered his pistol and started picking targets.

Crack. The top of a female zombie's head sheared away as the hollow point blasted through the skull.

Crack. A young boy dressed in a school uniform was hammered back as his face exploded.

Crack crack. Two rotten crawlers sprawled out into the dust, green pools spilling from their gaping mouths.

A huge zombie strutted forward, leaden grey muscles accentuated by an armless workout t-shirt with the words 'I flexed and the sleeves fell off' imprinted on the filth encrusted chest. Sidestepping the meaty arms, its bulky momentum carried the monster forward into the brown trunk. Holbeck wasted no time in pressing the muzzle to the side of its head and pulling the trigger. Fragments of skull and brain embedded into the dense bark and it crashed to the ground.

"Prick." Holbeck had always hated the puffed-up posers.

It was do or die time. With twelve bullets left, he could take out eleven of the creatures and save the last bullet for himself, or he could climb. With only fifteen feet between himself and the wall of encroaching horror, reloading would not be an option. The misty exhalations left him in no doubt of the likely fate if he was trapped overnight in the branches of the mighty tree. Hypothermia and death would claim him long before the sun peeked over the horizon the following morning. But at least it meant he could use every available bullet on the enemy below and help his troops at the same time. Securing the pistol and clipping the strap, he looked for a means of ascending.

Placing his toes into a circular depression where a branch had long ago been lopped off, Holbeck kicked upwards. Encircling the lowest outcrop of rough wood with his arms, he hooked a leg over a higher branch. Grunting with effort, he twisted his body until a deep rut in the bark was within reach. With a final pull, he slumped down, legs spread and back against the trunk. The assault rifle dug painfully into his spine, so he shifted position and retrieved the weapon before hanging it from a broken nub of timber to his right.

The dead had fully surrounded the tree, but Holbeck was several feet clear of even the longest arms. Doing a quick ammunition check, he had four full rifle magazines and two more for the pistol. One hundred and sixty-six rounds would put a hefty dent in the crowd beneath, but would still leave over a hundred eager mouths to feed. Repositioning himself to account for the recoil which would topple him from his precarious perch given the chance, he started to aim and shoot. There was no rush and he took calming breaths between each kill. One by one, the awful creatures fell at the base of the tree, coating the ground in brains and bone. Six bullets into his third magazine, he heard the dull crump of a grenade from his troops. Seconds later, the unmistakable screams of Walker took over from the shocked pause. Closing his eyes tightly, he mourned the young soldier. No other yells of pain presented themselves and he prayed the silence meant they had got to safety within the farmhouse. A last flash followed by a hollow boom to the south signalled the end of the artillery barrage, and with a sigh of relief, he knew it had been called off by one of his troops.

Unable to see the building from the angle and distance he had run, Holbeck's finger paused on the trigger. If they knew he was out here alive, they may be tempted to mount a suicidal rescue mission, despite his orders to the contrary. He was dubious if the sharp retorts would carry over the groans of the dead and then through the small apertures left in the sealed windows. Deciding the risk was too great, he placed the rifle back on its wooden hook and sat back against the trunk.

Reaching into a pocket, he removed the picture of his wife and their new-born child. They had separated over a year before the apocalypse by mutual agreement. Being an army spouse was exceedingly difficult with the six-month deployments and constant upheaval required by the role. Wherever they were, he hoped they had been together at the end. All he needed to do now was lay back, relax, and allow the unforgiving elements to reunite him with his estranged loved ones. Doing his best to ignore the dead, he folded his arms and closed his eyes, waiting for the last of the afternoon light to fade.

***

"I nearly gave up on that branch," Holbeck explained. "I'd give anything to see my family again in Heaven."

"We wouldn't have blamed you, Sarge, this whole world's an unending nightmare," lamented Petermann. The loss of his friend was hitting him hard.

"What made you keep fighting?"

Holbeck looked around the room slowly. "You did," he replied. "I'll see my own when my time is up, but until then I have to fight for this family and anyone still alive out there."

71

Tears welled at the sentiment, even from the sisters who dabbed at their eyes gently. Loss was something always hovering nearby in the zombie apocalypse, ready to snatch away those nearest and dearest in a welter of blood. The hatred borne of this unending threat was a tool they could use. A fire burning in their hearts to even the odds and retake the world for the living, no matter the cost.

Langham took a shaky breath, holding back the bubbling emotions. "We're glad to have you back in one piece, Sarge."

"Hell yes, we are. But I've got to know," Harkiss said, frowning. "How'd you survive the night? It was colder than a witch's tit out there."

"Simple. I lit a fire," Holbeck replied.

"You lit a fire… in a tree?" Carpenter asked, forming the words slowly to show her disbelief. The looks on the faces of the rest of the group were equally incredulous and Holbeck laughed.

"It wasn't that hard."

Eldridge raised an eyebrow. "I should imagine not. You were surrounded by wood…"

"Ok, look. You know I always carry my multifunction tool after Afghanistan," Holbeck explained, showing them the many bladed object of army legend. Caught between an encroaching Taliban force and a series of IEDs, he had used the tool to defuse the explosives to facilitate the patrol's retreat. With no time to wait for an Explosive Ordnance Disposal team, it had been a choice between certain death and almost certain death. His bravery had saved the lives of twenty-three soldiers that hot, dusty day.

"When it started to get dark I finally realised I couldn't take the easy way out. Two of the branches were perfectly aligned and where they met at the trunk formed a small depression. I lopped a load of the thinner wood from further up the tree and laid the pieces from one branch to the other to make a sleeping frame, before tying it off with cord."

"I wondered what that was when you jumped down. Fair play, Sarge," marvelled Petermann with a nod.

"I want to hear about the fire. How the fuck didn't you burn yourself and the tree to the ground?" Harkiss pressed.

"It was easy. The branches and trunk are far too dense and wet to burn properly, they just scorch and nothing more. I built a tiny fire with twigs in the depression and just kept it fed all night. It wasn't enough to warm me properly, but with the leaves I used as a mattress it kept the chill away."

"Another tale of the sarge's badassery," said Dougal with awe.

"Hardly. I was freezing my nuts off up there," Holbeck replied.

"We may leave that out of the story then," Eldridge added with a chuckle.

CHAPTER 10

ebbie dreamed of the board on the wall, except there were now three in a row. Between bouts of delicious clitoral teasing, she flayed portions of skin from the men shackled before her. Their screams of agony and pleading were as arousing as her probing finger and she closed her eyes, revelling in the power. Mike, Craig, and Wozniak were trussed tightly, streaming blood from bare patches of exposed muscle tissue. Peter stood to her left, nodding and smiling, while Winston stood to her right, passing other implements of torture as she required them. Taking the offered hacksaw, she stepped over to her rapist and smiled.

"I know I promised to bite it off, but this will work so much better," she cackled, running her finger down the blunt blade.

"I'm sorry for how I treated you last night. I don't know how to act around beautiful women," Wozniak sobbed.

"Please, Debbie. I never meant to hurt you. If you let me go we can be together forever," Mike pleaded.

"Shhh," Debbie replied, shaking her head sadly.

Lifting the flaccid penis and scrotum of her attacker, she placed the cold, tungsten teeth against the flesh. His eyes went wide as the inevitability of what was coming dawned. Without urgency, she commenced sawing at the cold skin. Being totally incapacitated, he could only shriek and vibrate on the board as she removed his member and balls. A torrent of blood erupted from the open wound and his eyes fluttered as the pain grew too much to bear.

"Debbie, I'm begging you..." Mike gasped as she turned her attention to him.

"I said shhh," she chided, forcing the severed phallus between his lips.

Suddenly, she was gasping and coughing. The icy water ran from her face and dirty hair, saturating her flat pillow on the prison bed.

"Wake up, cunt! Make me a cup of coffee!" Wozniak sneered.

The comforting fantasy faded. From head to toe, the injuries of the previous night blossomed to life. Licking at her lips, the splits in the soft tissue from his fevered kisses blazed with agony. Her breasts were two mounds of bruised meat and any adjustment in position caused her to wince as they shifted. By far the worst pain was between her legs. Both orifices had been brutally violated, and not just with his manhood. Objects littered the floor, still covered with blood and semen from when he needed to recharge his flagging libido.

"Get your ass moving or I'll use the wine bottle again!"

He sat down at the small table, lit a cigarette and nodded at the small barbecue stove and saucepan. Trying to roll over, Debbie had to stop midway. Her senses reeled at the countless aches and cramps in her abused body. Darkness danced at the edge of her vision until Wozniak fished a cup of water from the toilet bowl and tossed it over her. Unlike the first dousing, he had not used the fresh water in his bucket and the unmistakable stench of stale urine caught in her nostrils.

"Last warning or I'll leave you in pieces. Get your fat ass out of bed and make my fucking drink!" Wozniak screamed and it reverberated in the tiny cell.

Drawing on the deep well of hatred churning in her stomach, she managed to push some of the pain away and started to wrap herself in a bedsheet.

"Did I say you could cover yourself?"

"But I'm cold," she whined.

"Do you want me to warm you up? You took a lot out of me last night, but I'm sure I can manage a quickie before I go to work," he said, leering.

Shaking her head, she stood up on trembling legs.

"You think you're too fucking good for me? Is that it?" he demanded angrily, flicking the glowing cigarette at her. The hot tip hit her bare skin, sending sparks in all directions.

"No, I didn't mean it like that. I'm sorry," Debbie muttered, rubbing at the burn, "I'm just... tired."

"That's better," he growled, lighting a fresh smoke.

Checking the pan was filled with water, she turned the small brass valve and the ring started to hiss. With a flick of the lighter, Wozniak ignited the gas. Taking a mug, she tipped in a spoonful of instant blend and looked around for sugar or cream.

"I like my coffee like my women, black and bitter."

She ignored him and stared intently at the bottom of the stainless pan, watching the tiny bubbles rise as the heat started to spread.

"That was a joke. Why aren't you laughing?"

"Sorry," she repeated.

"You will be later, sweetheart," he growled. "I might even bring a few friends back to share you around. I wonder what surprises we can come up with in the workshop to fit inside that tight pussy."

Retching, Debbie doubled over and a stream of bile coated the grey floor. "Please, don't," she begged, swallowing hard to keep her gorge from rising again.

"But you loved it, I know you did," he grinned. "I'll think of something inventive, don't worry."

The water was seething, steam rising in the frozen cell. For a split second, she thought about launching the contents at Wozniak until he jumped to his feet, startling her.

"Here, let me," he said, knowingly. "Don't want you spilling any now, do we?"

Mixing the brew, the smell was delectable and, despite her awful predicament, she found herself yearning for a cup. Blowing at the boiling mug, he sipped at the contents, screwing his face up in ecstasy.

"This is probably the best cup of coffee I've ever had," he teased, sniffing at the rising aromas.

"Can I have some?" Debbie whispered.

"Fuck no! This is for important people like wing bosses and their crews." He scooped more water from the toilet bowl and placed it down in front of her.

"I'm not drinking that."

"After a couple of days without water, that cup of piss will look like nectar. Trust me."

"I'd rather die," she declared.

"Now we can't have my little plaything checking out early, can we? I'll just have to make you drink it. Now get on the bed."

She cowered away, whimpering. "Why?"

"Because I fucking said so!" He snarled and threw her onto the stained mattress.

Taking out a few short lengths of rope, he bound each of her arms and legs to a metal bedpost tightly enough to cut off circulation. Pulling at each binding, he nodded in satisfaction and covered her in the wet blankets. His prize would not be going anywhere.

"Get some rest. It's going to be a long night."

Raising his coffee in a toast, he winked and left the cell.

CHAPTER 11

Jason Rechtman was broken in all ways a man could be broken. His physical injuries barely had time to heal before one of the cruel overseers inflicted more punishment. Because of his value to the prison, Craig had banned the convicts from punching him, but they evaded the rule by slapping instead. A hefty palm with enough force left him bruised for weeks. These days his bare skin was more purple and black than the healthy colour he used to sport. In a matter of months, the once lustrous brown hair on his head had taken on a distinctive grey. Running his hands through the greasy strands, he felt the bare patches where it had started to fall out from the unrelenting stress. Sagging trousers spoke of his inability to eat properly and the skeletal figure which presented itself in the mirror every morning hardly seemed to be human.

Psychologically, he was in no better shape. Unable to sleep through the groans of the dead and the gibbering shrieks of the crazed inmates, he stared at the ceiling every night with only brief snatches of slumber when absolute exhaustion could no longer be denied. Any scream carried on the night ripped him from his bed as he tried to identify if it came from his family. He knew he was perilously close to losing his mind completely. Not even the promise of rescue from the stranger at the farm shop could hold back the dread. In the darker hours of the night he had even began to wonder if she was real at all or merely an apparition conjured by his fractured mind; like a lush oasis beckoning to people trapped in the baking desert.

"We've made thirty feet, Mr Rechtman," said Jacques, breaking into his introspection.

Looking at his watch, they had only just made the target and he had been generous with the time allowance. The rate his workforce was perishing in the gauntlet and on ill-conceived raiding missions would soon mean he was unable to fulfil his obligations. This would mean more beatings and unspeakable treatment aimed at his wife and daughter.

"Good work," was all he could muster through the anxiety and the man left with a nod.

The schematic drawings on the table fluttered in the cold breeze. Nothing registered of his calculations or the carefully planned directions and distances. Everything blurred together and he slumped into the chair, sobbing. If the lives of his family were not in the balance he would have gladly buried himself alive in one of the tunnels. Better still would have been if he could get Craig and a few of his henchmen down there at the same time. Oh, what a joy it would be to see their faces as the soil began to crush the life out of their black hearts. The fear of what may fill the power vacuum and what that would mean to the decent folk trapped inside the walls was another concern which prevented the alluring self-sacrifice being carried out.

Composing himself, he sipped sparingly at a cup of freezing cold coffee. The cruel embrace of winter was always eager to steal the heat from the abandoned mug as well as the unfortunate souls caught in the grounds of the prison. When had he even got the brew? He wondered. In his fragile mental state, short periods of time were often found completely missing from his memory. He could be stood by a section of tunnel one minute and the next he would be counting the materials left from Hombre's railyard run. Whether he had fallen asleep on his feet he could not say and no one ever mentioned it to him. So far, the mental blanks had not stopped him carrying out the tunnelling projects, but it could only be a matter of time before something went disastrously wrong on their account.

"How's the progress?" came a gravelly, Scottish voice to his rear.

"Slow."

"The boss won't be happy to hear that," Matt said, stepping into view.

"Well what does he expect? We're losing between five and ten prisoners a week, sometimes more. At this rate, he'll need to make the tougher convicts help as well," Jason muttered. He knew the Scotsman to be a reasonable man who understood the difficulties on running engineering projects without proper equipment or trained personnel.

"The boss won't be happy to hear that either, nor will the guys. You may find yourself even more of a target."

"I can't succeed. It's an impossible task," Jason sighed and stared into the cup. The black liquid swirled as he rotated the coffee and with a yell of defeat he threw it across the yard.

Matt stepped in close, grabbed him by the collar and hefted him to his feet. "If you don't keep to the schedule, I'll throw you in the fucking gauntlet myself! Do you understand?" he screamed, making sure everyone heard the exchange, then quietly whispered. "Clarissa's safe. She's staying with me now. Keeping's as dead as the fucks at the walls, so your wife won't be getting hurt anymore."

"You did this?" He gasped at news of the death.

Matt slapped him with a massive, open hand, pulling the blow at the last second. "I don't want your excuses! Get the tunnel finished or Craig will peel you!" He yelled as Jason's head rocked, then leaned in close to his ear, "Not a word to anyone. You're the only reason we're surviving in here and I want to keep it that way. I can't keep your wife off the list, but I hope that knowing your baby's safe will make it easier to bear. In time, things will change, I promise."

For a final display of faux aggression, Matt threw him to the floor and the watching inmates cheered. Without saying another word, he walked away and left the engineer on the cold, hard ground. Attempting to stand, Jason had to grasp at the metal table for support. His legs, already weak from malnourishment, were made to feel like jelly at the revelation his daughter was now out of immediate danger. To any observer on the watchtowers, it would look like he was bawling at the dressing down and physical abuse. In truth, for the first time in months, he felt a spark of hope in the bleak nether world that constituted his life.

CHAPTER 12

ow's the face?"

Mike gingerly pressed at the bandage holding his nose and shrugged. "It's getting there. The painkillers help."

"At least you've learned to think before you speak now. If it had been someone else I may have had to kill them, but I know Matt will leave it at the warning."

"I guess he didn't like being called out on it?" Mike muttered.

"Careful, little brother. These walls have ears and things can get back to people very quickly."

Mike stomped over to the governor's window and peered out, angry but powerless to act in any way. "So, on the one hand you peel and make the nonces run the gauntlet, and on the other you allow one of your lieutenants to keep a child in their room?"

Craig broke out in a wide grin. "Matt's as much a kiddie fiddler as you or me. He's trying to be clever and protect the girl and I'm happy to let him. As long as the others are still terrified of him, who gives a fuck what they think?"

"How can you be so sure?"

"Because every time he gets me alone, he pushes me to increase the age of those on the Rape Night roster, or abolish it altogether."

"Oh, I see. But you won't get rid of it, will you?"

"I can't. These men have nothing to occupy themselves, and without an outlet would butcher each other in under a month. You should've seen the uproar when we had to ration the tobacco."

"So, what does the future hold? Have you given any thought to long term planning?"

"The main priority was to survive the winter. Our food supply will last a few more weeks but we'll need to push out into Wick and Littlehampton soon and that's going to be dangerous. I was hoping Rechtman would have us closer to a solution but all he keeps whining about is that he can't tunnel under the river without the right equipment."

Mike frowned. "It seems logical. I'm fucked if I would want to walk through it and get drowned if the thing caved in."

"Yeah, I know. It doesn't stop it being frustrating as hell though," Craig grumbled.

"Why not just go over the bridge to the south? Remember the one we used to drive over to get into Brighton if we were doing a coastal pub crawl?"

"There's only one problem with that," Craig said slowly, "There are about sixty million festering corpses who want to eat us the second we set foot outside the walls."

"So? Am I really both the brains and the beauty in this family?"

"Not with your face all mashed up like that," Craig teased.

"Even with this crooked nose and two black eyes I'm prettier than you, brother."

"Ok, enough flirting. What do you have in mind?"

"You can't tunnel under the river, but what's to stop you tunnelling right up to the bridge itself?"

"Nothing. But again, I remind you of the sixty million mobile corpses who want to bite our nuts off."

84

"Forget them," Mike spat, "What is it you said about them losing interest?"

"The ones near the walls who follow us to the tunnels always end up coming back after a while, but I don't see how that will help when we are trying to bring back food and goods."

"Can I assume that somewhere in this prison you have a few guys who are handy with a trowel?"

"You mean builders?"

Mike nodded.

"Of course."

"And you have a structural engineer available twenty-four-seven?"

"You're killing me here. What's your point?"

"Secure the bridge completely on both sides; it's only two lane blacktop."

"And how do you suggest we do that while under attack?" Craig posed.

A knock at the door interrupted the discussion and both Hombre and Matt entered the office. The Scotsman eyed Mike warily and Craig ordered them both to apologise and get over it. An uneasy handshake was exchanged alongside a few mumbled words and the meeting continued after Mike briefly explained his idea. The two right hand men were even less enthused than their boss.

"Now listen! We need to get the engineer to pop up right in the middle of the road on our side as the bridge begins. There's a certain amount of tree cover on the approach road which will give us some concealment. Hell, you could probably fell some of them and make a semi decent obstacle to buy us more time. Then, when the coast is clear, we pop up and get the builders to lay as much in the way of fortification as possible before we're forced back into the tunnel by the zombies. We rig some kind of alarm system back at the prison and use it to lure them back to the walls. Rinse and repeat."

"It could bring even more in if we start ringing the dinner bell," said Hombre.

"These walls could hold a hundred thousand at bay, probably more," Matt replied.

"Exactly! From what Hombre tells me, the rail depot has enough material to cocoon both sides of the bridge and as soon as it's sealed off you can just start digging another tunnel on the eastern road. I'd say allowing for a half moon shaped wall for extra strength, you'd need about fifty to sixty feet of concrete blockwork. We can use sections of steel rail to reinforce it as well if we can find some acetylene torches to cut and weld it."

Hombre held up a cautionary finger. "There's one problem. How the fuck do we get the stuff from the rail yard back here? The last effort was a disaster and I'm still gutted about the pineapple chunks."

"Pineapple?" Mike asked and Craig waved the question away unanswered.

"Why go over land?"

They all turned and stared at Matt who had begun to see the merits in the plan. Beckoning them to join him at the window he pointed to the River Arun flowing merrily by.

"You want to take a swim with concrete blocks and shit loads of building supplies?" Craig teased light heartedly.

"No. Boats."

"I'm afraid to say we're all out."

"Then let me take some men and we go south towards the coast until we find some."

"You think you can sail between the depot and the bridge?"

"No. It'll need to be motorboats and I'll need your help," Matt said, gesturing to Hombre.

"I've never been on a boat in my life, you know that. I navigate the open roads to pillage and plunder."

"Ok, Blackbeard," Craig chuckled.

"I don't want to drown you. I need you to bring a petrol tanker back for us to refuel."

"Well why didn't you say so? I'll just pop across the road and get one while you collect your armada of rubber dinghies."

"Stop being a pussy. We're bound to find one if we send out scouting parties."

"Fuck it, why not. If you're crazy enough to risk your ass loading and unloading boats, the least I can do is keep the tanks topped up."

"Good man," Craig exclaimed.

"We need to get a full requisition list from Rechtman for the tunnel first. It's only a short run from the rear gates of the prison where you parked that truck to the edge of the riverbank. We'll need to kill the few hundred who were waiting and at the same time keep the largest group occupied at the front walls."

"They didn't behave too well the last time we tried it," Hombre warned.

"It's a bit different," Mike explained, remembering the hospital, "They don't herd well in great numbers as they just get bored and filter back to whatever had their attention. As long as we keep a low profile while we move the goods inside and the guards stay visible, they should be quite content to stay where they are."

"Plus, we can make plenty of noise to mask the sounds of the engines," Craig added.

"What if I can't find a tanker?"

"Then we start siphoning every car in the district," Craig shrugged.

"You always did like sucking on the hose, brother," Mike teased, but Matt and Hombre just glowered.

"Give him a fucking break, you two! It was a joke!" Craig snapped.

A polite rap on the door broke the simmering tension and one of the guards peeked inside. "Boss, Pesci's back."

"Good, let him in."

Walking through the door, the men wrinkled their nose at his stench.

"Fuck me, Pesci. Have you not washed yet?" Hombre hissed, covering his nose.

The man narrowed his eyes in confusion. "Why would I? Craig told me to come straight back with my report."

"And?" He leaned across the desk, yearning for the good news.

"They're all there."

A dreadful grin spread across Craig's face as he looked at each man in turn. "It appears I need to find a worse punishment than peeling for our friends in the castle. Pesci, get yourself washed, fed, and rested, I've got another task for you."

CHAPTER 13

"Stephen, thanks for joining us. Come and sit down," Kurt said. A fire crackled in the hearth of the small room, casting dancing shadows across the faces of the waiting group. On the large desk were differing ages of castle layouts charting the various adaptations and changes that had occurred over the past millennium since its original construction. Alina had made notes on a jotter detailing her own knowledge of the hidden nooks and crannies of the ancient fortress, but they were rudimentary at best. They all knew the greatest fount of information was locked away inside the curator's mind.

"Will you be ok?" Patricia asked from the doorway.

"Yes, thank you."

"I'll go and get a coffee while you chat. Back soon, sweetie."

She closed the door, sealing them in the warmth and Kurt offered Stephen a chair.

"I really don't need to be chaperoned at all times you know?"

"It's just a precaution until I'm satisfied you're really with us. I think you'll agree it's a small price to pay for being allowed to stay?" Kurt said, gauging his expression for any tells.

"Fine."

"Good. Now, Alina has been kind enough to show us a couple of the secrets of the castle including the sally port which drops down from the north-eastern wall. We can use that to get out and plot a safe route to the supermarket if the need arises. What I need to know from you is simple. Are there any other tunnels or tricks which we can use to our advantage?"

"What if I told you there weren't any more secret passageways?"

Kurt narrowed his eyes, "Then I'd be a little upset, because we both know that would be a lie."

"How would you know it was a lie? Are you part of the original construction or architectural team? My goodness, you've aged well."

Kurt ground his teeth and thought of DB's offer to extract the information, by force if necessary. It was the last thing he wanted to countenance, but if the obstinate man left him with no alternatives then pain would be their only option. Trying a different approach, he softened. "Stephen, I know we'll never see eye to eye, but my only concern is keeping everyone inside this castle safe, including yourself. You love this place, that much is obvious, and I can't blame you. I'm sorry that you see us as uninvited interlopers, but I want to protect this magnificent structure too. I want to keep it for the living, not as a shelter for the abominations outside to infest."

"The way you people treat this place it's like an infestation anyway."

"Explain," demanded Kurt with a scowl.

"The place is filthy. I've seen people urinating in the hallways. Litter is left where it's dropped and plates of half eaten food have been left to rot."

Kurt had to reluctantly agree with the way certain individuals were not pulling their weight and it must have been distressing for Stephen to see his life's work abused in such a way. "That'll change, you have my word. I'll organise a cleaning team who'll keep this place immaculate, just like it was before. And there certainly won't be any more instances of people doing their business in anything other than a toilet. How does that sound?"

"It sounds like a tall order when you can't even get everyone to work together to defend the castle. I find it hard to believe that Jasmine and her merry band of slobs would be willing to follow your orders and clean up after themselves."

"Perhaps," Kurt admitted. "I think I may need to be a bit more... persuasive, where they're concerned. Surely, it's worth a shot, though?"

"I think you put too much faith in your fellow human beings. From what I've seen, they will just ignore you and carry on regardless."

"That's my problem. Can we at least give it a try? I really do need your expertise if we're going to secure enough supplies to see us through until spring."

"If I help you, will you call off your watchdog?"

"Be careful with the insults, Stephen. Patricia helping us secure the castle is one of the reasons you may not be starving to death."

Ignoring the jibe, Stephen raised an eyebrow. It was clear this was to be his price for cooperation.

"Ok, I'll let you go about your business unhindered. Do we have a deal?"

"We do. Apart from the usual defensive additions which were designed for human sieges, not undead ones, there are three secret tunnels which may prove useful. I have no idea if any of them are still in one piece, but I can show you where they are if you'd wish?"

"I'd very much appreciate that," Kurt replied.

Stephen stood up and dusted imaginary fluff from his clothes, "Let's be to it then, I don't have all day."

Alina glanced at Kurt and neither could contain the buzz of excitement they felt at the coming revelations. As the trio left the small study, Patricia returned and started to follow.

"Change of plans. Stephen's helping us and for that he wants to be left in peace," Kurt whispered.

"Is that a good idea?"

"Not really," he admitted. "Go and relax for a while. We'll be with him the whole time anyway."

"Ok, sweetheart," she replied and headed back to the main hall.

Stephen was marching away like a drill sergeant, hands clasped firmly behind his back. "The first is in the crypts."

"Really? We didn't see anything."

"It wouldn't be a very good secret tunnel if you did, would it?"

"Touché."

"You may need your dark-skinned friend to help us," Stephen explained.

"Would you like me to fetch him?" Alina offered.

"Yes please, love. Thanks," Kurt replied, then turned to Stephen, "His name is DB. I don't think he would appreciate being called the 'dark skinned friend'."

"Duly noted."

Five minutes later, they had exposed the steps, descended into the tomb, and were all stood around the deepest sarcophagus.

"This is going to be difficult. I shouldn't imagine it has moved for centuries."

Stephen and Kurt took the head of the stone lid and DB clasped the foot. With a rocking motion and much grunting, they broke the seal free and lifted it up a few inches. Twisting the massive slab, they laid it sideways on the top of the tomb. Peeking inside, they could see a set of steps leading down into darkness.

"If this passageway is still intact, it will take you to the accompanying crypt within the Priory of Saint Nicholas

Arundel where great religious leaders have been laid to rest."

"That's really close to the cathedral! It would make a rescue so much safer," Alina said.

"We'll take a look later. Until then we need to make sure nothing comes crawling out of this thing," Kurt replied and they muscled the stone back into place.

"The second is in the Earl's bedroom, or what we would call the master bedroom today," Stephen explained and led them through the maze of hallways and up flights of stairs.

As they took in the opulence of the room, it dawned on Kurt how implausible a tunnel could be on the second floor of the building. Alina was expressing similar confusion as she stared around the windowed bedroom.

Stephen chuckled at their confusion. "I see you doubt me. All shall be revealed, I promise."

Curling a finger to follow, he led them over to the fireplace. Long dead ashes had crumbled on the hearth and the fire blackened stone revealed no clue as to what the curator was so fascinated with. Dropping to his knees, he pointed up the wide chimney. Kurt leaned in and looked upwards but could only see the faint daylight weakly illuminating the first bend which penetrated the top of the stack.

"I don't follow."

"Look in the stonework as it rises," Stephen said mysteriously.

Shining the torch in a rising circular motion, he could only see the poor construction. "I see missing stones. I'd call the builders back and give them a bollocking."

Alina leaned past, looked up and whispered, "They're patterned like toe holds,"

"Exactly, my dear!" Stephen clapped his hands. "Kurt, have a climb and tell me what you see."

"What?"

"Trust me."

Snorting his frustration at the outlandish request, Kurt pulled the fire grate out, scattering the grey debris all over the floor. Standing in the fireplace, he was surprised at how large it was. The opening itself would easily accommodate even his broad shoulders all the way to the roof. Finding the first nook, he placed a foot inside the gap and used a higher depression to pull himself upwards. After three metres or so he reached the angle in the chimney and the mystery was revealed. Partway up the stone, but safely out of sight of anyone who may peer upwards, was a large hole. Holding a hand over it, he could feel the supplementary draught of another opening. Carefully scooting himself up the incline, he used the torch to peer inside. The vertical bolthole was about two metres deep instead of the full height of the building and from that point, steps wound downwards in a spiral.

"Well, bugger me," he muttered.

"Impressive, isn't it?" Stephen called from below, delight evident in his voice. It was obvious he adored everything about the castle and in some ways, it transformed him from the brooding, whining, pain in the arse.

"Very."

Backing out and climbing down, Kurt was covered in soot and cobwebs. Alina giggled at him as he wiped sweat away and left a massive streak of grime across his face.

"Mind if I take a peek?"

"Be my guest," Kurt said, handing the torch over.

As the two men waited patiently, thin streamers of black dust fell into the hearth from her movements. An audible gasp could be heard and Kurt smiled, knowing exactly how she was feeling.

"It was designed to be a means of escape for anyone important," Stephen explained. "If the castle was breached, they would climb and retreat through the bolthole while a servant lit a fire. To any observer it would look like the person had fled and hidden somewhere else within the castle. By the time the fire died and if anyone even found it, they would be far away from danger."

"And where does this lead?"

"About a quarter mile across the fields to the south east. Because most attacks would be launched from the west due to the even terrain, it was felt to be the easiest place to evade capture."

"Genius."

"Indeed, they were," he replied.

Alina ducked under the mantel and she too was streaked with grime.

"The third one is the most fascinating, and also the most dangerous."

"Lead on," Kurt declared, grabbing a small hand towel from the adjoining bathroom to dab at his face.

Their final destination led them up the steeply climbing steps of the central watchtower. The well was located in the circular sentinel which provided the last line of defence in times of attack. Some of the protective bars, which were designed to keep the public from falling in, had been removed to allow the buckets unfettered access to the water below.

"How deep is it?" Kurt asked.

"One hundred and thirty feet to the water table," Stephen replied.

"So why are we here?" Alina looked around at the solid walls surrounding the well housing. Nothing lay on the other side except long drops to the ground below, that much she knew.

"The last tunnel is down there," Stephen whispered, pointing down the stone lined shaft.

"You're shitting me," Kurt gawped.

"Not at all. Take the torch and move as far to the left as possible, then aim the beam down directly below me, about sixty feet or so."

Kurt complied and, sure enough, the dark arch was right where he said it would be. "How the hell is anyone supposed to climb down there?"

"You don't climb, you're lowered."

Kurt was rocked by a sense of vertigo and he had to look away from the sheer drop. Alina asked for the torch and took up position where he had been standing.

"You wouldn't ever get me down there," she muttered and Kurt could only agree with the sentiment.

"You must understand that this was a last resort. If the defenders were beaten back, they would have water and provisions in this tower. A young scout would be tasked with breaking through the enemy lines and securing reinforcements. This tunnel would give him the best chance."

"And where does this one come out?"

"Due north, right by Swanbourne Lake which is the source of this water."

"What's to stop the enemy from just walking inside and poisoning the well?" Alina wondered.

"That's where it gets interesting. The poor lad would need nerves of steel as the outlet is submerged in the lake itself. He would need to swim underwater in the pitch darkness for about twenty feet before hitting the surface of the lake. Even in the event of capture, the chances of him being able to pinpoint where he had emerged from in the middle of the night would be next to zero."

"Ingenious. But I think we'll ignore this one for now," Kurt said, stomach still woozy from the view.

"That's probably for the best," Stephen agreed.

CHAPTER 14

"Hawkeye, this is Early Bird, are you receiving? Over."

"Hawkeye receiving. It's good to hear your voice, Sarge. Over," Morrow replied.

"Can you perform a sweep of the holiday park? Looking for an infiltration point with minimal resistance. Over."

"On it. Drone is five minutes out. Over."

Replacing the radio, Holbeck turned to the sisters. "Are you going to be ok for a while?"

"You do what you need to. We'll clear up as much of this mess as possible so the folks aren't treading in zombie guts when you bring them back."

"You're both remarkable," Holbeck said with a grin.

"Don't you forget it! How long do you think it will take?" Max asked.

"All strategic planning goes out of the window with the undead, you can't account for their behaviour like you can with human enemies. If we can do a smash and grab, then about four to six hours. It'll be a squeeze trying to get everyone back in one journey, but we're not going to be able to do multiple runs with the dead on our asses. We wouldn't have survived this encounter if it wasn't for the pair of you and I'm not getting bogged down again."

"Understood."

"If we can use the gas it's going to make a hell of a racket," Eldridge explained. "Please keep your eyes peeled for any dead the noise may draw your way until we get back with the big guns."

"We will," Angela said, hugging the young woman.

Climbing into the APC's, the soldiers waved at the farmers and their faithful hounds. Trundling away, they pulled up and sat idling at the eastern fringe of the farm. Holbeck watched the tiny dot in the sky as the Watchkeeper performed its reconnaissance run.

"Early Bird, this is Hawkeye. Are you receiving? Over."

"Go for Hawkeye. Over."

"You're in the clear all along the western edge of the park. The largest body of zombies are surrounding the main complex on all sides and there are only small pockets of them interspersed elsewhere. Groups ranging from two to six will be your biggest threat until you engage the main force. Over."

"Thanks for the sitrep. Over and out."

"What's the plan then, Sarge?" Eldridge called out over the grumbling engines.

"I think we're going to try and lay a trap if we can keep our heads down long enough. The caravans weigh several tonnes each, so if we can drag them into a circular formation it could be a good way of penning them in like cattle."

"How big are they?" Eldridge asked.

"About twenty-five feet long. With about ten side by side, I think we could herd most of the undead and then use the opportunity to get the survivors clear."

"And then we could always rig the gas cylinders to explode when they are caught inside," Harkiss replied.

"You really want to blow shit up, don't you?" Carpenter shouted from the driver's seat.

"I want to set the world on fire, baby!" he replied, banging on the cab roof.

"If we can ensure that it won't impact our own safety, or that of the civvies, then we can jerry rig something," Holbeck agreed and Harkiss punched the air.

"Let's roll out. Slow and steady, drivers. I want to come in on the north-western tip of the park."

Carpenter and Petermann gave a thumb's up and slowly accelerated towards the partly frozen morass. The tracks crunched through the crust and the vehicles were on their way, churning the boggy ground in their path. In the distance, hundreds of aluminium clad, static holiday homes came into view. The engines eased back to minimise the announcement of their arrival to anything nearby that may be listening.

Holbeck pointed to three small bungalows which were at the furthest northern edge of the grounds. Judging by the uniforms that hung from the washing lines, it was accommodation for some of the staff to use. Red shirts emblazoned with the parks logo swayed gently, while others had broken free of their pegs and were caught in bushes or partly submerged in dank puddles. Coming to a stop, fifty feet away they could see all three front doors were hanging off their hinges. The soldiers exited the Warthogs and gathered round.

"We're going to clear the buildings, but only use the axes or machetes the ladies gave us. Any gunfire will give away our position and the whole plan is shot, do you understand?"

"Yes, Sarge," they all replied.

"Langham and Petermann, bungalow one. Eldridge and Dougal, two. Carpenter and I will clear three. Harkiss, you're our eyes."

The silence was eerie. A place of vibrancy and youthful exuberance now lay as quiet as the proverbial grave. In place of the shrill laughter of children at play was the flutter of fabric which would never be worn again, and the distant groans of the massed dead.

It could have been assumed that any lingering zombies would have already left for the chance of a feast to the south, but assumptions were long past. They all knew the unpredictability of their foe and acted accordingly. Eldridge placed her back to the bare concrete render to the left of the shattered door and listened. When she gave the all clear signal, Dougal risked a glance through the large bay window. The morning light gave a clear view of the lounge and apart from the furniture and television, nothing lurked inside. Stepping carefully over the twisted door, the carpet squelched underfoot from the rain which had blown in through the opening. They both paused in the narrow hallway, listening more intently now the outside world had been largely shut off. Nothing.

Apart from the musty odour of mould and mildew, the scents of the dead were absent and they cautiously moved deeper. The internal doors had fared no better as whoever had taken shelter tried to keep the dead at bay. The weak, hollow shelled construction had disintegrated under the onslaught and, mixed with the fragments of cardboard and wood, were dried patches of brown and black.

Dougal shook his head in commiseration and the look on his face said; *poor fuckers.*

The second and third doors led to the sleeping areas and each room had three bunk beds. Mattresses had been shoved against the brittle doors in a futile attempt to keep the ravenous mouths away and these also bore the same dried arterial spray.

"Dear God," Eldridge whispered, pointing at the awful scene in one of the bunks.

A bloody human outline lay on the bottom mattress of the furthest bed, like a snow angel painted in red. Whether they had been fast asleep, or more likely had just tried to cover themselves like an infant hiding from monsters, the soldiers could only guess. It had been fruitless and whoever they were, they now undoubtedly walked among the damned.

The tiny bathroom was clean, but the kitchen was in a terrible state, though not from the attack. It was typical of any accommodation for youngsters or students across the world. Half eaten food, cigarette ends scattered around indiscriminately and a sink full to the brim of dirty dishes and saucepans. The balancing act of crockery and stainless steel was impressive.

"I'll wash, you dry?" Dougal whispered, trying to lighten the mood.

Shaking her head, she peeked out through the back door. The rear yard was full of more detritus; beer cans and broken bottles, even a toppled glass bong. Leaning over the fence, the vast fields stretching towards Chichester were empty which at least meant they could focus their vigilance on the immediate surroundings while they prepared.

"All clear," Dougal said after checking both sides of the small building.

"Let's get to it then."

They joined the others who all had the same story to tell. Evidence of a struggle, blood, and death. Putting the sadness to the back of their minds, the living beings a quarter of a mile away were the only priority.

"Those caravans form a small cul-de-sac." Holbeck pointed to the nearest collection of static homes fanning out like spokes on a wheel from a small, circular road with a patch of grass in the centre. "It makes sense to do our work as far away from the horde as possible."

"Can we move them by hand?" Harkiss asked.

"Possibly, but I don't want to risk any injuries. I'm glad the owners were greedy, because the small size of each pitch means we can use the Hogs to twist them ninety degrees and then butt them up against one another. It will be like circling the wagons back in the Wild West, except we will be the Injuns!"

Harkiss put his hand to his mouth and was about to whoop until Holbeck glared at him.

"Petermann, you see that building?"

"Yes, Sarge."

"It's one of the communal shower blocks for the tent campers. Get your ass up on the roof on lookout. Keep low and if you see anything coming, wave. One of us will be watching at all times."

"You got it," he replied and jogged away.

"That'll give him a full view of the area, so make sure to keep him in your sightlines. I want the rest of us to pair up and collect as many gas cylinders as possible. Don't get creative, turn the valve clockwise until it stops and cut the rubber hose with your bayonets, then bring them back here."

Splitting up, they all moved in different directions. Casting glances under the trailers ensured they wouldn't be taken by surprise by any lurking creature hiding in the shadows beneath. The propane tanks were held in place by a chain clipped to the caravans. After removing the links, they isolated the gas and severed the tube before running back with the prize.

Petermann was staying low on the roof, scanning the park but showing no signs of alarm. After ten minutes, they had requisitioned thirty of the large red vessels and placed them in the centre of the road for dispersal once the moving had been carried out.

"This is where it gets hairy," Holbeck explained, "We want to twist them on their central axle so they form an impassable barrier. I need you to keep the revs to a minimum and take it slow. We try it with one and see what reception we get."

Carpenter nodded, face set.

"I'll get the chain," Dougal offered, hurrying off and reaching into the back of the APC.

Carpenter fired up the Warthog and quietly manoeuvred it into position facing away from the caravan's towing hook. Fixing the chain in place, Dougal tapped on the side of the vehicle and her face stared back in concentration from the side mirror. Holbeck made a flat palm and waved it back and forth, indicating she should pull forward. A slight upsurge in the engine pulled the chain taut and the troops used their own strength as a counterweight on the back of the trailer to help it pivot. A dull grinding issued from the concrete levelling blocks as they were dragged out of position, the stacks falling with dull thuds. Holbeck winced at each sound and studied Petermann for any chance in body language.

"It's lining up perfectly," Eldridge said as it settled into position.

The troops quickly picked up the fallen bricks and placed them beneath the unsupported end of the trailer to stop it tipping. They all stared at Petermann and he must have felt their boring gaze as he turned to give them the all clear. Eleven more homes were rotated into place with only minimal movement required to shore up any gaps between them. The three-hundred-foot circumference sphere was complete, with a twenty-foot-wide opening left where the road entered the dead end. If they could draw the zombies in and trigger an explosion, the extraction of the survivors would be a much simpler affair.

Petermann was totally relaxed and had even risen to his feet, hands on hips. They all looked at each other with a sense of relief. After the disaster of the previous day, the soldiers had all felt a deep foreboding for the mission and fully expected further setbacks and pain. The fact that they had so far gone about their business unmolested was, hopefully, a sign of a change in fortunes.

"At least two gas cylinders per caravan, valves facing into the centre!" Holbeck ordered.

"How do we detonate, Sarge?" Harkiss grunted, hefting two into position.

"It won't be like you see in the movies, they're protected by flashback arresters even if they catch fire. Once we've ignited the hoses, we unload the HMGs through the walls and hope to penetrate the outer casing. Then we may see some fireworks. If not, then at least they'll fry."

"Sorry to be a dumb arse, Sarge. But how are we going to light the things? I'll be fucked if I'm going to stand there with a lighter."

"Stop your bellyaching, I'll tell you in a minute," Holbeck growled. Waving to get Petermann's attention, he waited for the sentry to return before explaining the plan. "We will have one shot at this and I don't want any fuck ups. Carpenter, you'll stay with the vehicles and keep watch. I don't want anything waiting to surprise us as we fall back. The rest of us will move between cover until we reach the entertainment complex. Once we make our move, we unload everything we have at them and try and draw as many back into the trap as possible. The layout of the grounds will funnel them towards us, we just need to hold our nerve and stay as close as possible until we reach safety."

"What about the gas, Sarge?" Harkiss piped up.

"Will you shut up about the fucking gas!" Holbeck shook his head. "I was just about to get to that part."

The soldier ignored the rebuke and started to bounce like an excited child in anticipation.

"When we arrive back here, everyone spreads out and opens each valve fully. Carpenter will lay out a box of flares in preparation. Once we're sure they've taken the bait, we duck under the trailers and start lobbing them over the top. Some will ignite, some won't, but as soon as the fifty-cals start chewing through the canisters we should see some explosions. As soon as they've blown, we circle down the western ridge of the marshland parallel with the park and clear a path for the survivors to bolt. I don't care if they have to cling onto the roof and side armour to start with, as long as we get clear."

"They may not have a choice if there're too many to fit in the transport cabs," Carpenter agreed.

"Ideally, we need to make contact with the survivors in the building first. I'm amazed that we've not been attacked yet and that gives us an opportunity to prepare them for what's coming. They can gather whatever they need and be ready to abandon the building at a second's notice instead of wondering what the fuck's been going on with all the gunfire and explosions. I wouldn't blame them if they're all cowering inside, terrified."

"How do you suggest we get past the rotters, Sarge?" Harkiss asked.

"I was going to say you should run naked along the beach to distract them while one of us snuck inside, but there's not enough down there for a meal," Eldridge teased.

Ignoring the banter, Holbeck continued. "We're going in blind from here on out. If we can approach and find a way to get inside the building safely, then good. If not, then we just execute the plan and bundle them out with whatever they have on their backs. If Morrow is correct, there are four thousand of the things, so it may be an impossible task anyway."

"What if one of us makes it inside but then can't get back out to help spring the trap?" Langham asked.

"Personally, I think keeping the civvies calm and ready is just as valuable to the mission as an extra gun," Holbeck replied and they all agreed. Humans by nature could be erratic creatures. Factor in hunger, exhaustion and the thought of being eaten alive and it was a recipe for disaster.

"Ok, magazine check."

After one final count of the ammunition levels and equipment, the soldiers were ready.

"Carpenter, get the flares laid out and get to safety. Use the bayonet or machete if any zombies turn up before we get back. Move out!"

Following closely behind their commander, they stayed tight to the concealing trailers. Coming upon the brick built shower block, Holbeck ordered Petermann to hop up and perform one last scout of the surrounding area. Lacing fingers together to make a toehold, Harkiss hoisted him up towards the roof with a grunt. After a few seconds, he carefully lowered himself back down.

"Nothing in the vicinity. I think I saw movement a few roads over, closer to the complex."

With a nod, they all moved off again, blades at the ready. Moving past row after row of bland trailers, they all noticed the signs of vacations which had ended in horror. Discarded bicycles, brightly coloured balls and frisbees, buckets and spades which would never excavate the sandy beach to make vast yellow castles. Fresh hatred swelled in their hearts at the abominations which had ravaged humanity to the brink of extinction.

Holbeck held up a hand and they hugged the wall. Pointing a thumb at the floor, he indicated the enemy was near. Eldridge crouched down and could see the tattered legs of the cadavers milling around between the next caravans. Holding up four fingers, the soldiers nodded. She picked up a small rock, looking to her superior for permission before throwing it. The sergeant nodded and with a careful aim, she tossed it over the roof and it fell to the ground with a soft thud in front of the group. Ducking once more, the undead turned to see what had caused the disturbance.

Chopping his hand down to signal the attack, the troops moved silently from concealment. Without compunction, they butchered the distracted zombies, spilling the brains on the overgrown grass. Wiping the weapons clean, they waited to see if the brief violence had summoned any more monsters. Nothing moved.

Spreading his fingers, Holbeck waved his arm to signal the team to move up. The faintly audible din of the dead had grown to a dull roar and it became apparent why their relocation project had been unharmed. Glancing under the last trailer standing in their way, it was obvious there was no way through the siege on foot. At least five deep as far as the eye could see, no one felt the need to skirt the building to check the other side. The survivors were surrounded, just as Morrow had informed them.

"I think I can get in," Dougal whispered.

"Where?" Eldridge asked with disbelief.

"Up there," he replied, blanching as he pointed to the overhead pylon and the large cable snaking towards the roof of the building.

"I didn't think you liked heights."

"I don't, but it's no different to the ropes above the training grounds. I managed to get along those just fine."

Holbeck gave it some thought and decided it was worth a shot. "Do it!"

"Shit, Sarge. I was hoping you'd talk me out of it."

***

Dougal tossed the duvet they had collected over the barbed wire and started to climb the chain link. The thick blanket shielded his hands as he hoisted himself over the top of the secure area.

"Shit. Shit. Shit," he muttered.

Looking up, the true scale of what he had volunteered for became clear.

"At least if you lose your grip it'll be the fall that kills you," he sighed to himself. Holding the access ladder so firmly his fingers ached, he took a deep breath and started to climb. The ocean breeze tugged at his clothes, bringing back memories of days spent sea fishing with his army buddies. The excursions often ended with more beer cans laying in the bottom of the boat than fish, but it was always good fun. It *had been* good fun, he corrected himself.

Reaching the maintenance platform, the transformers had ceased to hum with electricity at the same time the power stations went offline. Absurdly, he reached out and gingerly tapped at the insulated cable. Movement caught his eye and Eldridge was holding her arms wide in a *what the fuck are you doing* gesture. Harkiss had made a tube with his hand and was doing a good impression of shaking a cocktail. Dougal replied eloquently with a middle finger.

Aided by the angle of descent, it was possible he could have ziplined down the cable. Unlike the movies, however, a cloth strap or piece of clothing would swiftly disintegrate from the friction and send him plummeting to the earth. Given the opportunity, he would prefer to pop his clogs with his future family gathered round. His five sons and daughters, eighteen grandchildren, and sobbing quietly in the corner, his glamour model trophy wife who had vowed never to remarry or look at another man. Maybe women, though.

Heart jackhammering, he got a tight grip on the PVC conductor and swung both legs up. Hooking his feet over, he interlocked his boots and closed his eyes. Each breath was a ragged gasp and if he was unable to slow it down, he would pass out before navigating half the distance.

"These people are counting on you," he whispered, growing angry with his foolish anxiety.

Craning his neck, he stared at an extractor vent on the roof and forced out all other thought. Pushing away, he slid his legs along and over the void. Without the steel platform beneath, he imagined that gravity was a physical being, tugging on his uniform to dislodge him from the precarious high wire act.

"Stop it," he growled through clenched teeth.

Focusing on the grey vent, he continued shimmying along inch by inch and, with each second he lived, his confidence grew. After eighty feet, the cold had penetrated through the gloves and his legs were starting to cramp from the awkward position. The zombie army had started to converge below, straining to reach the dangling morsel. Laughing with joy, his view changed from rotting oblivion to the flat, gravel covered roof. Dropping from the wire, he hugged the stones to himself, cackling manically.

The layout of the complex had been explained in the briefing; it formed a large T with the three branches housing a different recreational activity. Dougal was currently on the roof of the auditorium, where shows and bands had been laid on nightly. To the south were the leisure pool, amusement arcades, and the variety of restaurants which serviced the huge camp. Standing at the edge of the roof, he called out, "Hang tight. I'm going to try and make contact." He expected no response and received none, except for the animated moans of the dead.

The stone lined roof of the stage had no skylights so he moved across to the swimming pool. The water had taken on a brown hue with algae blooms floating on the surface. From the raised lifeguard tower, to the bright green water flume, nothing moved. Figuring the most likely place would be near the source of sustenance, he jogged down the rain channel to the food court. Still nothing.

"They must be in the hall," he mused.

"Who the fuck are you?" demanded a voice and Dougal spun on his heels.

Three men and two women were glaring at him, wielding a mixture of bars, broom handles, and kitchen knives. Raising his hands, he stepped forward to explain the situation but one of the men swung a steel rod wildly in warning.

"Whoa, calm down. We're here to help!" Dougal snapped.

"Who's *we*?" asked one of the females.

"He's here to steal our stuff!"

"Why's he wearing an army uniform?"

The jittery man nodded. "Yeah, why are you wearing a uniform?"

"Because I'm in the army," Dougal replied.

"Bullshit! The army's gone. You stole it, didn't you?"

"No, I..."

"Is that gun loaded?" demanded the man, stepping forward.

"Of course," Dougal replied, raising the rifle and pointing it at his face. "Don't come any closer."

"I bet you stole that too, didn't you?"

"For fuck's sake, I didn't steal the fucking thing! My team and I have fought our way from Thorney Barracks to rescue you and this is the reception we get? I lost a brother yesterday for you people!" Dougal growled, dropping the gun and walking forward into range of the clubs.

Uncertainty passed over the man's face at the furious response.

"Christopher, leave the man be," came a new, soft voice.

Sighing, he slowly lowered the pole and moved out of the way. The source of the order was a lady in her forties, with shoulder length brown hair and glasses. She exuded a quiet confidence, which Dougal instantly warmed to.

"I'm Joan Macleod," she introduced herself, shaking his hand, "And who might you be?"

"Private Dougal, ma'am, but you can call me David."

"Come inside out of the cold, David, and we'll make you a cuppa. Then you can explain what you're doing dropping onto our roof like Tarzan," she said.

"I need to let my team know I've made contact first," he replied.

110

"Of course."

Moving to the edge again, he called out, "They're ok. I'm going in to explain the plan. Stand by for my signal!"

Joan held open the roof access door. "Come and meet the family."

CHAPTER 15

Seconds seemed to last hours until all sense of time and space became convoluted. Debbie watched the patch of light caused by the morning sun as it edged millimetre by millimetre around the wall of the cell. Like a sundial, it counted down towards the inevitable brutality which was coming. She found herself staring at the demarcation between light and shadow, desperately willing it to pause in its movement and delay the horror. It bore her no heed.

Head slumping back to the lumpy pillow in defeat, a wracking sob escaped through her broken lips. Pain blazed into life across her body from the spasms; a kaleidoscope of memories flashing back from each tortured nerve ending. The sadistic things Wozniak had done would haunt her dreams forever more. The multitude of cigarette burns around her most sensitive area. Gleeful eyes as he forced his huge member down her throat, refusing to let go even as she choked and thrashed, lights dancing at the edge of her vision. She could still taste the rancid phallus and retched, strings of bile pouring from her empty stomach.

Not even her father, who would creep into her room stinking of whiskey had treated her so appallingly. Slurred mutterings of love accompanied the abuse as her mother lay passed out from prescription medication in the next room. At six years old, Debbie had been unable to understand what was happening. Innocent of the ways of adulthood, she always cleaned herself before dawn and remained silent. Her heart fluttered with her father's threat of being taken away by the police if anyone ever found out what was occurring. By the age of ten, the midnight visits inexplicably stopped. A feeling of betrayal and jealousy had grown when her younger cousin started to stay over, revealing the reason. The unmistakable creak of the landing floorboards in the darkness as her abuser picked a younger victim filled her with hatred. An unfortunate accident in their swimming pool had ended those trysts. Debbie could still remember the girl's face as it stared through the water at her, hands pulling at the arms which held her under, the bubbles from her open mouth slowing as the struggles weakened. Her uncle had never forgiven himself for being inside the house drinking as his only daughter perished. A year later he took his own life.

Banishing the thoughts, Debbie felt a pang of envy. If she hadn't been such a coward, one fierce bite to her tongue could end her suffering. Nipping with her teeth once had been enough to end that idea. *How long did it take to die from the cold?* She wondered. A passive suicide would be far more favourable. The urine sodden sheet had taken on the chill of the day and her own body heat was unable to counteract the frigid temperature. If the attempt failed, however, it would mean several hours of even worse discomfort and the same abhorrent outcome when Wozniak returned. *Not worth it.*

Looking up at the grey, concrete ceiling, she wondered where Peter was. He was a weakling, boring, and easily manipulated, that much was true. But on the other hand, he had always been loyal and willing to put up with her contrariness and spiteful nature. Was he dead now? If she could get to the walls would she find him gawking up at her, flesh peeling from his bones? To her surprise, she hoped that he was safe even though he had forsaken her for that slut, Paige. Now that she was dead, all could be forgiven if he would see sense and take her back. Mike had been a mistake, he would understand. In her twisted mind, it all seemed so logical; if only she could get out of the cell and reach the castle.

Pulling at her bonds, most of the sensation had left her extremities. Only by a monumental effort would her fingers and toes flex. The rough ropes had already abraded the skin and the raw wounds leaked a mixture of clear pus and blood down her wrists. It was a niggling injury compared to the others and she ignored it. The steel frame was solidly welded; a way of ensuring the inmates were unable to take it apart and use the individual parts as a makeshift weapon. This left only the ropes themselves as her means of freeing herself. Wozniak had done a great job on the knots and no matter how much she bucked and strained, they held fast. *There must be a way!*

CHAPTER 16

How many people today?" Craig asked from the 'throne'.

"Only two so far; Wozniak and Rechtman," replied the guard.

"Show them in then."

Craig was in a great mood. Plans were in motion to bring about some much-needed retribution and he could barely contain his excitement. He would have started bouncing like Tigger if the risk of stabbing injury from the knife forged seat wasn't so high. Instead, he grinned mirthlessly and to most people this looked even more terrifying than his scowls.

Rechtman ducked away as a prisoner raised a hand to him and the room erupted in laughter.

"Enough!" Craig roared and silence descended, the only sound that of Rechtman's shoes on the polished wooden floor.

"Thank you for seeing me," whispered the engineer.

"What the fuck do you want? Shouldn't you be out finishing that tunnel?"

"Yes, of course. I'll be going straight back to it, I promise."

"Well..."

Rechtman coughed to clear the lump of fear in his throat. "I was hoping to discuss the workforce situation."

"What about it?" Craig asked through gritted teeth.

"I need you to stop killing my men," Rechtman declared, finally making eye contact.

"*Your* men?" Craig replied.

"While they are working in my tunnels, yes. They are *my* men."

Craig smiled at the sudden bravery of the put-upon individual. He knew it was likely down to the safety of his daughter, yet he felt a fraction more respect for him than before. "Go on."

"We are losing too many people to the gauntlet and suicidal supply runs. I know this could get me killed, but if this continues I simply won't be able to complete the tunnels."

"What do you suggest?"

Rechtman was taken aback. In place of the expected beating, Craig was leaning back and crossing his leg on the throne, waiting for his response. "Umm... I think we need to find entertainment that isn't as costly to our efforts as the gauntlet."

Craig stared at him, which could be a good thing or a bad thing. Finally, he waved a hand in a *go on* gesture.

"I was working on a construction project a few miles away. There's a mobile CAT XQ 425 generator there."

"And I'm supposed to know what that means?"

"Sorry. It's a diesel generator that you can hook to a vehicle like a trailer. If we could retrieve it, I can connect it to the main power supply and run a good portion of the cells again. We could get the stereos, televisions and other luxuries working."

"In case you hadn't noticed, the TVs don't work anymore because everyone's dead."

"Of course, but I meant for films, maybe even computer games. I've seen the consoles sitting idle in a lot of the rooms."

"Do you have a secret stash of diesel fuel tucked away somewhere that I don't know about?"

"No," Rechtman replied, "I would need some of your men to go and retrieve everything."

Craig jumped to his feet. "Oh, so now they're *my men* who need to risk their lives? It seems a bit unfair, don't you think?"

Rechtman's head fell, he knew it was hopeless. Their numbers would continue to dwindle and eventually the place would starve. Perhaps it was for the best. "I'm sorry to have bothered you. I'll get back to work."

Craig had been thinking during the exchange and it all seemed to fall into place. The old generator which kept their food fresh was dying, and they had to secure fuel for the construction project which would see them safely over the river to the bounty of Wick Town anyway. It might be possible to secure both a diesel and petrol tanker

"Wait!" Craig ordered and Rechtman turned wearily.

"Sir?"

"How much fuel would it use?"

"It depends on the load. If we stick to limited appliances and key lighting at night time only, maybe one or two hundred litres a day. I'd need to do some calculations."

"Do them. I'll make arrangements to get the construction site address and find the fuel you'll need. We're going to need every hand for the next tunnel I need you to build."

"Really?" Rechtman was dumbfounded. "What about the gauntlet, though?"

"I'll close it for now. The inmates will have to get their jollies from horror films for a while."

"And you mentioned another tunnel?"

"Forget that for now. Work out whatever you need to get the juice flowing and then we can talk in a few days."

"Ok," replied the engineer before walking away in a daze.

"Next!"

Wozniak was shown in and approached the platform. His smell reached the ruler long before his body did, but Craig ignored it as best he could. Filth and dried patches of God only knew what covered the man and the other guards grimaced at the spectacle.

"Wozniak, my friend. How can I help you today?"

"It's more what I can do to help you, boss."

Craig raised an eyebrow and leaned forward. "Well, now. You have my interest. Go on."

The disgusting inmate looked around the room for a moment, seeing the number of eyes and ears that watched over their leader. Frowning, he took a step closer and whispered, "I think this needs some privacy."

"You want to get me alone?" Craig asked warily. "I trust these men, so anything you have to say feel free to say it in front of them."

"Sorry, boss, but I don't trust them," he muttered and turned to walk away.

Craig's mood was souring at the ungrateful prisoner and the grin disappeared. "Ok," he growled, "But this better be fucking good. Everyone out!"

As the men with their guns and blades exited the hall, Wozniak paced back and forth. He was obviously agitated about something.

"So, what's the big deal?" Craig demanded.

"I'm not a grass!" Wozniak spat in anger.

"I never said you were," Craig replied, shaking his head in confusion. A grotesque, filthy creature, yes, but his prison honour had never been in question.

"I hate even being here, but you've been good to me and this place since everyone died."

Craig could see the conflicting emotions on the man's face and waited patiently for him to get to the point.

"Fuck!" Wozniak blurted, glancing around the empty room. "The Fowler brothers are going to make a move on you soon." His shoulders slumped in self-disgust. This went against every code he had ever lived by.

Craig mulled for a few seconds. "How are they planning to do that? They don't have enough people."

"All I know is that one of the other wings is involved."

"Who?" Craig's face was going scarlet as the rage took over.

"I don't know. As soon as I do, you'll be the first to know."

"Why are you telling me this? Not that I don't appreciate it, but didn't you and those scouse bastards do a couple of jobs once?"

"We did," he agreed, reluctantly. "They're just too unstable and don't have the brains that you do. I trust you to keep us secure more than they will."

"Thanks. See Ziggy on the way out and tell him I owe you a carton of cigarettes."

"You won't discuss this with anyone, will you?" Wozniak asked.

"Only Hombre and Matt, you have my word."

Satisfied with the reply, the grimy inmate started to leave.

"Keep me updated as soon as you hear more, I think there'll be a position coming up for a new wing boss soon."

Guilt at his betrayal prevented him from being happy at the prospect, so Wozniak simply nodded and pushed through the door.

"Fucking wankers," Craig growled to himself. Their deaths would be legendary, and very slow.

As the hall refilled with guards, no one dared to approach him. The look on his face was enough to tell them someone was getting murdered soon and the last thing they wanted was to annoy him and take an early place on the list. Several minutes passed in hushed expectation until the sound of an explosion rocked the building, dust streaming from the roof as it shook.

"What the fuck was that?" Craig roared. "Get to the walls!"

CHAPTER 17

S tanding in shocked silence, Craig and his men stared down at the torn figure of Wozniak. He was slumped in a heap after bleeding out against the opposite wall where he had been thrown by the blast. Shards of broken crockery were embedded into his body and face between the scorch marks of the explosion. Carefully stepping over the spreading pool of crimson, the men waved their hands around to clear the air. The fire had quickly died out from the lack of fuel in the sparse cell and only a cloying cloud of dust and remnants of smoke curled around their passing.

"What the hell happened here?" Craig muttered at the devastation.

The heavy cell door had been ripped off and lay halfway up the corridor, twisted and buckled. The rear wall of the cell had been blown out into the yard by the contained detonation and daylight peeked in, highlighting the swirling dust. A faint cough caught their attention and they stepped into the ruins of Wozniak's lair. In one corner was the mattress, soaking wet and torn in places. From beneath the bed, something stirred again, groaning in pain.

"Debbie?" Hombre whispered, stepping over the rubble.

Pulling it back, she was drifting in and out of consciousness. Her hair was mostly burnt off and blood was trickling from her ruptured ears. With her one undamaged eye, she looked up at him in a moment of clarity and smiled. Her broken front teeth and gums were a ghastly sight and he winced inwardly. Leaning down, he gently picked her up and could see what had caused the damage. The bedframe still had the remains of the bindings, covered with blood and fragments of tooth.

"She chewed through the ropes," Hombre said, filled with awe at the girl's moxie.

"And she rigged the cell to blow with the gas in his stove. She must've taken cover behind the mattress and waited for him to get back before igniting it. Clever bitch," Craig added, kicking the shredded vessel. It was an annoyance that his source of information was dead, but at least he was forewarned of the coming insurrection. They would just need to be more vigilant in the coming weeks.

"What do we do with her?" Matt asked.

"Take her to medical. There's more to this little lady than meets the eye," Craig replied.

Hombre nodded and proceeded down the hall. Mike came rushing around the corner, nearly colliding with them and reeled back in shock at the sight of his ex-partner.

Stepping around the pair, he approached his brother. "What the fuck happened here?"

"It seems your girlfriend had other ideas about our choice of accommodation."

"No shit," Mike blurted.

"I wouldn't worry too much. She probably won't survive anyway," Craig informed him.

"And if she does?"

Craig clapped him on the back, "I'd keep her away from naked flames if I were you."

CHAPTER 18

"Can I get you a coffee, sweetie? I've just brewed a pot."

Denise turned to her friend and smiled. "No thanks, I'm fine. Where's your pet?"

"Mr Vincent is currently helping Kurt with something," Patricia replied, taking a seat.

"He's helping? You're shitting me."

"Honest to God," Patricia replied. "It's why Kurt sent me away. Apparently, I was crowding the poor dear."

"I'd have locked him in the coldest, darkest room and let him rot."

"I think most of us would after the way he behaved towards us," Patricia agreed. "But at least we have new management now."

"Absolutely. I like Kurt and the others, they've got balls."

"You can say that again. I can still remember the crack of the first shot. Everybody damn near fainted."

"Did you see the look on Stephen's face when he thought bandits had come to kill us all? Fucking pussy," Denise grumbled.

"I hate to admit it, but I had a moment of worry too. They were heavily armed and looked fierce as hell."

"And what did I say?"

"You said they were just people trying to survive, like us. I'm still in awe of your ability to make judgement calls so quickly. And be right!"

"It comes from years of walking the beat. The second I looked through the binoculars I could see they weren't like that. They worked as a unit, the women and children as much a part of the fighting as the men."

"There can be bad women and children too…"

"Of course. But the way they fought…" Denise tried to find the words. "It was with love. I could see the apprehension written on their faces for one another. If it was just a ragtag band of miscreants trying to take our shelter, it would've been different."

"I'll take your word for it, honey. You were spot on with your analysis. I still feel guilty that I waited behind while you and the others charged out to help."

"I needed you to stay and keep the others safe, just in case. If any of those things had got past you and inside the castle, I hate to imagine how it may have turned out. You know how fast the infection takes people."

"I understand."

"And besides," Denise continued, patting her friend on the thigh. "I needed you to make doubly sure that weasel didn't shut the door on us."

"I wouldn't have put it past him. He was whining the whole time about 'those ruffians' and how they were tearing up the place. As if the zombies hadn't been doing a bloody good job of that anyway."

"He should be grateful. Those ruffians are the only thing standing between us and starvation."

"Exactly!"

"Has Kurt spoke to you about how he intends to get the food back yet?"

"No. I think Stephen's explaining some of the secret routes in and out of the castle," Patricia replied. "Once every possible avenue is explored, then I'm sure we'll start planning a raid."

"Thank all that is holy. I can't wait to eat something other than the leftover crap no one else wants."

"I'd kill for a pepperoni pizza and some popcorn."

"Mine would be a grilled cheeseburger with tomato, lettuce, mayo, and ketchup," Denise replied, salivating at the memory.

"Now you put it like that I've changed my mind. I want a Five Guys burger. Do you think any of the meat will be usable?" Patricia wondered.

"Not after all this time, but I'll settle for a pack of beef crisps," Denise said with a chuckle.

"We'll need to go with them when the time comes. They'll need as many people as possible with firearms expertise."

"I think guns will be for emergency use only. If I know Kurt, he'll want to try and get in and out with as little noise as possible. Plus, he'll probably prefer to keep some of us back at the walls in case the prison tries to make a move."

"Do you think it's likely?" Patricia asked.

Denise shrugged. "I had to deal with the scum of the earth for years. The one thing I've learned is they'll always surprise you, and not in a 'I'm turning over a new leaf and behaving myself' kind of way."

"You'd think with the zombies nearly wiping us out that people would be more concerned with cooperating. Fucking douchebags."

"Human nature lets us down every time. There will always be those who want power over everyone else and are prepared to do anything to achieve it. By the sounds of it, Craig and Mike are two shining examples of psychotic fucktards who should've been smothered at birth. The only problem is that there are bound to be two more psychotic fucktards waiting in the wings to take their place."

"Or in the case of the prison, hundreds."

"There'll be a high number, certainly. Some will be low level felons who are just trying to do their time in peace. My worry is that if we ever manage to take the prison, identifying who'll be valuable and who'll be eager to cut your throat at the first opportunity will prove impossible."

"Do you think we have a chance of saving the innocents inside?"

Denise considered the question for a few seconds. "I've been analysing it from every angle, and no, I don't."

"Have you told Kurt?"

"Not yet. It would be different if it was just a few prisoners holding the people, but we're talking hundreds of inmates. Even if we managed to get inside, they'd think nothing of using them as human shields. Best case scenario is that we add ourselves to the hostage tally, worst case is that everyone dies; us, the prisoners and the hostages themselves."

"What about infiltrating the prison?" Patricia suggested with a glint in her eye.

"How do you mean?"

"Who's in charge there?"

"Craig Arater, Mike's brother."

"And who's just turned up here after fighting at Mike's side?"

"Winston, but he abandoned them because he was scared of the prisoners. Are you suggesting we send him back? I'm sure he'd love that."

"No. I'm suggesting that if the time ever comes, we can ask him how he feels about the possibility. I was chatting to him in the kitchen and it turns out he'd developed a close bond with Mike. That could be his way in."

"I thought he hated Mike and Debbie?" asked Denise.

"He fears them, but Mike stood up for him. I think he took the lad under his wing a little."

"Kurt needs to hear this," Denise said, brow furrowing. "If he's concealing this kind of thing it could be dangerous for us all."

"It's not like that, sweetie. He told me because he felt so guilty about lying in the first place. Winston won't betray us, I can assure you of that."

"And what makes you think he'd betray Mike?"

"I don't. It was just a silly idea, anyway. Forget it."

"Don't get me wrong, I think it has merit. The only problem is that he knows exactly what Kurt and the others will do if they ever got hold of them. I don't think it's fair to put that on the poor lad's shoulders."

Patricia nodded, sipping her coffee. "They're already in prison, though," she suggested.

"Huh?"

"What if we could guarantee their safety and just lock them away as punishment?"

"I think the feud's gone beyond simple incarceration, but it wouldn't hurt to raise it as an option."

"In all honesty, I've no idea what he could do even if he did get himself inside," admitted Patricia.

"I think that young man could be quite inventive if he set his mind to it."

"You may be right. Who'd have thought to steal a crane and trundle across country?"

Denise winked. "Indeed."

CHAPTER 19

Entering the dark stairwell, Dougal was nervous about being directly in front of the erratic defenders and stood to the side as they passed. Joan smiled and waited with him, understanding his hesitation.

"When we get into the hall, you'll understand why they're a little protective," she said mysteriously.

Green smears lined the bare concrete walls of the rooftop access and it was obvious what had left them. Handprints, some incomplete from lack of fingers, were visible along its length and she could see his confusion.

"I'll tell you all about it later. Let's get you that cup of coffee."

Reaching the main complex, the door was held open by Christopher who still regarded him with wariness. When the world ends at the teeth of monsters, trust of strangers is the first casualty Dougal surmised. In hindsight, he could not blame them for their reaction. In the brave new world, people trying to gain access to your shelter by climbing across thousands of undead would seem unhinged to say the least. Factor in guns and it was even more understandable.

The drab utility stairs gave way to the corridor and true holiday spirit. Bright colours and smiling bears were painted across the walls, promising fun and frivolity for the children. Posters with the latest night time entertainment and prices of discounted alcohol were taped between the innocent, cuddly animals, promising the same for the adults.

"Joan, would you mind showing him around a bit first? I'd like to calm the others down and explain everything's ok before he sees them," asked Christopher.

"Good idea," she agreed. "Let me give you the grand tour!"

"I don't fancy a swim if I'm being honest. I think your pool monitor needs to be fired."

Joan laughed at the quip. "Indeed, but I'm the pool monitor. I can give you the details of head office if you'd like to make a formal complaint. They may be a little slow in getting back to you, though."

At this, the others checked if she wanted an escort. "I'll be fine. I have a good feeling about this gentleman."

"I've never been called a gentleman before," Dougal admitted as the lady linked arms and led him away from the auditorium.

"If you are genuinely here to help us, then that makes you a gentleman. I must admit I was shocked to hear that someone was swinging across to us like a monkey in combat uniform."

"I didn't mean to scare anyone. It was just the safest and easiest way to try and make contact with you all."

"Safest?" she asked with a wry smile.

"Well I'm terrified of heights, but more scared of being eaten. So, yeah, it was the safest way," he replied.

Joan took him on a tour of the facility, beginning with the reception and pool house. Sections of steel cladding had been welded to the front doors, completely isolating them from the dead.

"We were very lucky. The holiday park had been meaning to rebuild this structure last year in a different location. It was to have been constructed using a great deal more windows to give a brighter interior, but the builders went bankrupt a month before they were due to dig the new foundations. If the outer wall had been made of glass instead of the cheap metal cladding from the eighties, we would've been overrun in the first few days."

"Thank God for recessions, eh?"

Leaving the muffled groans carrying into the lobby, they passed through the changing rooms of the swimming area. A pleasant, soapy fragrance was trying to fight off the noxious stench coming from the main pool. Leaning inside one of the shower cubicles, Joan turned the valve and water started to flow. No steam accompanied the cascading liquid and Dougal reached out and put his hand in the flow.

"It's freezing cold!" he hissed.

"It's from a rainwater system I helped to install a couple of years ago. Yes, it's cold, but at least we can clean ourselves. I could've rigged a heater, but it was felt the fuel would be better used to cook, keep us warm and to kill any contaminants by boiling the water we drink."

"That makes sense."

After closing the valve, she showed him the fire exit which had also been welded closed. Blackened paint had peeled away from the searing frame as the acetylene melted the metal.

"Who's the welder?"

"I am. Among other things."

"Really? You'd be a tremendous asset to Thorney Barracks."

"Is that where you and your friends are from?"

"Yes, ma'am. There aren't many of us left, but we're trying to change that and bring back any survivors that we can find."

"I'm not altogether sure everyone will want to leave."

"Why?" Dougal wondered. "Do you have enough food to last for years?"

"Oh, goodness no. We have enough for a few months, but that's all."

"So why would you stay?" He was having a hard time understanding.

"You'll see soon enough."

They entered the arcade and familiar memories flooded back from Dougal's childhood. Flashing lights, the alluring beep and buzz of games machines and scrolling penny drops now sat in silence. It was an eerie sight to see the once manic visual treats masked in shadow and he hurried through. An old friend caused him to stop in his tracks and stare.

"Would you look at that," he whispered.

"It was one of the biggest earners. Ironic, isn't it?"

The large machine had two plastic guns holstered near the coin slots. In trickling, blood red font, the words *House of the Dead* stared back. The blank screen showed their vague reflections where once the players would do battle with hordes of pixelated horrors. Now they could do so in 3D, complete with a true Game Over if they should be bitten.

"I used to love that game when I was younger."

"As did a lot of people. I played it myself on occasion."

"I bet the creators didn't realise how prophetic their game would become."

"I should imagine not. Come, let's see the food hall and then I'll take you to meet the others."

Three fast food franchises had counters side by side, offering pizzas, burgers and fish and chips respectively. Surrounding the premises were easy wipe plastic tables and leather chairs bolted to the floor. A set of doors lay to their right and Joan pushed through, leading the way.

"This was the main restaurant for people who wanted fine dining. Well, as fine as you can get in a holiday camp, anyway."

The contrasting decors separated by a single set of swing doors was remarkable. Each table had a small lamp

131

to provide mood lighting and stainless-steel cutlery laid in preparation for a meal that would never be delivered. The kitchen and bar area were of a far higher standard than the quick fix establishments outside, but bore the age worn feel of the building itself. Several years past due for a refurbishment, the owners had probably held out to save money for the new building. Dougal looked at the bar and its faded varnish, replete with small burn marks from a time when smoking cigarettes had been allowed inside. A fine layer of dust had settled on the glass display shelves to the rear, giving it an air of grubbiness and neglect. The childhood memories of joy in places just like this brought a tear to his eye and he turned away. Beneath his feet, the carpet shifted with a brittle crunch. Among the dark thread was a darker patch of dried blood and he looked at Joan.

"It was bad during the outbreak," she explained.

"At least you managed to fight back and save people."

"Not enough," she sighed. "Not nearly enough."

***

"Your work?" Dougal asked.

"I felt better knowing we had a safety net if the dead got inside somehow," Joan replied with pride.

Freshly cemented into the walls were heavy duty hinges carrying a patchwork of plate steel welded together to form a door. Expecting a piercing creak, Dougal was surprised when it glided open effortlessly.

"We keep it oiled," Joan said, reading his mind.

Once through, it was closed and three lengths of thick wood were wedged against the metal and dropped into recesses in the floor.

"How did you find the metal?"

"I borrowed it from areas that were no longer important."

"Wait," Dougal stopped mid step. "How would this help if the dead got inside? You'd be trapped."

"We're trapped anyway."

"I know. I meant what would you do if you couldn't get to the food and water."

"You mean how would we fare dying of dehydration or starvation?"

Dougal nodded.

"I made up a concoction from the first aid room. We'd fall asleep and never wake up."

Dougal shook his head. "What an awful world we live in."

"Indeed," Joan replied sadly. "Now listen. I need you to be careful with how much information you give the others. Most of them didn't see the fighting and think there has just been a bad accident."

"I don't understand," Dougal muttered, completely dumbfounded.

"Come and meet everyone and you'll see."

Pushing through another set of doors, the truth revealed itself. Sat calmly in three rows facing them were over thirty children, ranging in ages from six to twelve. Their expectant faces gazed up, mouths wide open in shock at the appearance of a real soldier and his gun.

"Children, I'd like you to say hello to Private Dougal. He's a soldier in the British Army."

The children waved and greeted him as only children could. The synchronous drone of *hello, Private Dougal* would be familiar to anyone who had spent time in a classroom. Circling the young were Christopher and the other adults, faces set, the threat behind the eyes obvious if he should try and endanger them.

"Now you can see why they were afraid of you and your intentions," Joan whispered.

"Where are their parents?" He whispered from the corner of his mouth.

133

"Outside," she replied and shuddered.

"Oh."

"Now that you see our quandary, we can discuss your plans," Joan said, before turning to the children. "We're just going to have a chat and a cup of coffee. If you're good and do your worksheets, I'll see about making something special for dinner tonight. Deal?"

Special always meant a freshly made pizza dough with plenty of cheese and delicious toppings. The cold had been their saving grace in food preservation. If it had been coming into summer, most of their supplies would have long ago fallen into decay just like the creatures at the wall.

Dougal went to follow Joan until a small hand took his own. He looked down into the angelic face of a blonde boy. "Are you here to bring our mummies and daddies back to us?"

"I... I don't..." Dougal could barely speak. The wide, misty blue eyes had such trust and hope in them that his stomach twisted into knots.

"Come now, Robert. Let's get those math questions worked out," Christopher said and gently led him away.

Grief was painted across Dougal's face and he looked around the cavernous theatre, lost. Joan squeezed his shoulder and smiled warmly. "Let's get you that drink."

***

"Can you see why I'm reluctant to leave now? These poor darlings would be forced to flee past their dead parents."

"Jesus," Dougal muttered at the thought.

"We're safe in this facility. If the army could see their way to supplying us with food, we could remain here indefinitely."

"It's not that simple, Joan. We don't have an army any more, just the last few fools who didn't try and reach their families."

134

"Did the others make it to their loved ones by any chance?" she asked, hopefully.

"I can't see how. Those things are everywhere."

Lowering her head, she sighed. "Then it seems we are in debt to your foolishness. I understand the dangers of trying to come over land, but is there any way an aerial drop could be arranged?"

"We don't have any capacity for that, I'm afraid. We're down to the last few helicopter crews and they're working flat out to resupply the forces which are trapped in the mountains."

"I see."

"Do the children know nothing of the outside world?"

"No. They were part of a holiday club that was playing in the hall when it all happened. We managed to keep them from the horror, even the ones who were bitten and rose again."

"I understand why you did it, but hiding from this isn't going to help them. We need to get them all to safety, real safety, and that's the barracks."

Joan sat in quiet contemplation for a few moments. "If we were to leave, how would it work? There are only fifteen adults and that's not enough to protect the young ones from the hundreds of monsters outside."

"Our team has set a trap to the north of the park. When the time comes, my friends will draw most of them away and destroy them. The stragglers will be far less concentrated and with the firepower on the Warthogs, we can clear a path to get you all loaded."

"Warthogs?"

"They're armoured personnel carriers. Impenetrable by explosives, let alone the dead. You'll be perfectly safe while we head back to Ham Farm, then onto Thorney."

"Why Ham Farm?"

"You must've heard the battle from yesterday and this morning?"

135

"So, it was you that woke me up?" she replied and they both laughed.

"My apologies, ma'am. We fought a couple of thousand zombies from Witterings and Almodington. During the melee, I lost a brother."

"I'm truly sorry to hear that." Joan reached out and patted his hand. "I'm sure he was a fine man."

"He was. I'll tell you about him some day."

"Let me bring the others in and we can take a vote."

Apart from Christopher and one other lady who was leading the studies, everyone joined them. The vote was eleven to two in favour of leaving for the sanctuary provided by the island and its fearsome soldiers.

"Joan, how can we keep them from panicking when we head outside? They'll be terrified and freeze," asked one of the men who voted no.

"We get them to link hands and keep their eyes closed, Colin."

"We can't do anything about the noises," he continued. "What if they look to see what is making them?"

"We can't do anything about that. It doesn't change the fact we don't have a choice if we want to survive though."

"But if the soldiers are going to kill the zombies, why do we need to go? We could find a way to scavenge for food if the area is clear."

Dougal shook his head. "More will come. They always do."

"We need a haven with a future," Joan declared. "I know you are just trying to protect our children, and I love you for it. Their best chance is with people who can fight the dead."

"Ok," Colin sighed. "You've kept us safe this far. I'll do what you need me to."

"One thing, though," said the other lady who had expressed reluctance. "How do we get out with the doors sealed?"

"I can get them to ram the doors. Ten tonnes of armoured vehicle will punch clean through," Dougal explained.

"So be it. We'll need half an hour to collect their belongings and prepare them for the ordeal."

Dougal rose to his feet and thanked them. It was a great relief to know the innocents would be secure in a few hours. "I'll let my team know to prepare for the assault in thirty."

Retracing his path through the maze of the building, Dougal finally reached the edge of the roof. Nothing had changed in the behaviour of the horde below, they still milled around the walls. Wherever the team were, they were invisible.

"We're go for mission. We need one of the drivers to bust through the main doors as they've been welded. Give it thirty minutes and then give them hell!"

A solitary torch flash came from a trailer window, two rows away, safely out of sight of the gathered dead.

***

"Set your watches. Thirty minutes and we go," Holbeck whispered. "Langham, you'll hold position here. Petermann and I will take the east of the complex, Harkiss and Eldridge the west. We'll open fire first, trying to peel them away from the front doors and get them to follow us around the sides. We'll join back up here and keep picking them off while maintaining a safe distance until they're in the trap. Is everyone clear?"

"Yes, Sarge."

"Let's get into position."

Separating at the front door of the trailer, they wished each other good hunting and moved off in silence. Dougal could see the stealthy movement and yelled for all he was worth to distract the enemy. Leapfrogging between the

137

concealing shadows, they reached their respective destinations.

Eldridge looked out along the park's esplanade in horror. Human remains lay rotting where they had fallen, torn and scattered like confetti. Washed up on the pebble beach were the bloated corpses of the drowned. Forced into the water in an attempt to escape, exhaustion had taken them one by one. As the sea closed over their faces and their frantic struggles ceased, the currents broke them against the submerged rocks of the sea floor before returning them to dry land. Unable to gain their feet, the zombies flopped like fish out of water, rotten lungs coughing up brackish water which refilled with each tide.

"Just when you thought you'd seen it all," Harkiss whispered, barely audible.

Eldridge could only stare in disgust.

Many hundreds were spread along the outer wall of the complex, clinging to the cladding like putrescent lichen. The sharp slaps of fleshless palms on metal sounded like the pattering of rainfall on their tin roofed billets from basic training. After twenty-five minutes, it had grown intolerable. Quite how the people inside had endured the noise was a mystery to them both. Glancing at their watches, the last sixty seconds ticked away towards the inevitable confrontation. Adrenaline flooded their systems, heightening their senses as zero flashed on the timer.

"Now!"

Breaking cover, they stepped over the festering remnants of the dead holiday makers.

"Come on you bastards!" Eldridge screamed.

"Dinner's served, mother fuckers!" Harkiss yelled.

Holbeck and Petermann's shouts carried from the opposite end of the building. Unable to shoot at the horde due to the risk of hitting each other in the crossfire, they fired into the air. Taken by their insatiable cravings, the zombies split away like Moses parting the sea and flowed towards the soldiers to the north and south.

"Fall back to the next row of caravans!"

Taking up position, they shouldered their assault rifles and waited. Preceded by rapturous groans of anticipation, the swarm of dead poured around the corner and from between the separate plots. The inhuman din was drowned out by the crackling, automatic rifle fire. Raking the bodies, bullets tore through ribcages and stomachs. Until the soldiers converged, the decision had been made to simply keep their attention instead of killing them with head shots. A pile of bodies in the narrow alleys between the static homes could create a barricade which would scupper their plan. The main road back to the waiting trap was much wider and the undead could more easily navigate around any that were shot during the retreat.

"Next row!" Harkiss shouted when the creatures were almost close enough to touch.

Repeating the tactic, most of their loyal following were still engaged when the separate groups of soldiers joined forces once more.

"Single shots and pick your targets from the sides. We need to funnel them!" ordered Holbeck.

Individual streams of the shambling horrors converged into a solid mass of leaking corruption on the road. Surging forward, the troops let loose their hatred from the barrels. Heads burst apart, throwing the bodies against the trailers, coating them in green gore and brain.

"Magazine!" yelled Langham, reloading.

"Watch the flanks!" shouted Harkiss, swinging to the right.

A small contingent of zombies had bypassed them and attacked from between the trailers. Before he could get a shot off, the creatures barrelled into them, knocking Langham to the ground. Holding up an arm to defend her face from the gnashing teeth, she screamed as a chunk was bitten off, uniform and all. Holbeck and the others had pulled their side arms. The pistols bucked in their hands, slugs destroying brains at point blank range as the main swarm approached. Petermann and Holbeck reached into the struggling mass, pulling their battle sister free.

"Fuck!" screamed Eldridge at the sight of her shredded limb.

With no time to spare, they pushed away or shot the remaining monstrosities and fell back into position.

"I can still fight!" Langham cried, grimacing from the pain. "Give me your gun!"

Passing the Glock, Eldridge quickly took aim with her rifle again. Each shot sent a wave of agony through Langham's arm from the recoil, but she kept firing until the magazine ran dry. Pressing the release, it fell to the floor and she tried to pry a fresh one from her vest. The damaged arm was unresponsive, hand curled in paralysis from the poison which flowed through her veins.

"Here!" Harkiss growled, holding a magazine upright in his palm.

Slapping the pistol grip down, it locked and Harkiss racked it for her. She started firing again, scoring a kill for each bullet. The creeping cold had reached her shoulder and sent icy tendrils towards her neck. It would not be long before she succumbed.

"Petermann, get up on the shower block roof and see how many are following!" Holbeck barked.

Like a whippet, he complied and scurried up the iron drain pipe. Backing towards the entrance of their trap, Eldridge cast a glance upward as he scanned the enemy.

"Most of them are falling for it, Sarge!" he yelled. Some were breaking off and heading back, but the bulk formed a procession thirty wide and over a hundred deep.

"Good. Everyone get back to the entrance on the double!"

Helping their brother down, they bolted towards the gap in the caravan blockade. Facing off against a shambling wall of filth, the troops glowered their eternal hatred. It was so palpable they could feel it emanate from them in a black wave.

"Hold your fire and get the valves open," Holbeck grunted. "I'll stay here to keep their attention."

Langham was fading fast. The cold fingers of death were clamping around her mind, dulling her senses. For a second, she considered eating a bullet and making a quick end of it, but that was not her way. Living a life of excitement and thrills, she decided to go out in the same way and staggered to the rear of their trap.

"Give me…" she croaked, shocked at the weakness in her voice. Summoning her last reserves of energy, she cleared her throat and tried again. "Give me your grenades," she shouted with more force. "Bring a couple more of the gas tanks to me."

"What're you planning?" Eldridge called back, opening one of the vessels.

"They want a meal? I'll give them a fucking meal they'll never forget!"

Arguing was moot. Eldridge knew the wound was fatal and felt immense pride at her friends' bravery. "Are you sure?"

Her throat had gone numb and it took every ounce of her remaining will to stay on her feet. Nodding instead, she was heartened when Harkiss and Petermann dragged two tanks over. Leaning against the closest, she was glad of the support the heavy cylinder provided. The open tubes hissed, spraying the rotten egg smell of the compressed gas over them.

"Will you be strong enough to pull the pins?" Petermann asked as she swayed.

A lethargic shake of the head indicated no.

"I've got an idea," Dougal said, holding back the tears. Kneeling, he unlaced one of his boots. After threading the shoelace through the pins of the deadly balls, he stowed them inside one of her pockets and secured the clasp. Tying the loose end to the upright canister, he kissed her on the cheek. "All you need to do is sit down and it'll pull the pins for you. I'll see you in Valhalla, Mel. We'll drink a toast to our brothers and sisters together."

A bone-weary smile formed on her lips and she winked. It was time to go.

"All ready, Sarge!" called Eldridge.

"Ok, get your asses under the trailers to safety!"

Dropping to their knees, the troops retreated and scurried through the dark underbellies of the caravans.

Holbeck watched them go and turned to Langham. Offering a crisp salute, he said, "You'll be a legend, private. People will talk about your bravery for a thousand years after this war."

A twitch from her unbitten arm was all she could manage in returning the salute, but Holbeck knew what it meant and squeezed her shoulder once before ducking out of sight.

She heard the final order from her sergeant, yet it sounded a million miles away. "Fall back to the APCs, ignore the flares! We'll wait for detonation and then light them up!"

Her vision was starting to fog as the infection commenced shutting down her mind, one neuron at a time. Their plan had worked better than they could have imagined with nearly every zombie shuffling into the kill zone, unaware that the meat on offer came with a steep price. Marching towards her like an all-conquering army, the undead growled their jubilation at a fresh meal. Swarming Langham from all directions, they raked at her with tattered fingers and tore flesh with decayed teeth.

None of the pain registered, only a sense of relief that her last act would be to kill thousands of the abominations.

Fuck you! she screamed from the last, uncorrupted corner of her mind and slumped to the ground. The extracted pins tinkled against the steel cylinders; a chime signalling the end of her life. Then nothing.

***

From the rear of the Warthog, Eldridge watched carefully. With an almighty crack, the grenades ruptured the first cylinders and a searing column of flame rose into the air. Thin aluminium walls were no match for the blast and the nearest trailers peeled open like sardine cans, showering them with smouldering furniture and insulation. Like a row of dominos, the initial explosion sent shrapnel tearing through the next vessel and they added their own fuel to the eruption one by one until the whole perimeter was an inferno. Contained within the hellish fire, the zombies who had survived thrashed around in confusion. Skin peeled and flesh melted under the intense heat, streaming from their bodies and hissing like a joint of meat on a griddle. Hunks of charred flesh rained from the sky, sending the soldiers ducking for cover in their vehicles.

When the last of the zombie remains had hit the ground, Eldridge called out, "Sarge, shall we open fire, just to be sure?"

"There's no need," Holbeck shouted in reply. "They're cooking."

Poking her head through the turret housing, the stench of burning, rotten meat hit her full in the face. Holding a hand to her mouth to still the churning stomach, she watched as thousands of creatures flailed futilely against the all-consuming flames. Senses fried, they could only stagger around within the confines of the trailer shells until their bodies succumbed. Each creature added its clothing

143

and fats to the grateful conflagration. *This is what Hell must look like,* she thought with a shudder.

"Everyone aboard!" yelled Holbeck. "We do this now!"

Carpenter fired the engine and Harkiss followed suit. Leaving the roiling blaze, they swung west and crashed through a wooden fence, dropping down into the muck and mire of the marshland. The two Warthogs churned their way south, their wide tracks easily guiding them along the boggy ground. A well-trodden footpath snaked off from the campsite and the drivers gunned it, careening up the steep slope in a shower of mud and dead brush. The beach was in sight and only a small concrete wall stood in their way. A juddering crash accompanied the contact, but neither APC slowed down this close to the most critical part of the mission.

Holbeck came over the radio. "Hold position at the south-western edge of the building. We need to have a clear line of fire along the front of the complex to kill the last undead. It's the only way we can ensure none of the survivors get hurt by stray bullets."

Pulling up, Eldridge aimed the heavy machine gun and opened fire down the long, steel clad wall. The wide barrel coughed out its bullets in steady bursts, chewing through the last cadavers which went cartwheeling away down the esplanade to join the other shredded bodies.

"Carpenter, move to ram the front doors. Petermann, on me!"

Holbeck jumped from the vehicle with Petermann and took up position to guard the flanks; their mobility made it an easier job than the gunner in her mechanical turret. The Warthog accelerated forward, mashing anything that lay on the paved surface. The two soldiers were carrying on the clear up with double taps on any zombie not fully dead.

Carpenter paused, the rear compartment directly in line with the sturdy doors. Holbeck banged on the steel plates. "Stand clear! We're going to break through."

Even over the noise of racing engines and gunfire, he could hear voices inside ushering people to safety. With a final wave, the armoured vehicle leapt backwards at speed, crashing through the barricade with a rending shriek of buckled metal. As Carpenter cleared the way, Holbeck carefully inspected the damage to make sure nothing was in danger of collapsing and injuring anyone. Harkiss moved up and into position alongside her, eager to collect their human bounty.

"We're all clear. Dougal, move them out!"

"Yes, Sarge!"

Both rear doors were flung open and the soldiers could only stare incredulously as two lines of young children poured from the building, eyes closed and holding hands.

"That's it, my darlings," Joan coaxed, "You're nearly there."

Holbeck could see the logistical nightmare looming. "We won't be able to fit you all inside, ma'am. I'll need the adults to climb onto the top of the cabs and hold on."

"That's fine. A bit of excitement never killed anyone which is more than I can say for those bloody things!" Joan snapped, shooting a glare of disgust at the dead who had skirted the building.

"We've got company!" Eldridge shouted and swung the gun around.

Snapping a fresh belt into the chamber, she pulled the charging handle and let loose. Meeting a wall of devastating lead slugs, the corpses crumpled into mounds of twitching flesh before taking more than two paces. To her rear, she could hear the gasps and grunts of effort as the previously trapped people clambered aboard.

"It's great to meet you!" she shouted, unleashing another stream of bullets into the monstrosities.

"Is everyone on?" Holbeck yelled over the din.

"That's everyone accounted for, Sergeant," Joan confirmed.

Before closing the rear doors on the children, Petermann leaned inside the transport cab. "There's going to be some bouncing around, so everyone should hold on tight, ok?"

Despite their terror, they all agreed and he locked them inside. Standing on the rear foot plate, he gave a signal to Holbeck that everything was good to go.

"Ok, everyone, get ready! We're leaving as fast as we arrived and it's going to get bumpy!"

Harkiss fell in behind Carpenter as she drove back towards the smashed wall and the marshland beyond. In the side mirror, he could see the people clinging on for dear life to the vehicle and it reminded him of an old picture he had marvelled at as a youngster. It was of an Indian train and, because of overcrowding, every square inch of the roof and sides were covered with people. This endeavour, though smaller, was no less fraught.

"Hold tight!" Holbeck shouted as they reached the embankment.

Everyone braced themselves for the shift and, thankfully, no one was thrown clear as the heavy Warthogs dipped down. The noses met the quagmire with a squelch and churned up a mass of wet mud before righting themselves.

Letting out a long, shaky breath, Holbeck looked around at the new faces. "Not far to go now. By nightfall you'll have clean beds and hot showers."

Shaken deeply by the sudden upheaval to their lives, they could only grimace and nod from their precarious perches.

***

"Ok, children. You can come out now."

Joan ushered them into the home and each face lit up as the dogs made them welcome, tails wagging furiously and tongues working overtime on kisses. When they were all inside, Angela started to prepare a fresh pot of beef stew from a box of cans which the twins had been saving for a special occasion. The others gathered outside to discuss the next leg of the journey.

"How long do you think we'll be here, Sarge?"

"Not long, maybe an hour or two. The kids have had quite a morning and it won't hurt to let them stretch their legs a bit."

"I'd advise keeping them to the front of the farmhouse and the barn area," Max added, pointing to the rutted tracks.

The sodden, green tinged ground had been churned by the sisters as they used an old excavator to push the bodies. Thankfully, they had chosen to clear the area around the front door where the worst of the fighting had taken place first. A short walk around either corner would have revealed a grotesque crush of piled corpses.

"I haven't heard them laugh in so long," Joan said quietly.

Between friendly chuffs came the musical giggles of the youngsters as they frolicked and petted the dogs. Touched by the sounds, the group fell silent and listened, soaking up the innocence. Two had fallen, but Holbeck knew that they would be looking down with pride at what their sacrifice had achieved. After a minute, everyone was wiping away tears. Sadness interwoven with a glimmer of hope for the future filled each of them.

Christopher broke the silence. "Thank you. I'm sorry I was so aggressive when you arrived."

Dougal smiled. "I don't blame you, mate. They were your only concern."

"And now they have a chance at a real future because of your bravery," Joan added. "We can never repay that debt."

"No debt is due," Holbeck replied. "In this Godforsaken world, they're the only chance we have of longevity. Everyone on the base will die to keep them safe."

"I hope it doesn't come to that, Sergeant."

"So do I, ma'am."

Angela peered through the door. "Lunch will be ready in half an hour. The oldest children have asked about coming outside."

"That's fine, let them out," Holbeck said.

A mad rush of small people tumbled from the doorway, quickly gathering around their mistress. The excitement was written on each face and even the dogs joined them, sitting obediently and listening intently to the human.

"You're only allowed in the hay barn. If you should climb, be careful and don't go too high. Do you understand?" Joan explained.

"Yes, Miss Macleod."

Buzzing with excess energy, a single nod sent them racing across the grounds and through the huge opening.

"I know we've done a sweep, but I want Petermann, Harkiss, Eldridge, and Dougal to each take a corner of the barn. I will maintain visual on the eastern marshes in case the zombies make it across before we leave. Carpenter, you're on the western fringe."

They all moved off to their assigned positions, scanning the horizon for threats.

"Is there anything we can do?" Joan asked.

"Feel free to move around the area and help us keep watch. But if anything should attack, come and get us, don't try and tackle it alone."

"We can fight too, you know," declared Christopher. It wasn't a challenge, merely an observation.

"I know you can," Holbeck replied. "But after what we've been through to get you here, there's no point in taking unnecessary risks. When you've been on the barracks for a while and have been given weapons training, you'll be more than welcome to join the fray alongside us."

"Ok. I just didn't want you to think we weren't pulling our weight."

"Not at all. There'll be plenty of time for you to fight back over the coming months, I can assure you."

The children shrieked their enjoyment, bunching the spilled hay into piles and jumping into it from on high. The dogs leaped and bounded, caught up in the games with their new friends. It wasn't long before Angela called out that lunch was ready and the children filed back from the barn, coated in chaff and dust. The setters emerged to chaperone the children, sneezing madly and shaking themselves.

While the survivors ate their fill, the soldiers rotated on sentry duty. Nothing emerged from the surrounding area in the time it took to fuel themselves. Even the last of the undead who were trying to reach them from the holiday park had become trapped and harmless.

"We're going to be travelling back through villages that were full of the dead," Holbeck said to the adults. "There's a chance that some of the bastards will still be loitering around, so some of you will need to sit by the turret and the rest will be on the roof at the rear. I don't need to warn you to keep your arms and legs inside the ride at all times, do I?"

A couple gave nervous chuckles at the weak attempt at humour.

"No, Sergeant. I was wondering, though, how do we get to the island itself? I expect you have your own welcoming committee waiting at the gates to eat you?" Christopher asked.

"We're going straight across the ocean to the barracks. The old girls float despite their size."

He was astonished. "Bugger me, I never knew that. The wonders of modern technology."

"Indeed."

Once everyone had eaten their fill, the loading began. With more time to arrange the seating, most of the group could be squeezed inside the two separate cabs of each vehicle. Max and Angela took their dogs in the gunnery section, making them lay on the floor and providing a thick, rawhide bone for each to gnaw on the journey. The children were seated in the back with any supplies and a couple of adults to supervise. When it came time to roll out, only four had no seat but climbed up onto the roofs without complaint. A little discomfort was a small price to pay for the safety the base provided.

"I've left the key in the lock," Angela said to Holbeck in the turret. "You never know when someone may need the place."

"Good idea."

Looking to the shelter, she had bagged and tied it to keep moisture from penetrating the mechanisms. The house stood proudly, bearing the blood of battle on its walls. Angela's arm reached from the window, giving a final wave to their beloved home.

"When this is all over, I'll help you move back in," Holbeck offered.

"You're a darling, thank you."

"Don't think I'm a saint. I'm getting Harkiss to lift all the boxes."

***

A radio transmission had been sent to inform Thorney of their imminent arrival before leaving the farm. The further loss of Langham had been met with sorrow, but the news of

150

the survivors brought some comfort to their captain. She and Walker would receive a full military funeral with honours. Neither Holbeck or Hayward needed to mention the coffins would be empty.

Bobbing across the broad stretch of water, the drivers kept a wary eye on the surface for any of the floating monsters. Whether it was luck or just the tides, nothing presented itself and they made excellent time. Waiting on the shoreline was practically every soldier on the base except those on guard duty or other essential posting. Jubilant cheers rang out from the crowd, welcoming their comrades home. The sergeant raised a hand in greeting and the troops erupted into chants of *Holbeck, Holbeck, Holbeck!*

It was a bittersweet moment and, turning to look at Eldridge in the other vehicle, her face told the same story. Neither felt like conquerors and when the celebration started later, they would probably excuse themselves and pay quiet respect to their fallen brother and sister.

Captain Hayward stepped forward as the Warthogs came to a standstill, the stones crunching beneath the wide tracks. "It's good to see you, Sergeant. Damned fine work out there."

"Thank you, sir. We have some visitors you may like to meet."

Doors were flung open and the new arrivals gingerly stepped onto the beach. Like a breaking wave, the ecstatic soldiers rushed forward to say hello to the newcomers. Hands were shaken and backs patted in greeting. The children were hoisted onto shoulders and grinned madly as they were spun around. For the first time in months, the inescapable feeling of dread receded a little. New life had been brought to the barracks and each man and woman felt a renewed sense of purpose. They were no longer just waiting to die; they had a future to build for every little one who had made it to their sanctuary.

CHAPTER 20

With only a limited selection of modern blades at their disposal, it was decided to reclaim as many of the antique weapons as possible. Richard, a resident enthusiast, had joined them to explain the dangers of the swords which stood proudly on display. The variety was staggering and he detailed the age and use of each type for the uneducated. Short bladed steel with heavy leather handles. Long, elegant rapiers, ideal for piercing. Two handed behemoths which could cleave a man in two. Scimitars, imported from the middle east.

The group stood in silence, fascinated by the history surrounding the lethal weapons. Some bore the deep nocks of past battles, but Richard explained that it was mostly just Hollywood perpetuating the myth of epic sword clashes. In reality, slamming forged steel against forged steel was frowned upon and the best way to parry was to use the flat edge, or even better, a shield.

"It doesn't look quite so exciting, though," he admitted with a chuckle.

"Which ones are going to be safe to use?" Kurt asked.

"In my opinion, very few," he replied honestly. "You must remember some of these are hundreds of years old and more likely to fall to bits instead of cutting into a skull. The ones from the shop are utterly useless as well. They are cheap imitations and not designed to be swung."

"Damn. I was hoping for an arsenal," muttered Kurt. The survivors who had helped them take the castle must have been exceedingly fortunate to grab blades which had stood up to the punishment.

"My advice? Let's take a selection to the courtyard and test them against the trees. After a few swings, I can inspect them and see if they may be useful in a real fight."

"It can't hurt to be careful. Until we can raid a hardware shop for some more machetes and hatchets we'll just have to make do."

Richard pointed to Kurt's belt and the war pick hanging there. "Those don't suffer from the same issue. A lot of the maces, morning stars, and some axes are primarily made of solid steel. If a person can handle the weight, they can be quite devastating when used properly."

Winston stepped forward, mouth agape. A double-bladed battle axe was mounted by two hooks, impressive in its brutality. Looking towards Kurt, his eyes asked for permission. Sam, and to a lesser extent, Braiden, had vouched for him earlier in the day. He was just a victim of unfortunate circumstances. They had been ordered to remain on guard in his presence nonetheless. Braiden subtly touched the sharpened screwdriver to show he was prepared for any betrayal. The rotund lad would have no chance of swinging the weapon before being taken down. With a nod, his request was granted.

Lifting it, he was mesmerized. "Now I feel like an orc warrior from World of Warcraft." he whispered, hefting the weapon to judge the balance.

"Nerd," Sam teased and the younger members giggled.

"I was always more partial to a blood elf priest personally," remarked Pauline Ennis, one of the younger staff members.

"Holy or Discipline?" Winston replied, grinning.

Pauline rolled her eyes. "Shadow priest, of course. I'm no healer."

"Good choice," he said, gazing between his prize and her eyes.

"What the hell are you on about?" Braiden muttered.

"Nerd stuff," they replied in unison, before breaking into fits of laughter.

The others shook their heads and started to load up the wheelbarrow. Several of the hilts fell off or crumbled at the first touch, which lent credence to Richard's warnings. Jodi and Peter had both picked up a wickedly pointed morning star and gave them a few test swings.

"These iron spikes would crush a skull easily," Jodi explained, fingering the sharp tips.

"It's a bit heavier than your bat," Peter replied, following the main group as they left the room.

"I'm going to give it a try. The bat is good, but I've had a few times where it has just stunned them. With this, I know it will penetrate to their brain first swing which saves my energy."

"You'll need to be precise, though."

"I'm going to have a practice after the others have blooded themselves. Care to join me?"

"Absolutely."

DB helped Kurt to manhandle the fully laden barrow down the winding staircases, while the others carried two or three items each. Reaching the small group of trees, the weapons were tossed to the ground, clattering against each other.

Stephen winced. "Must you really do this? Those antiques are a priceless part of this country's history."

"I'm afraid so," said Kurt. "We need to be able to fight back as a whole group. Without these, half of us wouldn't have a way of defending ourselves."

"But what about the guns? Surely, they're keeping us safe," he complained.

Jonesy shook his head. "We've only got a few thousand rounds left. There are more zombies than that in this town alone. They're too valuable to use except in an emergency."

"What about the bows and arrows?"

"Three problems with that; Reclamation of the arrows outside the walls, the low number we have, and lastly, the lack of accuracy," Stephanie added.

"This is a disgrace. What's the point of surviving if we have nothing to cherish? Our culture is the one thing the undead can't destroy, unless we let them."

Kurt could see the curator was conflicted about what he saw as desecration of his legacy. Taking him to one side, he tried to reason with him. "Listen, I can understand your feelings, but we need to prepare people for any possible attack. What if I got Richard to do a preliminary check of each weapon and any that are obviously not going to withstand a strike, we carry back up and place them back on the display?"

Stephen looked across at the expert. "Can you do that?"

"I can only give my opinion based on what I've seen over the years. I may be able to save a few though."

After a moment of reflection, he replied, "I'll be waiting inside. When you're finished, can you please send someone to inform me and I'll return the weapons left behind to their rightful places."

"We will," confirmed Kurt.

"Such a waste," muttered Stephen as he departed.

Shaking his head, Kurt turned back to the group. "Those of you with solid weapons can have at it straight away. Those who would prefer swords can stand to the side and wait for Richard to hand you something you'll feel comfortable with. I've got to say it again; don't try and be a hero with a weapon that's too heavy. If you tire, you die, so select something that won't exhaust you too quickly."

Winston, Jodi, Peter, and some of the survivors moved away to a thick trunked Birch tree. Swinging their chosen clubs through the air a few times, Peter and Jodi began hammering at the wood. The points embedded deeply into the grain, and the only way to remove them was to twist and wrench until they freed themselves.

"What if that happens to a skull?" Peter wondered.

"It won't. The bone will crumble as it goes in and because of the taper on the steel it will come straight out again. It's the density of the timber that's the problem," Jodi replied.

"I suppose we can test it shortly on a real zombie and then see what happens."

Winston maintained a respectable distance while he limbered up. After the running debacle, he knew the value of stretching out and rotated his arms at the shoulder to warm them up. The morphine had dulled the pain in his forearm, but he knew he would be suffering for the fun later. Everyone had taken an interest and watched furtively as he got a feel for the long-hafted axe. The blade was dull and would need some attention, but for practice it was fine.

"Stand back just in case I miss and take my own head off," he warned.

Keeping a firm grip on the weapon, he took a deep breath and swung it behind and then over his head with a yell of hatred. The curved blade hit with a thud, rending the bark and biting deeply. The upper branches shook from the force of his blow and drops of moisture rained from the dead leaves. A round of applause rung out in appreciation of his strength.

Blushing, Winston took a bow. "Thank you, I'm here all week for your entertainment. Probably next week too, and the week after."

"Don't push your luck!" Kurt chipped in with a sly grin.

"It appears my show may be cancelled at some point, so make sure to get your fill of me while you can, folks!"

156

Pulling the axe out, he swung it in a wide arc from behind his back like a baseball bat. Once again, the steel cut into the trunk with ease.

"That'll be really useful. Hack their legs away from under them and the rest of us can finish them off," Braiden said from behind, startling Winston.

"You trust me to fight with you?" Winston had seen the secret signal between father and son.

"We'll see, won't we?" It was both a warning and an opportunity.

"Meet us after we've killed the frozen ones at the gate. We've something to discuss with you. Then we can put it to the other students," Sam added with a wink.

"Let me guess, you want an in-depth discussion on the merits of World of Warcraft."

Braiden pulled out the screwdriver. "Did you want to get stabbed?"

"Fine! Remain oblivious to the greatest game that's ever existed."

"I think we'll survive," Braiden replied.

At the sword inspection, Richard had picked two dozen which looked resilient enough to swing. The young and old picked their preference and spread out around the trunks.

"The rapiers are meant as a thrusting sword," Richard explained to those with the thin weapons. "Think of a fencer; that is how you must attack. A swing will just as likely lead to the blade shattering as a clean kill."

Without training, none of those wielding them could get anywhere near their point of focus. Holes pierced inches from the section of bark they were staring at, realistically meaning death if they had been facing a zombie. It quickly became apparent that they were too awkward with such a small target as the brain. Factoring in the adrenaline rush and subsequent tremors as a result, they were dropped in short order.

"Try the scimitars and short swords," advised Richard. "They can still stab, but the thick blades will allow you to slice too."

"There are only nine of them," said Anja, one of the female staff. "And I think the two handers will be a bit too much for me."

Jonesy stepped forward. "Here, take my hatchet. It's sharp enough to shave with."

"Thank you. I'll take good care of it."

"Everyone with a sword, please listen. Don't attack with all your strength or the blades will be damaged because the trunk has no flexibility. Hit it just hard enough to cut, but feel for any movement in the hilts or anything else that feels off."

A few minutes later, and with everyone huffing and puffing in the crisp morning air, the testing was complete. Only one of the nine swords had broken from a previously unnoticed crack in the blade itself. Out of over forty people, two thirds were now armed with more than foul language. The children had taken a back seat from the proceedings for the most part. Having already faced the monsters in the winding corridors during the first battle, they felt comfortable with destroying them. Or as comfortable as possible when fighting a rotting, undead foe. Conversely, it was down to the adults to prove themselves now.

"Is everyone ready?" Kurt shouted.

"No, but it needs to be done," replied Anja.

"You'll be fine," Jonesy whispered to her.

"Ok, move to the main entrance. Richard, would you mind fetching Stephen and helping him return the rest of these to the armoury?"

"Not at all. I hope I've been helpful."

"Very much so. Thank you."

As the older gentleman headed back inside, the group made their way to the portcullis housing. Three of the students had raced off to the chain room, ready for the signal to raise the massive steel construction. Overnight, the youngsters had formed a human chain and poured hundreds of litres of water through the sprinkler system. Every zombie in the courtyard was frozen, icicles hanging from their fingertips and chins, rime covered skin glittering in the morning sun. A single row, numbering around fifteen corpses, had missed the drenching from their sheltered position against the steel latticework. Two more were run through, pinned against the stone floor, thrashing like speared fish. DB ended them with two swipes of his machete.

"The rest of you stand back while we destroy the ones who're still moving," Kurt ordered.

"Watch closely and see how we do it," Gloria added.

"Raise it!" Kurt yelled.

Chains rattling, the gatekeepers obeyed. Inch by inch, the protective grille was hoisted until the unfrozen dead tumbled forward. Darting in and hacking down, the seasoned fighters butchered the creatures in seconds. Green blood started to flow over the bare stone towards them, causing the greenhorns to back away.

"Who's got the hooks?" Jonesy called and Holly stepped forward, handing them over.

In the back of the huge larder, three old butcher's meat hooks had been found. DB took one in each hand and thrust the points up beneath the ribcages of two of the zombies, dragging them clear of the archway. Kurt took the other and repeated the procedure until only a pool of emerald gore and skull fragments remained.

"Did everyone make sure to wear the shoes we prepared last night?" Sarah asked.

"Yes," replied Pauline, tapping her soles against the ground with a metallic clink. The rest of the group did likewise.

Bob the repairman had found a few boxes of tiny, self-tapping screws which had been left over from the kitchen ductwork installation. Their length meant they were unable to pierce through the solid, rubber soles and the heads themselves gave excellent traction. Each shoe had been drilled with twenty of the rough, steel fixings to ensure no accidents occurred as the slayers moved further out onto the ice-covered stone.

"Right, everyone needs to listen," Kurt yelled, commanding their attention. "We're only going to clear half of the area and leave the rest alone. At the moment, the ones frozen close to the drawbridge are holding back the larger horde outside. If we kill too many, they'll swarm us."

"Then we let them defrost and repeat the process?" Pauline asked.

"We've talked about it, and no. Once everyone has destroyed some of the zombies, we're going to seal it back up and leave them be."

"But why?" asked Anja.

Jonesy stepped forward to explain. "The prison has the same issue, but it works in their favour as well. Not only does it keep the hostages compliant, but it makes an infiltration that much harder. We can assume that at some point the prison inmates will try and breach our walls, which is why we'll use the same tactic. I know it is awful listening to them day and night, but until we get some certainty about their intentions it's for the best."

Kurt looked at the faces as they processed the information. "Because of our low number and the size of the walls..."

"Not to mention our infamous rebels who have weakened us further," added Gloria.

"And them too," Kurt agreed. "We've got to ensure we can cover as much ground as humanly possible within our limitations."

"What happens when we're safe from the lunatics at the prison?"

"We still remain vigilant. If anything, I was surprised to find survivors at both locations. It means there may well be a lot more people alive than I first thought. They may be friendly, they may not, but you can be damned sure we'll be ready for anyone who tries to take this place," growled Kurt.

The vehemence in his words filled the group with hope for the future. Warnings about the possibility of other, malevolent survivors gave them all an appreciation of how lucky they were that Kurt and his extended family had arrived first. Now all that remained was for them to prove their worth and kill the blasphemous frozen mannequins that stood only ten feet away.

DB gave the final order. "I want you to behave as if they were fully mobile. Complacency can mean death, and these bloody things will surprise you if you let them. You saw the way we maintained our distance; dart forward and slash, then retreat and repeat. I don't want any accidents, so also be aware of the man or woman at your side at all times. Fight as one unit. Begin!"

The veterans all kept a close eye on the dead as the others lined up. Safeties were switched off on the rifles and handguns, ready to put a bullet in any threat. If they caught a twitch of a thawing limb, the attack would be immediately abandoned and the steel would be dropped rapidly to seal them off once again. A panic amongst the uninitiated would be fatal.

"Oh God, this is disgusting," muttered an older woman, grimacing at the pocked, rotten face in front of her. Even the worms and maggots were brittle and immobile. Others joined in the grumbling, scant breakfasts churning in their stomachs at the vile sights.

"It's no worse than when we cleared the grounds," Kurt replied.

"But these things are staring at us."

"Better than trying to eat you," said Sarah.

"Ok, here goes," snarled Pauline, swinging her scimitar down. The blade went wide, shearing the side of the girl's skull off, cheek, ear and all, before plunging through the collarbone. The mushy, frosted blood started to drizzle from the wound as she withdrew. She looked back apologetically.

"Don't worry. It's just your nerves. Try again," Winston said.

Steeling herself, she lashed out. This time, the remaining face parted in the middle, one half cracking off at the neck and falling to the ground. Fragments of flesh and bone broke off, skittering between their legs.

"Good job. Now the rest of you!" DB barked.

The front line gibbered and hollered, flailing wildly as they shredded the undead. Thankfully, no one got hurt in the melee, and the bodies fell to the ground with dull thuds.

"It wasn't pretty, but good work everyone. Now let us get them cleared while the next row forms up," Kurt said, hooking the ribcages and pulling them inside.

With only enough space for six people side by side, the newbies had to rotate until they had cleared the archway and made progress into the open courtyard where they could finally spread out. Following each kill, the shaking hands became steadier as their confidence grew. Dozens of zombies had been slain, their remains forming a growing pile within the castle. A couple of the survivors were holding back which Kurt picked up on immediately.

"Nick, Freya, what's the problem?"

"I don't feel..." grimaced Nick, looking across at Freya who had gone deathly white.

"I..." she choked, before a stream of vomit burst forth, coating the body at her feet. This triggered Nick's own sickness and he added to the warm puddle of bile and bran flakes. Two more of the group retched at the sight and sound, before a torrent of liquid poured from their own mouths.

162

"That's so gross," muttered Anja.

"I think you should go back inside and compose yourselves. We'll finish up," Gloria offered and the four gratefully hobbled away, wiping at their lips.

"This is why it was so important to get you out here. If we were in a real fight, they would've overwhelmed us," Kurt explained. They looked at him and nodded weakly; it was a valuable lesson in the realities of their new existence.

"My Viking ancestors would be proud of me," Anja beamed, revelling in the killing. Turning back to the task, she buried the hatchet into another decaying forehead, ripping it free with a yell of rage.

"I think we're nearing the tipping point," Kurt warned, seeing the surging mass outside push against the ice encrusted meat barricade. It would take very little for the remaining zombies to topple like skittles.

"Everyone back inside!" Sarah ordered.

Winston coughed politely, holding his axe up. "May I?"

"Ok, but hurry up! Everyone else, get back now!" Kurt shouted.

"One swing, I promise."

Facing off against the wall of filth, he got into a comfortable stance and hoisted the battle-axe onto his shoulder. Rotating his hips, he swung with every ounce of strength in his possession. It was devastating. The steel blade smashed through five skulls before slowing down, finally coming to rest in the neck of a sixth.

"Holy shit," blurted Braiden, eyes wide.

A feeling of raw power flowed through Winston's body, making him feel invincible. He was death personified, the doom bringer, a warrior without equal. Raising the axe overhead, he roared his triumph. The dead outside responded with their own guttural cries, redoubling their efforts. The dam gave way, bodies tossed aside or to the ground in the crush as the horde advanced.

"Shit!" Winston shrieked. Turning tail and bolting back to the castle, he ducked under the falling steel. With a clang, the portcullis dropped into place. "That was close!"

"Dumbass," Sam said with a chuckle, punching him on the arm.

CHAPTER 21

"Thanks for coming, everyone," Sam said by way of getting the meeting started.

Sat around their bedroom were the students and a couple of the younger staff, all eager to hear the secret plan which had been mentioned earlier. They picked at a lunch of spam and stale crackers with disinterest, as much because of the excitement as the lacklustre fare.

"Don't leave us hanging. What did you want to see us about?" Holly begged.

"It's always been the case that the adults were meant to keep us safe, right? I think what we saw earlier didn't bode well for us at all," Sam began.

"They didn't do too badly."

"Really? What about the breakfast all over the floor outside?" said Braiden.

"You can't blame them for blowing chunks though. The zombies are bloody awful; the way they look, the way they smell, the green blood. I mean, what's that all about?" Holly remarked, pulling a disgusted face.

"The difference is that when we arrived to take the castle, you all stepped up without complaint and fought by our side. From the watchtower, and then in the corridors, you didn't hesitate."

"We were all scared out of our wits," Pauline admitted.

"Of course, you were," Braiden shrugged. "You were taking on a bunch of rotting corpses for the first time. I'd be more worried if you weren't afraid."

"You weren't scared, though. I saw you kill them as if they were nothing."

Pauline nodded eagerly. "You were actually enjoying it!"

"Not as much as Winston was earlier. Six kills in one swing is amazing," Sam remarked.

The teenager blushed at the praise and turned away.

"Are you ever going to tell us the plan or do we need to pin you down and tickle it out of you?" Holly demanded, holding up her fingers in threat.

"Winston will explain everything," Braiden replied. "This psycho was breaking out of his sanctuary in the middle of the night to forage for sweets. He went out alone, unarmed, against the undead. Can you imagine that?"

Mouths gaped at the revelation and Winston rolled his eyes. He had told the boys that in strictest confidence and now the embarrassment burned even deeper.

Sam saw the discomfort and jumped in. "What my brother was trying to say is that out of everyone in the castle, this guy is the bravest of us all."

Braiden nodded, staring at him with a growing respect. "Exactly. Sam and I had the protection of my family and two soldiers when we travelled across the south coast. Winston had to overcome every danger alone, without guns."

"You're going to make me cry," Winston said, dramatically wafting a hand to dry his eyes.

"Cut it out, you idiot," Braiden chuckled, pushing him.

"Ok. We've been talking and we think it would be a good idea to take a bigger role in the defence of the castle. We're younger and can adapt far better to what is happening; that includes our speed, strength, and if I can lose this," he patted his belly, "Stamina."

He waited for a few moments while the youngsters digested the idea. Slowly, they all looked at one another and agreed.

"We've seen the divisions already appearing between the grown-ups. Kurt is a warrior and protector, but he'll need us behind him, fully prepared for what's coming."

"What do you mean? The zombies?" Holly wondered.

"They are a threat, of course, but the biggest danger is from the prison. All three of us have spent time with Mike and Debbie and they're as crazy as a box of frogs. They have an army at their disposal and they'll come for us. It may not be for a while because of the winter, but make no mistake, they're plotting as we speak."

"What can we do to prepare for it? We're stuck inside these four walls," explained Pauline.

"The first thing is maintaining our fitness regime. When my legs stop aching, anyway," Winston replied.

"Jonesy said we need to keep going through the pain," said Sam.

"That's easy for you to say, you're a skinny bastard. Try carrying Braiden on your back and jogging around the grounds. You'd soon change your tune."

"I've been carrying him ever since we fought in the classroom during the outbreak."

Braiden grabbed him in a headlock and they started to wrestle, laughing madly. "Bollocks! I was the one who saved you while you threw math textbooks at the zombies and shrieked like a girl."

"You hid behind Miss Blume the whole time!" Sam retorted.

"I think we all did," Braiden gasped, letting his brother go. "She was amazing and so brave for a teacher."

"If you two are finished cuddling, I'll continue," Winston snickered.

The room erupted in mocking oohs and the boys sat down, grinning and panting.

167

"Secondly, DB and Jonesy have offered to train us to use their pistols and rifles. We begin in the next few days when they find the time."

The students were unable to hide their excitement and Winston held up a hand to quieten them.

"We're going to be limited on the training by the amount of ammunition that they have, but they want others to have some experience in case something bad happens to them. Personally, I think we'll do better with the bows and arrows, especially when we set foot outside the walls."

"Did you know there's a sporting goods store just on the outskirts of town? I saw it as we drove in," Holly explained.

"So? We don't need trainers and golf clubs," Braiden teased.

"How about the bows and crossbows that I saw advertised in the window, smart ass?"

"You'll have to show us on a map. That'll be a fantastic haul if we can get to it," Sam admitted.

Pauline leaned forward, brow creasing. "Did I hear you say *when* we set foot outside the walls a second ago?"

"Yes. And this is where it's going to get complicated and extremely dangerous. None of you can truly understand what it's like out there until you've lived it. This brings me onto the third point. Sam and Braiden are going to ask Kurt if we can go outside and fight them."

"Are you nuts?" Holly demanded. The others shared the same opinion and voiced their disapproval.

"I know you think it's a crazy idea, but we'll need to eventually take them on face to face on their ground. I'd rather control the time and place that it happens. Silence and subtlety is going to be our friend. I'm not suggesting we open the portcullis and battle through the thousands at the main gate. We can either open one of the back gates where there are fewer, or drop from the wall on ropes and kill small numbers at our leisure before retreating to safety."

"But what if something goes wrong?" Pauline asked. She could understand the logic but her fluttering stomach would not relent.

"You can feed me to them. With my size, they'll be gnawing on me for quite a while which gives you time to escape," Winston replied with a wink.

"Stop talking about yourself like that," Pauline admonished, swatting him on the arm.

"Sorry, force of habit, but I mean what I said. I'll hold them off while you retreat if the worst should happen."

"I'm not even sure my dad will let us do it anyway. I wouldn't if I was making the call," Sam added.

"We'll convince him," said Braiden. "Or we'll just have to sneak out and do it anyway."

"Fuck that!" Winston blurted. "I've only just got here and he's looking for an excuse to mistrust me. How'll it look when I help to sneak you all outside the castle? I'll be lucky if he just tosses me from the tallest tower."

"You leave my dad to us," Sam assured him. "We'll take the blame if we need to."

"That's easy for you to say. I've heard what he can do with that axe of his and I prefer to keep my most important parts attached."

"Pussy," Braiden teased.

Sam broke in. "It doesn't matter anyway until we've had the talk. And we won't have the talk unless you're all on side."

The nervous teens stared back at the three boys, contemplation etched on their faces. For a long while they sat in silence, with only the crackling of the fire popping in the corner. Turning to each other, Sam and Braiden looked unsure until finally Winston was tempted to speak up and cleared his throat.

Holly nodded slowly and stood up. "I'm in. I want a future with happiness, not fear. I want children and grandchildren who don't have to look over their shoulder for a shambling monster."

Pauline joined her and, one by one, the others fell in behind them.

"It looks like we have an army of our own," Sam said.

"It's more like a squad or a small platoon, really," Winston replied. "Our army typically had about one hundred to one hundred and fifty thousand soldiers."

Braiden shook his head. "Nerd."

CHAPTER 22

The soldiers worked in silence, neither needing, nor wanting, to talk. The rush of battle and the dizzying high of rescuing so many people in a world thought lost to the dead had faded. Replacing it was a feeling of melancholy. Unburdened of the need to be on guard at all times, the peace and quiet allowed bad memories to inveigle their resting minds. The screams of Walker as he was dragged into the mass of zombies. Langham's last, heroic stand which might have single-handedly assured the mission's success by ensuring the gas tanks exploded. Like robots, they cleaned and oiled their weapons, the sounds of springs and mechanisms being stripped the only noise in the vehicle hangar.

Corporal Hague entered, flanked by two of Baxter's men. The prisoners were dressed in blue overalls with high visibility jackets to show their low status. Once surly, they now meekly stared at the floor, dragging the heavily laden pallet movers across the grey painted concrete. Crates of grenades and various calibres of ammunition had been stacked carefully on the lifting aid. Two L16A2 81mm mortars had been added, along with fifty greenies; the name given to the plastic cases which carried a pair of shells. Explosives had been woefully ineffective so far, but it was decided it would be worth having them just in case.

The Royal Engineers were going over the battered APCs while maintaining a respectful distance to the grieving team. They carried out their checks with an almost reverential care, as if the camouflaged beasts were a symbol of humanities changing fortune. Many of the soldiers on base had passed through to pay their respects to Eldridge and the team for their losses. Those that found it hard to express themselves would raise a beer to the fallen during the evening's festivities.

The six soldiers lined up, facing the freshly washed down armoured carriers. Tomorrow they would be returning to the fray, hoping for an uninterrupted run to the prison and castle. With the undead teeming across the land, it was a fool's hope.

"Is everyone still ready to move out at first light?" Holbeck asked, quietly.

"I'd be happy to get a bite to eat and head out right now," Dougal muttered. The last thing he wanted was to spend the night sharing stories of Walker and Langham, it was still far too raw.

"We need a night's rest."

"I don't think I'll be able to sleep," Petermann admitted.

"Me either, buddy, but we need to at least try."

"We won't be doing ourselves any favours by going out frazzled. I want to get to our brothers in one piece," said Eldridge, squeezing Petermann's shoulder.

"That's the last of it!" Dougal said, pushing the empty trolley out of the way.

The tannoy crackled into life. "I share your enthusiasm on this joyous day, so drink and be merry tonight. Before that, I'm afraid we have more pressing issues. I want everyone mustered in the main hall in thirty minutes. Hayward, out."

As the noise died away, Eldridge turned to her fellow troops in the vehicle hangar. "What do you think he means?"

"Fuck knows, but it didn't sound good. Let's grab a brew and go and see what's going on," Holbeck replied.

***

"Ladies and gents, thank you for coming. I know you want to get back to the celebration as soon as possible, so I won't take up too much of your time. I can't sugar coat this; our situation has gone from bad to worse."

"What do you mean, sir?" Holbeck asked when the captain paused.

"Twenty-four hours ago, our only concern was wresting back a vast city from the clutches of the undead to facilitate the docking of Her Majesty's Royal Navy at Portsmouth Dockyard. Now, we have something even more dangerous to undertake."

No one balked at the news.

"Our forces in the Chiltern Mountains are under siege and it won't be long until they fall."

The whole room erupted with worried conversation at the thought of their fellow soldiers in mortal danger.

"Dauntless has been closely monitoring the situation in London on the off-chance contact is re-established with the government. Unfortunately, radio communication with the Prime Minister and the cabinet remain out of commission."

"Thank God for small mercies," muttered a soldier at the back.

"I have to agree with you in some small part," replied Hayward. Politicians had no clue about military matters and the only reason contingents of the Army, Navy, and Air Force still lived was because they had ignored suicidal orders. "If that was our only problem, we wouldn't have an issue. However, satellite imagery shows the undead are leaving the city by the thousands and the exodus is showing no signs of slowing. Whether they are migrating because of the lack of... stimulus." He almost said food. "We don't know. Irrespective, the reality is that in the past few weeks hundreds of thousands of the zombies have left the city. By the end of the week, it will be millions. The same pattern is repeating from every population centre across the country."

"And they're attacking the mountains, sir?"

"Not quite yet, and that's the biggest dilemma we face. Some unknown instinct is driving them straight towards any remaining pockets of life. That means we have a massive horde headed south towards the coast as well. Our forces are close to breaking point with the relatively small number that are already attacking. When the wave of zombies from London and the surrounding area hit, they'll roll over them as if they're nothing. Current estimates put contact at twelve days."

"We need to evac them now!"

"Extraction still isn't an option. As soon as we weaken their front lines, they'll be overrun by the remaining undead. Ammunition and food supplies are nearly all gone because the last chinook crews are trying to bolster several different fortifications at once," explained the captain.

"What can we do then, sir?"

"We have two choices; We can sit here and pray for them…"

The shouts of outrage echoed from the walls.

Holding up his hands, the yells diminished. "Or we can saddle up in the remaining Chinooks and help them to repel the vile bastards."

"Once we land, there won't be anywhere to fall back to will there, sir?" Holbeck asked.

"No, Sergeant. This is a one-way ticket. Once we get there, it'll be a fight to the death. If we win, we can buy ourselves a window to withdraw and bring our boys and girls home in safety. If we lose? Hell, we'll give the bastards a good kicking first."

"What happens to Dauntless and the other ships if we fail?"

"Admiral Wright has given us the go ahead under the assumption we may not succeed. The battle group in the Solent still has a chance of finding another way if we fall. It may just need a leap of faith and an all-out attack on Portsmouth Naval Base from the water, even if it means losses. What's certain, however, is our troops *will* die if we don't reinforce them. That's something I can't ignore."

"We're with you, Captain!"

The whole room agreed in unison.

"I'll be liaising with command on the logistics and as soon as I know more details I'll share them with you. Dismissed!"

Eldridge caught Holbeck's eye, raising her hands to say *where does this leave us?*

"Captain, can we have a word?"

"Of course, Sergeant. Follow me to comms."

***

"What's the status of our mission, sir? We were hoping to move out at first light."

"For now, the mission is on hold I'm afraid. Because you've been out there and faced the things, I need you and your team more than ever. You'll be heading the convoy with me."

Holbeck was taken aback. "Convoy, sir? I thought you said we were going by air?"

"If we ever hope to hold them back, we're going to need some hardware. We have the personnel to take the Challenger tank, two Warriors, two Warthogs and four Mastiffs. They're all operational and ready to roll out. The remaining soldiers will be airlifted to bolster the front lines in readiness for our arrival."

Holbeck nodded. "I know the team will be disappointed, but we'll do what's required, sir."

"Sir, may I speak freely?" Eldridge asked.

175

"Of course, Private."

"We need soldiers with experience against the undead. There may be two mean sons of bitches who have fought the monsters on foot across land and captured a castle. Those guys are not a million miles from where we stand."

"I can't risk it, Private. If you get bogged down out there, we lose some of our most vital assets."

"If we leave at dawn we could be there by nightfall. I know the others will fight all the harder having Jonesy and DB at our side, sir."

"What makes you think they'll want to leave their new friends?"

"With all due respect, sir, that's not even a question. As soon as they hear of the trouble coming from London, they'll be on our side. And if I may be so bold, how many soldiers will be remaining at Thorney?"

"A bare minimum of essential personnel. Communications, reconnaissance and troops to patrol the gates and perimeter."

"Sir, we promised the folks at the farm and holiday park a sanctuary. If we can't deliver that until we make it back, then the castle may be a safer place. We'd just have to get them there."

"What do you suggest?" Hayward posed, stopping outside the communications room.

"Let us go and make contact with the prison and the castle…"

"Not the prison," Hayward shook his head. "It's strategically irrelevant for now and the detour would add unnecessary risks."

"Ok, we head straight to the castle. We make contact with Privates Jones and Mutanto and explain the situation. If they're secure, we return to base and load the civvies into one of the choppers. Should the worst happen and we don't make it back from the mountains, at least they'll be in a safe place. We all saw how close the undead were to swarming us during the cull. If the London horde reaches the base, they'll eventually clog the river and flood across the barracks."

"That's a sound plan, but we need the birds to help the Logistics Corps. If we don't get enough food, water, and ammo on that mountain we'll all die."

"It would only take an hour, sir," Holbeck interjected. "And if I may also speak freely, I'd feel better knowing the people that we'd saved were somewhere fortified. Fifty feet of water and a chain link fence just doesn't have the same impact as solid stone walls."

"I've got no problem laying down my life out there, sir. Nor did Langham or Walker, but I think we'd be doing their memory a disservice if we rescued the civvies only to let them die on this island," Eldridge added.

"Dishonouring their sacrifice was never my intention, Private," Hayward replied in a clipped tone.

"Sorry, sir."

"That being said, I understand that emotions are running high and I can appreciate your sense of responsibility towards those people, especially the children. Leave it with me. I'll make sure to leave a window open in the schedule should you find our wayward brothers at the castle."

"Thank you, sir!"

"Tomorrow we'll be running drills and I need you here for that. You can move out at dawn in two days' time."

The soldiers came to attention and saluted the officer.

"Dismissed."

CHAPTER 23

"Hi, Joan," Eldridge said.

"Private Eldridge, please join me. I still haven't had a chance to thank you all in person."

"Call me Beth. Do you have a drink?"

Holding up a beer, she smiled. "Yes, thank you."

"I was surprised that you aren't with the others at the party. Christopher said you'd gone to the library to gather your thoughts."

"I just needed some quiet time and it's too cold to be wandering around outside. As much as I love the fact that we're safe now, it just reminds me of all those people we couldn't save and I didn't want to sour the mood. Those poor children will never have the chance to say goodbye to their families."

"Sadly not, but they have a chance at a life now. All because of your group's bravery during the outbreak."

"It didn't feel like bravery. It felt like a few hours of unending terror and bloodshed that I can't stop dreaming about."

"I remember it well," Eldridge shuddered. "No one would believe what was actually happening and we lost a lot of good soldiers. Then things got much worse."

"I know what you mean," Joan commiserated.

"How did you keep them all safe. If you don't mind talking about it, that is?"

"It may help me to get some of it off my chest. It all happened so quickly I was acting on instinct and adrenaline for the most part. To the west there's an old church which was both a blessing and a curse."

"I don't understand. How could it be a blessing?"

"Because it was so close, we were hit by the newly resurrected monsters within the first hour. If we'd been caught unawares by the swarm that came from Selsey town later in the day we wouldn't have stood a chance. Their... incompleteness... Is that even a word? It meant they were a lot slower because of the bits they left behind. It gave us a chance."

***

"Trailer thirty-eight F?" Joan said into the phone. "I'll be there asap."

"Problem?" asked Maisey, the assistant receptionist.

"There's a leak in one of the trailers. It's the one we've had a couple of antisocial behaviour complaints about so I expect they've been messing around with the plumbing. I was going to get Xander to have a word later, but I can do it myself."

"Probably better that you go. If they get mouthy, you can be a bit more diplomatic."

"Pardon me," said a young lady, approaching the desk. "Is this the right place for the Teddy Club?"

"It certainly is," Joan replied. "All I need you to do is fill in this form with your details."

Offering the clipboard across the counter, the woman took it and began fishing for a pen in her handbag.

"Here, take mine," offered Maisey.

"You're a lifesaver, thank you."

"You're welcome. What's your name, sweetheart?" Maisey asked the child who darted behind her mother's skirt to hide.

"It's Penelope," replied the mother. "Say hello to the nice lady."

The red-haired girl peered from behind the pleated camouflage and whispered, "Hi."

"Do I need to pay now?"

"It's all part of the holiday. There's no charge," said Joan.

"Really? That's amazing. I didn't even see that on the pamphlet," beamed the mother.

"It's not. We had an issue with our last marketing manager who has since left us. If you notice any other parents looking like they could use a break, send them our way and we'll entertain the children for a few hours."

While Maisey played peek a boo with the young girl, the mother shook Joan's hand gratefully.

"You go with the nice ladies, Penelope, and I'll be back to pick you up at two o'clock."

"I don't want to, Mummy."

Joan was a dab hand with children and moved from behind the counter, kneeling by the cowering girl. "What's your favourite thing to do in the whole wide world?"

Looking uncertainly up at her mother, she pulled the skirt around her like a protective cloak.

"Penelope, the nice lady is talking to you."

"I bet I can guess," Joan coaxed, smiling warmly. "Is it… playing football with the boys?"

The little girl turned away, burying her face into the fabric.

"I don't blame you. Boys are icky. How about playing armies?"

The head shook slightly. Joan caught sight of the Jurassic Park motif on her t-shirt. An unusual interest for such a young girl, but she went with it.

"Really? You look like a soldier. Ok… Is it… playing with dinosaurs? I love how scary they sound," Joan said, mooing like a cow.

180

Penelope giggled into the skirt.

"What? That's how dinosaurs sound, isn't it? Or is it like this?" Joan whinnied like a horse.

The girl giggled again and turned towards her. "That's a horse, silly."

"Penelope!" gasped the mother.

Joan winked to say it was fine then raised an eyebrow at the girl. "Are you sure?"

"Yeah. Dinosaurs sound like this," she replied meekly, making a cute attempt at a roar.

"That doesn't sound right," Joan replied, "I'm sure they sound like this." She clucked like a chicken.

"That's a chicken," giggled the girl.

"All this time I've been getting it wrong." Joan threw her hands up in frustration. "Would you mind teaching me?"

"Mummy, can I?" asked Penelope.

"I think that would be wonderful."

Taking Joan's hand, the girl led her past the reception desk. The initial reticence was completely forgotten in the excitement of teaching a grown up. "It's really easy. Have you ever heard the noise a lion makes?" Almost as an afterthought, she turned around and waved, "Bye, Mummy. See you later."

"Bye, sweetheart. I love you."

Chatting excitedly, they moved through the building to the auditorium. Seven children were already playing in the hall. Seeing the new girl, they all rushed over to greet her.

"Everyone, this is Penelope. She's been teaching me how to sound like a dinosaur," Joan explained and they both roared.

The youngsters clapped and gathered around to say hello.

"Do you like colouring?" asked one boy.

181

"Yeah, I guess so," replied Penelope, feeling a little overwhelmed. She moved towards the familiarity of her new friend, pulling on her leg.

"Sweetie, that's Christopher." Joan pointed at the friendly looking man. "He doesn't know how to roar, either. Would you mind showing him too?"

"Yeah!"

Joan grinned as the beautiful girl scurried off to play.

"Are you ok with them? I've got to do a couple of jobs and I'll be back," Joan asked Christopher.

"Are you kidding? We're going to have a great time and I'm going to learn to roar!"

***

"Maisey, are you ok holding down the fort while I fix the leak?"

"Sure. It's still early, so the only people coming through are the kids who your new friend can round up."

"New friend?" Joan asked.

"Mrs Glenmoore. She's over the moon with you and how you handled her little girl. She's going to write a letter of thanks to the bosses."

"That's nice of her. I'll be back in a jiffy!"

Pushing through the double doors, the wind tugged at her hair. Dark clouds were gathering overhead. The passing holidaymakers all looked downcast and Joan pitied the poor souls. The British weather was a gamble, and they had lost.

"Good morning," she said to an elderly couple as they passed.

"Is it?" grunted the old man.

"You've got your health and the love of a beautiful woman. I'd say that's good."

He refused to answer, but Joan felt a warm glow as his hand sought out his wife's, giving it a squeeze. Opening the back of the maintenance van, she checked the tools were present. Gary had left the bloody things in the pool room the last time and she had made it all the way across the park before having to come back. It looked unprofessional and she hated that.

"Excuse me?"

Joan turned to see a gathering of parents and their excited children. "How can I help you?"

"Is it true that the kid's club is free?"

"Absolutely. It doesn't cost a penny. I'm sorry for the misunderstanding."

"That's ok," replied one of the fathers. Turning to his son, he asked, "Did you want to go?"

Joy lit up the young faces with thoughts of getting out from under the dank and dreary summer weather.

"If you pop in and see my friend, Maisey, she'll help you with the paperwork. It runs every day from ten in the morning until two in the afternoon."

Thanking her profusely, they hurried inside. As Joan turned the van around, the smiling adults emerged. They stood around for a few moments, seemingly lost and unsure what to do with their newfound freedom. One of the women made a suggestion and the heads all bobbed in agreement. Joan moved around the building and lost sight of them just as they headed off on whatever activity had them so delighted. It probably involved a local pub and alcohol.

***

"What took you so fucking long?" demanded the tattooed man who ran up to the van window.

"Mr Lord? I came as soon as I got the call, sir."

"Well that's not fucking good enough!" he growled, blocking the door.

"If you move out of my way I can fix the problem and see about getting you an upgrade on your accommodation," Joan said, trying to maintain her cool.

"You'd better," he yanked on the handle, pulling the door open aggressively. "I want compensation as well. This has completely ruined our fucking holiday."

"I don't have that power, sir. You'll need to write to the owners and make a complaint. Where's the water coming from?"

Ignoring the request to see the plumbing issue, he grabbed her by the arm. "I'm not writing no letter. You get your supervisor on the phone and get him over here. Now!"

"Take your hand off me and show me the problem. Sir!" Joan replied, pulling away.

"Who the fuck do you think you are, you uppity bitch?"

Joan fronted him up, glaring. "I'm the person who decides if you stay in this sodden mess. Or I can just have you thrown out of this park, physically if I feel in the mood. By real men who don't try and act tough by accosting women. If you touch me again, not only will you have a broken hand to deal with, but you'll be sleeping on the street with the rest of your parasitic family. Do you understand?"

Taken aback, the man's face reddened. "I'll have your job for this. No one speaks to me like that."

"I don't think so. The small print of your contract states that any physical or verbal abuse directed at any member of staff is grounds for immediate expulsion from the holiday park. But I expect you're too dumb to have bothered to read that before you paid, aren't you?"

"I..."

"One call and you're gone," Joan declared. "Try me and see what happens."

A woman came to the door, cigarette dangling from her lips. A screaming baby was cradled in her arms. "What's the fucking holdup?" she shouted.

Ignoring her, Joan stared at the man. "I'm going to get my tools. You're going to go inside and tell your wife to stop swearing. We have nice people here and I won't have you ruining their one short break a year with your foul attitude. If I hear of any more instances of abusive behaviour, you'll be gone before your wife can even light another smoke to poison your child's lungs. Now get out of my face."

A faint scream came from the western edge of the park and Joan paused, listening intently. The sound lacked the excited quality of general holiday shenanigans. There it was again! It was filled with pain, a great deal of it.

"Are you coming or not?" asked the man with a bit more respect.

Joan ducked under the trailer and switched off the water at the inlet valve.

"I'll be back soon. I think one of the patrons has hurt themselves."

"But..."

"Five minutes, sir. The water is off so it won't leak any more. While I'm gone I'll put in the call for a gold trailer, ok?"

Looking sheepish, the surly man relented. "Ok. I'll get the area cleared for you to work."

"Thank you."

Leaving the man to argue with his wife, Joan drove away. Twisting and turning through the carbon copy roads, she estimated where the yell had emanated from. A small group saw her coming and started to approach. Some were covered in blood and as she got closer, their injuries came into stark relief. Lagging behind the wounded guests were the source of the damage. Dozens of... corpses, lumbering along.

185

"Oh, my God!"

Maggots and grave worms dropped from their ruptured carcasses. The insects writhed on the ground, the cold concrete far less accommodating than decaying flesh. The newly turned holiday makers surrounded her van, hammering on the bonnet as she braked in shock. Crimson hand prints smeared the glass and bodywork, obscuring her view of the horrific wounds. Mentally shaking herself, she sped forward, sending the creatures flying. The repulsive abominations from the crypts burst apart when the vehicle ploughed through. Limbs held in place by the last scraps of meat and tendon went sailing off to the sides of the road and at least one head bounced twice on the roof before splitting apart on the ground like a ripe melon.

Chaos raged all around. The undead were breaking through the hollow doors of the holiday trailers in seconds and ravaging the cowering occupants. Each new corpse added strength to the growing army of rot. Weaving through the dead bodies, a cold chill tingled at every nerve ending when they started to get back up again. Partially chewed chunks ripped from their own bodies lay at their feet. The dead flesh was no longer alluring to either the near fossilised or fresher zombies, so they ignored it and sought pulsing meat.

The children! That single thought blew away the cobwebs of disbelief which were weaving their way around her traumatised mind. They were totally oblivious to the horror unfolding only yards from the walls of their playhouse. If the monsters were inside, she had to move fast. Pulling a handbrake turn, the large vehicle juddered and squealed as it skidded around the corner of the building. Seeing the abominations pushing through the entrance doors, her heart sunk. Poor Maisey was totally defenceless. Slamming through a group who were drawn to the faint screams within, the van came to rest on top of their thrashing forms. Stepping around the arms, she pulled open the rear doors and quickly jumped back as tools and equipment cascaded onto the floor. Screaming as a hand lashed out and clutched her ankle, she reached inside for a shovel. Stabbing the blade down, it hit the tarmac with a resounding clang, severing the hand completely. Prising the fingers loose, she saw another zombie's shadow pass the driver's window.

Taking a crowbar in her other hand, she slammed the door and jabbed at the grey face. Stunned, it staggered back a few paces and Joan barged past, sending it crashing to the ground. Seeing the front door was swinging closed on the pneumatic hinge, she quickly sidestepped through the shrinking gap. Untouched by the ocean winds outside, the smell was nauseating in the confines of the small reception. Faeces and decomposition mixed with the coppery scent of blood which trailed across the carpet. Maisey was whimpering, trying desperately to avoid the grasping hands of the zombies beneath. Upon seeing them, she had jumped on the counter and tried to climb above the ceiling void. The weak, aluminium cross struts were only designed to hold the plaster squares aloft. Hooking her knees and elbows over the braces, the thin bars begun to split under the extra weight.

"Hold on!" Joan shouted.

Using the crowbar to secure the entry door handles, she turned back to the undead, brandishing the shovel. Swinging it down, the first zombie was swatted like a fly, forehead crumpling. The gong of metal on bone sounded like the chime of an old bell tower. Slashing sideways, the shovel blade sunk through the side of the skull and stuck fast. As it fell, the weapon was pulled from her hands. A series of twangs preceded Maisey's startled yelp as the whole ceiling collapsed, showering the area in dust. Winded from the fall, she could only lay there gasping as they pounced. Covered in white powder, the ravenous zombies added tones of crimson to the scene. Screaming in desperation, Joan wrenched the spade free, taking the top of the head off at the same time. The horrific, wet sounds of tearing and eating had replaced the girl's weakening wails. Joan still hacked at their backs and heads to try and force them away in the vain hope of saving her. Catching sight of Maisey through the melee put paid to that. Her neck was mostly gone, only the thick spinal column preventing full decapitation.

"I'm sorry, love," Joan whispered, giving up the fight.

Her only concern now was the children and the staff deeper in the building. Slipping into the pool house, the water was crystal clear and still. The lifeguards would not be in until noon and the absence of swimmers made the search much easier.

"Is anyone in the changing rooms? We have an emergency!" Joan yelled at the top of her lungs.

Nothing. Turning back to the corridor which led to the food and entertainment wings, one of the satiated corpses lumbered through. Covered in the blood of her friend, Joan felt a wave of revulsion and apoplectic rage. Using the shovel like a spear, the blade caught it in the face, embedding deeply into the mouth. Ripping it back, the jaw lolled from the severed muscle and bone. Jabbing at the chest, she drove it towards the pool. One of the feet slipped from the curved stone rim into the water and the body toppled to the side, cracking its already damaged face on the edge before slipping beneath the surface. The water churned, spreading a pink cloud that rapidly deepened to red.

Christopher came running down the hall. "What's going on, Joan?"

"You won't believe me, but it's zombies! Get back inside the auditorium and seal the doors!"

"Very funny," he replied. "But seriously, what's all the racket about?"

"Does this look like a joke?" Joan said, holding up the gore coated spade as she passed him towards the entertainment wing.

As if on cue, the gurgle of blood filled lungs came from behind her. Maisey staggered into view, head lolling against her back, clothing and flesh hanging in tatters. The shredded tubes of her throat coughed up bubbles of claret.

"Holy fuck!"

Joan pushed him forcefully towards the hall, "Now do you believe me? Get back and barricade the doors! I'm going to kill these things and seal the building!"

"I'll come with you, you'll need my help," he argued.

"No. I need you to protect the children. Get those doors barricaded and call for help!" Joan was adamant and Christopher could see she would accept no argument.

"For God's sake, be careful."

"Make sure they don't see anything. Some of those things used to be their parents."

"I'll make sure of it. If you need me, promise me you'll shout?"

"I will," she lied.

As he raced off to secure the doors and summon the police, Joan pushed through into the arcade. Chirps, beeps and shrill tones came from the machines. The same temptation that lured innumerable punters to the slots now worked on the dead. Their vacant eyes watched the flowing graphics and flashing lights. Taking full advantage of the distraction, Joan staved in their heads, spraying the screens with brain matter. Frantic cries were coming from the food court, drawing them away from the dazzling colours with the promise of a meal that was not for sale.

"Joan, help me!" Antonio shrieked.

Beating at them with a ladle, he was taken down in seconds. A young girl was backing away from a heavyset zombie behind the burger bar, begging him to spare her life.

189

"Keep away from it! I'm coming!" Joan cried.

The spatulas and assorted salt and pepper shakers within reach were useless. Using a saucepan, she scooped out a few litres of bubbling fat from the frying trough. Tossing the seething liquid over the zombie, its skin started to blister and peel away. Unfazed by the horrific injury, it advanced. Foot slipping on the oil, its legs flew out and it hit the ground hard.

"Here! Come on!" Joan urged, holding out a hand to help her over the counter.

"They killed Josh. They were eating him..." muttered the girl in shock.

"Forget that for now, honey. I need you to follow me and stay quiet. I'll keep you safe."

"I tried to offer them a free meal, but they just kept on shovelling him into their mouths" she said, voice faltering.

Seeing that she favoured her left leg, Joan looked down. The bite mark on her calf was bleeding profusely. Hooking an arm over her shoulder, Joan helped her through into the main restaurant. Seating her in one of the booths, she turned towards the bar and kitchen. The chefs and kitchen staff stared fearfully through the swing doors.

"Everyone, get a weapon and get out of there! We have an unbelievable situation and I need you to trust me."

The sound of clattering utensils carried through the serving hatch. Men and women exited the kitchens wielding knives, cleavers and tenderising hammers.

"What's wrong with Sandra?" asked one of the busboys, moving to help her.

"She got hurt, but she's going to be ok," Joan replied.

"She's passed out, that's hardly ok," he argued.

Sandra was unresponsive and lolled in his arms. The level of anxiety was far beyond anything warranted for a casual acquaintance. He cared for the girl.

"Someone help me," he pleaded.

"I'll get her left arm, Elliot," offered Felix, the head chef. "You get the right."

"What's going on, Joan?"

"Zombies. They're real and they're killing people," she said, risking a peek through the restaurant door.

"Bullshit!"

"Take a look for yourself, but keep your head down. We're going to need to fight our way through them and get to somewhere more secure."

The staff laughed, trying to convince themselves she was playing some kind of prank. When they looked, the hisses of shock and furious backpedalling convinced Joan they were now believers.

"Sandra, stop it! I'm trying to help you," Elliot complained, struggling with the girl.

"Fuck!" snarled the chef. "She bit me!"

Looking back, the girl's eyes had taken on the vacant glaze of death. The orbs had turned almost as white as the surrounding sclera, only the faintest outline of the iris remained.

"She's one of them!" Joan shouted. "Get away from her!"

It was too late. Felix had let her arm drop to nurse his own bitten limb. Unrestrained, she lunged at Elliot and they went down in a tangled heap of snarling and shrieking. Clamping on his neck, she tore his carotid artery out, spraying the tables with blood.

"Jesus Christ!" croaked a girl, throwing up her breakfast.

"Joan, they're coming!"

"Everyone get back, I've got to take care of her. Make sure they can't get through those doors!"

Lofting the shovel, Joan cracked it onto the top of her head. The skull crumpled beneath the blonde hair and she collapsed onto the twitching body of her friend. Or boyfriend? Now, they would probably never know.

191

"Is he going to turn into one of those things?" demanded Felix. "Am I?"

"I don't know how this bloody thing works," spat Joan. "Fifteen minutes ago, all I had to worry about was a burst pipe."

"He's moving."

"He might be ok. The bleeding has stopped," said one of the waitresses hopefully.

The peeling back of his eyelids banished any notion of things being ok ever again.

"Oh shit. I'm dead," sobbed Felix, slumping into a chair.

"I'll take care of him, love. You've done plenty already," said Gerry, the older chef, holding her back.

The swallow tattoos on each hand showed his military experience and his calm eyes told her he had seen things just as bad, or worse. Out of the group, he was the only one to not flinch when she had destroyed the girl. Trapped underneath the body, Elliot moaned and writhed. Holding him down by the forehead, the man stabbed him through the eye.

"I'm sorry, son," he whispered, wiping the blade clean.

"Thank you, Gerry," Joan sighed.

Nodding, he moved over to his boss. "Felix, we need to take your arm off."

"What are you talking about? Get away from me!"

"It's the only way to stop the infection from spreading," Gerry said, taking a cleaver from one of the others.

"It won't work, anyway. I can feel it in my veins like a drug."

"It works in the movies," he urged. "We need to try something."

"This isn't the movies," Joan whispered in his ear. "We don't have the medical supplies to patch up a severed arm."

"If we can apply a tourniquet, it'll buy us enough time for an ambulance to arrive."

"If what I saw outside's getting worse, the ambulance won't be able to get close enough to help us. They'll be killed too. Our only hope is the armed response units from Chichester Police Station."

"We could cauterise it to buy us some time?"

"Whatever you're going to do, do it quick. I can't hold the doors much longer."

The man was holding an upturned table against the wood, but each new zombie added their weight and he was losing the battle. Felix stood up on shaky legs and joined him.

"Felix, what the hell are you doing?" Joan demanded.

"I'll hold them off while you escape out the back," he slurred, barely able to stand.

"Didn't you hear the lady?" asked Gerry. "They're already outside and it's getting worse."

Felix blinked slowly a couple of times, like a drunk trying to process a simple order. Without warning, his eyes closed and he fell face first to the carpet, nose crunching.

"Everyone get back to the other side of the restaurant!" Joan yelled.

"We can't leave Felix like that," Gerry replied, stepping forward.

"He's already turning. Look," said Joan, pointing at the body which was twitching in the same way as Elliot had been minutes before.

The member of staff holding the table let it fall to the floor, jumping away from the former chef who was now trying to grab his leg.

"Get behind me, now!

193

Following Joan, they all moved to the far corner of the seating area, moving tables and chairs to lead the zombies. With nothing else to do, they waited for the abominations to clear the door. Feeling the trembling of those pressed closely around her, she tried to calm them. Everyone needed to be focussed in spite of the dire situation if they were going to survive this.

"They're vicious, but slow. We move around them and then head for the roof!"

"Why the roof? We'll be trapped."

Joan held out the shovel and nodded at their makeshift weapons. "One way up and one way down. It means we can't be surrounded and we can pick them off from above."

"And how many of them are there? If this is all over the park, we'll need to fight thousands."

"I've secured the front doors temporarily. Once we kill everything inside the complex, we can see what's happening and seal them completely if necessary. Everyone get ready."

Felix led the charge with his new family, the brilliant chef's whites contrasting with the bloody, ravaged creatures behind.

"They're falling for it!"

"Wait for it," said Joan, wanting the zombies to get as close as possible. "Ok... now!"

Darting to the left, the group circled the line of tables and chairs. Unheeding of the obstacle, the monsters fell amongst the furniture, buying them a few minutes to make good their escape. Barging through the swing doors, they weaved through the undead staff of the food court. Everyone tried to ignore the ruined faces of the people they passed. They had once been friends and colleagues. They had sat together in team meetings, drinking coffee and discussing the park and its future. Now they had no future. In the back of her mind Joan wondered if the same applied to the park itself, if not the whole world. Apocalypse. The word had such finality to it. Please let the world go on, she begged to anyone, or thing, that may be listening.

Reaching the branch in the winding hallways which led to the roof, Gerry asked the obvious. "What about the hall?"

"Christopher has blocked the doors to keep the kids safe. We only get inside once we can ensure their safety," Joan explained.

"Good. Let's go and get ready, I want to get some payback."

"You go, I'm going to make sure I have their undivided attention," she replied.

Propping the stairwell open with a metal bin, she watched the others run up the stairs and open the upper door. Using the shovel, she started to hit the steel handrail with the metal blade. Each clang echoed through the building, like a dinner bell being rung.

"I hope we aren't on the menu," she whispered to herself as the zombies rounded the corner.

The die had been cast. For good or ill, only time would tell. Taking the steps two at a time, the others were waiting for her at the top. Their faces had changed from scared to terror stricken.

"Have you looked at the park?"

Gerry nodded slowly.

"That bad?"

He nodded again.

"I need to see."

"We'll hold them here if they make it up, love," Gerry replied.

Moving to the roofline, the screams and shouts told her everything she needed to know. Small fires had broken out and people ran for their lives between the increasing numbers of undead. Cars raced to and fro on the small roads, their terrified occupants skidding and crashing, adding to the feelings of pandemonium. The sight of a surrounded family was too much. Moving to protect his loved ones, the father faced off against thirty of the lumbering horrors and Joan had to turn away before the inevitable bloodshed. Filled with a growing fury, she clenched the tool until her knuckles went white. Her aching muscles were forgotten as she moved back towards the roof access. The others were relieved and stepped respectfully out of her way when they saw the look on her face.

"Come and get it, you bastards!" she screamed.

The ascending zombies filled the stairwell, sliding against the walls as they jostled to be the first to feed. All they tasted was the steel of Joan's weapon as it cleaved through their ranks.

***

"Wow," gasped Eldridge. "And you managed to keep the place safe during that craziness?"

Joan sat back, sipping on her drink. "It was easy once I'd welded the front doors and the fire escapes. They had no way to get in, and we had no way to get out."

"You're amazing."

"It would've been for nothing if you hadn't shown up. Eventually the food would've run out and we'd have starved. Now the children can get a little part of their lives back. Fresh air, exercise, learning, and an even bigger family."

"I needed to talk to you about that," Eldridge replied.

Joan listened intently as she explained the gravity of the situation on the mountains. After the team had risked their own lives, it was only right she should do the same.

"I'm going with you to the castle."

"Captain Hayward won't allow a civilian to go with us, I'm afraid."

"I served my twelve years on the Versatile Engagement before getting into maintenance. I can still run and gun with the best of them."

"Really? When did you get out?"

"I was discharged in March 2005."

"Any reason you didn't stay for the full twenty-four?"

"Three tours of Iraq were enough for me," Joan replied quietly.

Eldridge knew the feeling all too well. The things she had seen on her tours of Afghanistan would stay with her forever.

"I'll talk with the captain and get you cleared. I know the others will be glad to have you on board after the way you handled yourself."

"When do we leave?"

"The day after tomorrow at first light most likely. Did you want to come with me to the range and I'll show you the ins and outs of the new rifles."

"I've been drinking," Joan warned, holding up the half empty bottle.

"Half a beer? I think you'll be ok," Eldridge replied with a wink.

CHAPTER 24

Hombre wiped at the moisture streaked mirror, revealing himself once more. Checking for nicks and cuts on his freshly shaven head, he looked this way and that. Satisfied he had removed the annoying fuzz, he rinsed the razor in the warm bowl and used a damp towel to wipe away the remaining foam. Pulling back his lips, he admired his white, even teeth. Reaching into the roof of his mouth, he pulled the false tooth out which had replaced the one lost against a fearsome Romanian fighter four years ago. It had been one hell of a punch and, for the first time ever, he had been rattled.

"Still lost though, didn't you?" he grumbled, scouring the tooth in his palm with the brush and paste.

An uneasy feeling had settled into his stomach in the recent days. Ever since the arrival of Mike and Debbie, things had been going south. A tension had crept in and pervaded the dark hallways of the prison. It was partly the knowledge of the impending attack by the Fowler brothers; the way he would catch certain glimpses of knowing eyes or scornful glares. He had noted down every name and, if given permission, would learn their secrets with his fists. No such order had been given which was out of the ordinary. Craig was normally unshakeable, with a single-minded pursuit of his hold on power, but too much time and planning was being devoted to revenge on Kurt. What good would retribution be if the Fowler's seized control in the confusion? Not that he was afraid, far from it in fact. The violence and mayhem would be legendary. It would mean fighting his way clear of the prison and forging a new path on his own, which may not be a bad thing. Being alone was safer in many ways, and perhaps even a single companion could join him, if she survived.

"Debbie…" he whispered.

Following Mike's betrayal against her, he had done his duty and kept his mouth shut for the good of the prison. A woman like that was touched, that much was obvious, but she had just as much moxie as Hombre himself. Rigging the cell to explode had been a brave move and as he had carried her limp body away, his admiration blossomed into something deeper. It was not love, at least not yet, but he was unable to deny the fierce attraction.

Leaving his room, he made his way to the medical wing. The doctor looked up from his task briefly to glower and then finished bandaging the arm of the prisoner. Seeing Hombre, the young man turned pale.

"What happened?"

"Nothing, boss. I fell over and cut myself."

"Are you likely to fall over and cut yourself again, or have you sorted your differences with the offending inanimate object?" Hombre growled, crowding the man. The rules on inter wing violence were for everyone's good and any transgressions had to be nipped in the bud.

"No, boss. It's all sorted now."

"If I hear anything different, I'll pay you and this object a visit. Do you understand?"

Nodding, he hurried out of the room.

"Must you always be so aggressive?" asked Dr Feeley.

"Yes," Hombre replied bluntly. "How is she?"

"She still hasn't woken and that isn't necessarily a bad thing. It's giving her body time to heal. Her eardrums are badly damaged which may lead to either permanent hearing loss or at the very least a bad case of tinnitus. I was surprised at the lack of damage to her lungs from the pressure of the blast itself. Normally, haemorrhaging is to be expected, but she must have held a hand over her nose and mouth. Even the burns are only first degree, superficial, and should leave little in the way of scarring. The gas burned itself out so quickly that it couldn't penetrate to the deeper layers of dermis and epidermis. Her teeth will need some work, and without a dentist to hand, extraction would probably be the easiest solution. Apart from needing a good trim to tidy up the burnt hair, I see no reason for her to not recover fully in time. I can give you a more detailed diagnosis when she wakes."

"Ok."

"If her hearing is a lost cause, the library has books on sign language," Dr Feely called out as Hombre entered the private room.

"I'll write notes. I gave up learning at twelve and it never did me any harm."

"Wait! Can I have just a moment of your time?" asked the doctor, trying to follow.

"When I'm done. Now fuck off and leave us before I get angry."

"Of course, thank you," he replied, dodging backwards as the door slammed in his face.

Approaching the bed, Hombre sat down on the edge and picked up Debbie's hand. For some reason, he expected it to be cold and clammy, but instead it was warm and dry. Stroking the brittle, scorched hair from her brow, she looked serene. Her beauty shone despite the blisters and encrusted scabs from the explosion and previous injuries. The throbbing in Hombre's chest grew; an unusual feeling that was alien to him. It could very well be the first stirrings of love, or could just as easily be lust. Rape served a need, but sex was always more satisfying when the other party was a willing participant, paid or unpaid.

"I'll look after you now, you sexy, crazy bitch," Hombre declared, squeezing the unresponsive hand.

How the relationship would work, Hombre could not say. He was not even certain she would want him, anyway. Common sense dictated he should steer clear because of his love for Craig and the complications which could arise. While she belonged to Mike, he had honoured that rule, but now she was free. Time would reveal the truth.

"You might not even make it back," he admitted to himself.

The mission was a simple one; reach the construction site and tow the generator back to the prison. This time he had opted to go alone and refused all offers of help. Most of the prisoners were too useless to do anything other than serve as zombie food. Matt was the only other man who he would have taken, but he had his own task in finding suitable vessels to ferry the building materials up and down the river. Scouts were already scouring the surrounding area for fuel tankers and as soon as the generator was safely within the walls, he would be heading out on the road again. After many weeks of inactivity, it was good to be busy, even with the added danger. Looking at his watch, the day was young and he had at least eight hours of daylight to use. Moving cautiously, he should be at the building site in just over two hours. Allowing a further hour or two to clear the area of zombies, or draw them away should there be too many, he would be eating dinner by the days end. The vehicle and its cargo could wait outside the walls until a safe plan could be devised to get it past the dead. Standing, he kissed Debbie's forehead, catching the acrid stench of burnt hair.

"I'll be back for you. I promise."

Dr Feely was poised outside the door and started complaining as soon as Hombre left the room. "You must tell Craig that I can't be involved in any more of the vile executions. It's barbaric and I won't be the cause of any more pain. I'm a doctor for goodness sake."

"Discipline has to be maintained or this place would descend into chaos."

"Peeling the skin from a man isn't discipline. It's pure evil."

"With the dead rising from the grave and eating every living thing, the word evil loses much of its meaning. Isn't it better to sacrifice a few lives to save the hundreds within these walls?"

"Why not just lock them in solitary? Surely that's more humane?"

"Doesn't have quite the same deterrent value, though, does it?"

"I won't be a part of it anymore!"

Hombre sighed. "I'll tell him. Then he'll ignore me. When it happens again, he'll threaten another of the children and you'll cave in. Why must we go around and around in circles, Doc?"

"I won't do it!"

"Fine," Hombre muttered. Walking out, he called over his shoulder. "Keep her safe for me or you'll be the one tied to the board."

"You can't threaten me!" yelled Dr Feely.

"It wasn't a threat, it was a promise!"

***

Craig pulled Hombre into a tight embrace. "Are you sure you won't take a few extra pairs of hands?"

"No. I want to move quickly and quietly."

"And what if you get into trouble?"

"I'll fight my way out of it. Don't worry about me, I won't do anything stupid."

"You don't need to do anything stupid to get hurt out there. Those bastards are hiding around every corner."

"Aww. Anyone would think you love me, boss."

"Get the fuck out of here, you big lug. I'll see you for dinner!" Craig pushed him towards the tunnel and walked away.

"Keep your head down out there, brother," Matt grumbled and followed their leader.

"You too, mate. Good luck on the coast."

Left alone with the tunnel guards, Hombre made a final check of his provisions. The ice axes hung from his belt and the slight bulge of the pistol in his jacket went unnoticed by the others. Water, food and tools were stowed in a small leather holdall, carefully wrapped to minimise the noise of his travel. With a firm nod to the prisoners, he descended the steps into the dark passage and fired up the torch. A lantern burned a short distance down the tunnel and the man on duty unlocked the door as Hombre approached.

"Be safe, boss."

"Always," Hombre replied, ducking through and striding away as the steel clanged shut behind him.

The beam of light illuminated the sturdy supports spaced evenly along the length of the passage. Insects skittered and fled under the vibrations and scrutiny, burrowing into any available crevice. Trying his best to breathe through open mouth, Hombre wrinkled his nose. He had always hated the earthy, moist smell below ground. The footfalls echoed both in front and behind, bouncing from the walls. A vice seemed to tighten on his chest, causing short, sharp gasps to escape his lips. Concentrating on the number of paces he had memorised, he fought through the burgeoning claustrophobia. It never affected him as deeply when he had fellow travellers in the darkness because of their distraction. But alone, with nothing but his own thoughts and the companionship of many legged creatures, it was nearly crippling. Several tortuous minutes later, the circular beam picked out the reflection of the aluminium ladder ahead. It was like a release valve opening on his anxiety, bleeding out the pressure which had been building.

Pausing at the foot of the steps, he listened carefully for any moans or shuffling of dead feet. A chill wind had sprung up and tugged at the loose board, whispering through the cracks and masking much of the noise of the outside world. Climbing up, he pressed both palms against the damp ply and raised it a few inches. Twisting, he repeated the procedure for all directions. Apart from the frigid draught which stung his exposed face, nothing else was topside. Heaving the sheet aside, Hombre quickly hopped up and replaced the heavy cover over the tunnel mouth and raced for concealment. The entrance to the farm shop was dark, providing a good vantage point to scan the area. The fields at each side had a small smattering of zombies wandering aimlessly. Either he could kill them, or just walk around and ignore them. The alleyway towards the main shopping promenade was completely devoid of life, or unlife.

Opening the small map, Hombre held it out into the daylight. The route would take him through open fields, an expanse of woodland and then directly into a town where the construction site was based. The town itself was probably swarming with the dead which is why he had opted to go solo. Any fuck ups would be on his shoulders alone. Stowing the map, he left the shadows and rounded the metal clad farm shop. Heading west-south-west, he hopped a fence and dropped into the field beyond. The ground was solid and crunched beneath his heavy boots. Sensing the warmth of the living, the zombies turned in his direction and started their laborious approach. Pausing to destroy them would waste valuable time, and ignoring them would mean he had a few eager followers.

"Fuck it!"

Making a beeline for the closest threat, Hombre unsheathed the ice axes. Beneath the filth and gore, a police officer's uniform could just be made out.

"Well, well, well. Hello, pig," Hombre snarled.

Slashing the ice axe up between the man's legs, it embedded deeply in the groin. It was purely symbolic; a sign of his deep-seated hatred for the law. Wrenching upwards, the creature was pulled off balance and fell onto its back. Standing on its throat, he raised the second axe and swung it downwards through the temple. Wrestling the blade free, he lifted a heavy boot and stamped down repeatedly on the grey, decayed face. When the head was nothing but mulch, he began rifling through the utility belt. Attached was a retractable baton, handcuffs, pepper spray and a newly issued Taser with three cartridges. Packing the items away and sliding the baton into his belt, the next zombie got within grabbing distance. Instead of a warm, shrieking meal, all the festering man got was a broken jaw from Hombre's left hook. Knocked off balance, it composed itself and lunged forward again into two lighting jabs which mashed its blackened nose flat. Attempting to dance around the corpse, the uneven ground made it too awkward and he gave up the boxing practice.

"Let's see how much use this thing is," he muttered, extending the baton.

Swinging the metal down, it cracked into the forehead, tearing the skin. Sideswiping, aiming for the weakened bone around the ear and temple, still the monster came on.

"Fucking useless, that's how much!"

Dropping the weapon, he punched with all his might into the seeping forehead, crushing the bone back into the brain. It was known as a bull hammer in bare knuckle fighting circles and had left many a fractured skull in its wake. The weakened bone of the undead made it even more devastating. Kneeling, he wiped the gore from his thick leather gloves onto the only patch of clean clothing available. Knowing he was wasting time, he put the baton in his bag just in case. As his absentee father had always said in the rare visits; *it's better to have something and not need it, than need something and not have it.*

Marching across the field between the remaining zombies, he butchered them unceremoniously and forged on towards the next farmstead. The old building was abandoned, with windows smashed and the doors hanging from torn hinges. No mark adorned the outer wall from the raiding parties. Each building which had been cleared was painted with a simple white cross to prevent time wasting. Given more time, he may have been tempted to search within the walls for any booty, but the mission was far too important and he made a mental note for the scavenging crews.

Movement caught his attention as he made to leave. Stumbling from the darkness came the farmer, replete with plaid shirt and dungarees. Pushing past him were two young girls, no older than eight. Their bodies were horribly torn, but the brown pigtails swung from their heads, blue bows fluttering in the wind. Having no interest in breeding, he still felt a small twinge of regret that the man had been unable to protect his family. *Jesus Christ, I'm going soft,* he thought. Debbie's appearance had been like pouring oil into the dry engine of his heart, and it scared him. For a man who had strived for emotional solitude his whole life, this new predilection for attachment was troubling. Maybe it would be better if she had perished in the explosion, then the decision would have been taken out of his hands. He could have gone back to the uncomplicated existence of violence and rape.

The twins, for that was what they were now that he could see them up close, moved faster than their obese father. A heavy toe punt snapped the first girl's head back, lifting her from the floor and sending her sprawling. Her sister was destroyed with the point of his blade piercing through the top of her skull. Laying her gently to the ground, Hombre quickly dispatched the other girl before she could regain her feet and laid them side by side.

"Come on, daddy," Hombre hissed, swinging a heavy kick at the man's closest leg.

The knee shattered, dropping the creature at the feet of his dead children. Dodging out of reach of the flailing arms, he darted forward and hacked at the upturned face, cleaving it in two. In the aftermath of the assault, the only sounds were from birds chirruping in the branches and the wind sighing through the leaves. Sipping from the water bottle, he gave some thought to collecting a blanket and covering the bodies properly.

"You really are turning into a little bitch, aren't you?"

Turning his back on the slain corpses, he forced himself to stride away. The forest lay before him at the edge of the farm, dark and foreboding. From within came the rustle of disturbed vegetation, the snap of twigs as something heavy moved in the shadows. Figuring that after a few minutes his night vision would combine with the stray beams of light breaking through the almost impenetrable canopy of evergreen branches, he pushed on. The gloom swallowed him whole.

CHAPTER 25

Sarah draped her leg over Kurt's knee and snuggled into the warmth of his chest. The locked door of the Earl's suite ensured their privacy, until something urgent came up anyway. It had been so long since they last had an opportunity to be alone. The intimacy would come again in time, Christina told her. The trauma and stresses of the past few weeks had taken a toll on her husband and it was only to be expected that his libido would suffer from all the horror. Sarah was desperate to make love, but would patiently nurse his mental health until he felt ready again. It was partly the need to be physically close to him, yet also a way to say fuck you to whatever forces had killed the world.

"I'm sorry, babe," Kurt whispered, shame reddening his face.

"It doesn't matter, love. I'm just glad to steal a few hours with you."

"Bob would happily take my place," he tried to joke.

"Bob would get a swift kick in the nuts if he ever tried," she replied.

"Did you ever think we'd get the chance to just lay in a bed and relax again?"

"Yes," she said, sincerely. "If anyone could get us to safety, it was you."

"And Dad."

"John too," she whispered, taking his hand. "You two are so alike."

"Bollocks. He was a stubborn old bugger," he said, affectionately.

"And you're not?"

"Maybe a little bit. I'm better looking though."

"I wouldn't be so sure. He had the whole silver fox, brooding older man thing going on. It was quite hot."

"Gloria thought so," he said, sadly.

"I think she saw something deeper than the looks. She saw his true soul and loved him for it. "

"It's such a shame they'll never get to see what could've happened given the chance."

"I know, sweetheart."

Falling silent, they stared up at the intricately plastered ceiling, following the swirling patterns. Feeling the creeping chill, Sarah pulled the duvet up to her chin. Kurt pushed it back and stood up, buck naked.

"What're you doing? Get back into bed."

"I'm going to stoke the fire and put some more logs on."

"Save the wood, I'll keep you warm," she purred.

"In a minute, love, I like the fire. It reminds me of when we were all tucked up in our old house."

Kneeling at the hearth, he picked up the iron poker and prodded. Topping the glowing embers with fresh logs, he watched as the flames blossomed back to life. Tendrils of yellow and orange licked eagerly at the dry fuel.

"I can still remember Braiden feeding Paige," Sarah said, kneeling beside him and wrapping the duvet around his shoulders.

"I remember that," he smiled. "And when she finally came back to us. She scared the life out of Braiden when she stroked his hair."

Sarah chuckled and pulled him close. "I know they're up there watching over us."

"I try and picture it that way. It makes it a bit easier, you know?"

"Of course."

Their faces started to burn from the radiated heat, so Sarah led them back to bed. It was impossible to miss the flex of his taut muscles and she felt a tingle of desire flood through her body. *You'll have to take care of yourself later. This is for Kurt.* A whine came from under the door, putting paid to the romance even if he had been capable. It was followed by an insistent scratching and excited panting.

"I'll get it," Sarah offered.

Turning the key and pressing the handle, Honey was pushing her nose through the gap to get inside. Licking Sarah's outstretched hand to say thanks, she ran into the room. Looking between the fire and the bed, the canine conundrum of warmth or strokes paralysed her. Kurt patted the sheets and her mind was made up. Bounding across the rug, she leaped and landed on the duvet. The cover slid across the bed and took the poor dog with it before Kurt could catch her. Falling to the floor, she quickly regained her feet, shook herself and tried again.

"Are you ok?"

"Silly girl," Sarah cooed, scratching behind her ears.

Rolling onto her back, she pawed at them until they rubbed her exposed belly. Catching her in the tickle spot, her hind leg kicked furiously. Moving into a better position to take advantage of the attention, her back legs spread apart.

"What a hussy. I wonder where she gets that from?" Kurt teased.

Sarah slapped his arm. "I'm a lady, I'll have you know!"

"Lady of the night maybe."

"You cheeky bastard!" she snapped, tickling him around the ribs.

"No!" Kurt choked through fits of laughter. "Get off!"

Unimpressed, Honey snorted and jumped down from the silly people and curled up by the fire. Her look of doggy indignation caused them to both burst into hysterics. Deciding they were crazy, she yawned and closed her eyes.

"We even bore the dog. I guess we're not cool anymore."

"I'm still cool," Kurt said, feeling insulted.

"You haven't been cool since you started to grow your beard."

He raised an eyebrow. "Is that a hint?"

"If you want me to shave," she replied, pushing his hand between her legs. "I want you to shave. It's only fair."

"How can I argue with that logic?"

"You can't," she grinned. "Now shut up and cuddle me."

Pulling her close, they turned on their side and watched the dog enjoy the fire. It was a good lesson in life, but Kurt was certain he had heard the phrase somewhere before.

"Enjoy the little things," he whispered into Sarah's ear.

"I don't have much choice, babe," she teased, giving his genitals a playful squeeze.

CHAPTER 26

Kicking at the dried patches of blood on the wood, Craig waited patiently while the prisoners gathered below. Fond memories flashed through his mind of the pain inflicted on the platform, the pleading and begging of his pathetic victims as he flayed them. Seeing the Fowler brothers emerge from the corner of block D, he smiled inwardly. It would not be long before they were shrieking their torment on the board, his knife severing through countless nerves as their skin peeled away. A shudder of pleasure passed through him and Matt caught it.

"You ok, boss?"

"Yeah, just someone walking over my grave."

"Lot of that going on lately," Matt replied drily.

Most of the prison had arrived, with only a few trickling out in dribs and drabs from whatever work duty they had been pulled from. Annoyed mumbles carried across the crowd at being summoned out into the freezing cold. Mouths blew into cupped hands to ward off the encroaching chill. Staring down, the crowd fell silent.

"I expect you wonder why I've called you together on this glorious winter's day. Don't worry, I won't keep you any longer than necessary. Times are changing and we have to make some sacrifices if we're going to survive in the long term."

He waited through the brief surge of questions the crowd posed to each other until they returned their attention.

"First things first. The gauntlet is closing its doors for the foreseeable future…"

Protesting voices interrupted, arguing about the loss of the only entertainment on offer.

Matt stepped forward and bellowed, "Shut your fucking mouths or you'll answer to me!"

"Thank you, Matt. The second order of business is the suspension of the rape night roster," Craig shouted. As the men screamed their frustration, Craig burst out laughing and held up his hands.

"I'm only joking about the second thing," he called, face setting in a sneer. "But the next man to whine will be peeled here and now. Do you fucking hear me?"

Eyes looked away as he regarded the cowed men. The Fowler brothers had folded their arms, leaning back against the grey stone, unimpressed.

"The continuing losses from the gauntlet are leaving the tunnel teams short staffed which means if it continues, you'll all be digging in the dark. I'm assuming you'll happily forego the show to ensure you avoid back breaking labour?"

Nobody disagreed.

"I thought so. Now, I'm not a tyrant, so I've come up with an alternative that I think you'll all like. I have a team out there right now securing an industrial generator which will be brought back and hooked up to the power supply of certain parts of the prison. Minimal lighting will be provided through the night, and on top of that you will all be able to use your TVs, consoles and DVD players for several hours a day."

The earlier complaints turned to fresh excitement. Games, movies and porn would assuage some of the boredom in ways a weekly show could not. Cheers echoed within the walls until he held up his hands again.

"I'm glad we're on the same page. The raiding parties have brought back a massive selection of material to borrow which will also be tracked carefully by Bennie Baverstock when everything is up and running. The reason this change is so important brings us onto the main business at hand. My brother and I have formulated a plan to safely reach the spoils of Wick town, including the food in the superstores and supplies of their industrial park. The tunnel team are going to dig towards the southern bridge and from there we'll be building a fortification around the entrance and exit. To this end, I need to know of anyone with building experience; labourers, bricklayers, metal workers. If you leave your names with Harry at the end, we can work out shifts."

The men looked at each other, worry evident in their eyes.

"It isn't as difficult as it sounds. We've worked out a way to ensure no one is in danger which I'll explain later."

"Do we have enough supplies to build anything, boss?" called out a face in the crowd.

"Not yet, but the rail yard has a huge amount of bricks, sand, cement and all the good things we'll need."

"Is that wise after the last attempt?" asked another, bravely. It was a legitimate question following the debacle, so Craig ignored the temptation to punish the man.

"It won't be going down the same way, and that brings me nicely onto the next order. Matt is going to lead an expedition towards the coast to secure a number of light vessels to bring back upriver. Those things hate the water which will mean you can travel in safety, ferrying the materials back and forth between the yard and the bridge. I want anyone with knowledge of motor propelled boats to also give their details to Harry. If I find out anyone has been trying to avoid their duty, you won't need to guess how I'll repay your idleness and cowardice." Craig gently stroked the stained board like a lover.

"How do we hold the yard against the dead fucks?"

"While Hombre was loading up, they were only attacked by a handful of zombies. All activities will be closely guarded with guns and blades. Should a sizeable number appear, everyone will retreat to the boats and head back to the prison until they disperse. We have enough food to last until the new year, but if we don't do this, we'll all starve to death come the spring. Does everyone understand?"

Hundreds of heads bobbed in unison. Even the Fowler brothers grudgingly agreed while whispering to each other.

"Good. If anyone has any questions, you can catch me at one of the meetings. Now get back in the warm and start planning how much porn you're going to watch, you dirty bastards!"

The cheers were deafening.

CHAPTER 27

Winston, can I have a word?" Kurt asked.

Winston turned and smiled nervously. *Fuck! What have I done? Sam hasn't even asked about going outside yet.* "Of course," he squawked. *Idiot! He'll know something's up.*

"Are you ok?"

"Yes. Fine. Never better, thanks for asking," babbled Winston. *Keep this up and you're going to learn how to fly!*

Kurt stared at the youth for a few seconds and Winston could feel his cheeks flushing as if someone was turning up a dial.

"You don't have to be scared of me," Kurt said slowly. "Unless you have a reason…"

"I'm not scared. Well, I am scared. But it's not for any particular reason. Ok, maybe that war pick on your belt is worrying me a bit," Winston replied, seeing Kurt finger the deadly weapon.

"I could get my hatchet if that would be better?"

"No, it's fine. Honestly," Winston stuttered, backing away. "How can I help you?"

"I've asked the others and no one else can help me with this. I want to bring the crane inside the castle walls, and you're the only one with knowledge of how to drive it."

Winston sighed audibly. "I can do that."

Kurt was surprised at the lack of objection. "Are you sure? There are a lot of the dead outside."

"As long as you can draw them away so I can get in the cab, it should be a piece of cake. I can see two problems, though."

"And what're they?"

"The old girl is running on empty. I'd need time and space to put some fuel in the tank before starting her up," he explained.

"I'm sure we can arrange that."

"Actually, that would make it three. Getting some diesel would be number two."

"No problem. We can siphon the vehicles in the castle. I've seen some jerry cans laying around in the maintenance building. And number three?"

"The bloody things keep stealing my shoes. I'd need some spares to replace the ones I'll lose out there."

Kurt chuckled. "Come on, let's make the preparations."

***

"Should we really be asking him to do this with his injured arm?" Sarah asked, kneeling beside Kurt as he filled up the fuel can.

"What an idiot. I didn't even think of that," Kurt replied, rolling his eyes. "He didn't say anything to me about it."

"Of course, he didn't. He wants to impress you, and this is another way for him to do that, even if it's extremely dangerous."

"Where is he?" Kurt mused, looking around the grounds.

"He's with the other kids. Let me go and get him," Sarah said.

Kurt watched her as she strode away, full of poise and confidence. God, how he loved her. Trapped in a living hell, she was a light in the darkness. She would sit with him through the long nights, comforting him as he wept for John, until falling asleep in her arms. Kurt analysed why the loss of his father had affected him so deeply. Following the loss of his mother, they had been drifting apart like ships passing in the night, vaguely aware of each other but with differing destinations. Gloria suggested that it could be the bond forged in their struggles against the undead. Adversity had a way of bringing people together and making the frivolous quarrels of the past irrelevant. Lacking a better explanation, he accepted it.

The hose gurgled as it drew the last dregs of fuel from the car. Kurt pulled the tube and replaced the filler cap to keep the legendary English rain at bay. There was no point damaging the vehicle unnecessarily. Sloshing the can, it contained at least ten litres which should prove enough to trundle through the gate to safety.

"You wanted to see me?" Winston asked, nervously.

"I wanted to apologise, mate. I never even asked if your arm was up to the task."

"You know me, I'm as strong as an ox. The same size too," he replied.

"You aren't that big. And if I'm not mistaken, your clothes seem to be a couple of sizes too large for you now."

Winston looked down at the sagging trousers and replacement belt which was buckled tighter than his previous one ever had been. "Do you think so?"

"I know so," Sarah agreed with Kurt. "Give it a week or two and you'll need to bin those baggy tops and find something that fits better."

"If only I'd known about the apocalypse diet and fitness regime before the dead came back to life. I may not have been such a loser."

218

"I've known losers, and you aren't one of them," Kurt proclaimed.

"You certainly aren't, sweetheart," confirmed Sarah. "Now, is your arm hurting? We can put this off until you're fully recovered if you want."

Winston flexed the fingers and moved the limb around. "It's not that bad. I'm off my face on morphine, which probably helps."

"Even more reason to delay it then," Sarah cautioned.

"Honestly, it's fine. I was only joking about being high as a kite. Apart from some itchiness, the medicine just dulls the pain. I don't feel sleepy or sluggish like I thought I would."

"I don't want to risk hurting you. If you want more time, just say," Kurt offered.

"No, we need to do it now. I didn't disconnect the battery with the switch when I arrived. If we wait much longer it may not start at all."

Kurt stood up and placed a hand on his shoulder. "I'd sooner lose that machine than you. Everyone in here speaks up for what a good soul you are, and I'm starting to believe it myself."

"Even Braiden?" Winston laughed, trying to deflect the awkward praise.

"Especially Braiden. I'm sure you can appreciate that he used to be the type of person who was your worst nightmare in school. There was a time I'd have run the little bastard over for what he did to Sam. Now we love him as if he was our own child. The fact that he speaks so highly of you is enough of an endorsement for me."

"He really says that?" Winston said with surprise. "Most of the time he's threatening to stab me."

"He likes to project this image of being a rebel. Deep down he craves the affection that never came from his real family."

"So, he wouldn't really stab me?" Winston asked.

"Oh no, he'd stab you. But only if you threatened his family. If you're part of the family, he would kill *for* you," Kurt replied.

"We all would," Sarah said.

"That's good to know... I guess." Winston gulped.

"What I've just told you about his past is in strictest confidence, do you understand?"

"Of course."

"And are you sure you want to do this today, honey?" Sarah asked.

"Yeah. A bit of excitement never killed anyone."

Kurt was impressed at his bravery. "Ok, let's get everyone ready."

***

Standing atop the wall, the men and women looked down on the silent machine. Hundreds of zombies still surrounded the crane and the nearby stone fortification.

"We can pick them all off if you can give us twenty minutes," DB offered.

"We need to do this quietly. The noise of the rifles will just bring more of them down on us."

Braiden nudged Sam in the ribs, "Now's our chance," he whispered.

"Dad?" Sam called.

"What's up, mate?"

"We've been thinking. We could go out there and pull them away across the fields."

Kurt shook his head. "No, it's too risky. I don't want to put anyone in danger."

"But you'll let Winston go out on his own? That's a bit unfair."

"I don't mind, honestly," Winston piped up.

"It's not really a danger, Dad. They can't move fast enough to catch us, and if they manage to cut us off from

220

the castle walls we can just hop onto the canal boat," Braiden explained.

"I don't know..."

"We can cover them from the wall," said Jonesy.

"See, Dad," Sam exclaimed. "We'll be fine."

Kurt looked at Sarah who slowly nodded. "Who're you going to take with you?"

"Ian Pringle and Anthony Christopher," Braiden replied and the two teenage boys stepped forward.

"They're a dead shot with the bow and arrow," Sam explained. "And with my slingshot we can pick them off all day long if we needed to. I've got pockets full of bearings and stones."

"What if the gate gets surrounded when the crane goes through?" Kurt was looking for any excuse to keep them safe, even though he knew it was selfish.

"We've been practicing on the ropes. We can climb them like monkeys now."

"If I didn't know better, I'd think you've been planning something like this for a while," he suggested, suspicion evident from his narrowed eyes.

The students all shuffled their feet, looking at anything other than Kurt.

"I thought so, you sneaky buggers. We'll talk about this more afterwards," Kurt muttered.

"Is that a yes?" Sam pressed.

"It's a yes, but don't be surprised if I put you over my knee later and give you a bloody good spanking!"

"I'm too old for that!" Sam hollered, running off with the boys to get their weapons.

"You're never too old for a thrashing!" Kurt called back, grinning.

"They'll be fine," Sarah whispered. "They just want to prove themselves and show off to the others. I remember a time when you did the same with me."

"I don't know what you mean."

"I take it you've forgotten the first holiday we took? The balcony hopping in our hotel complex?" Sarah replied, eyebrow raised.

"That sounds far too dangerous. Only an idiot would do something so foolish just to impress their new bit of skirt."

"I was your fiancée by then, asshole," Sarah slapped his arm. "And yes, it was stupid. I could've kicked your ass for scaring me so much."

"It all worked out, though. Didn't it?"

"This will too."

***

"How many are there outside?" Sam called up to Patricia.

"Six at the gate. There's eight more of them fifty yards to the south."

"Ok, let them in," Braiden growled.

Peter drove the vehicle away from its position against the gate. Denise slid the bolts, backing away as the weight of the dead pushed it open. Before the first zombie could take a step, an arrow whistled forward, burying itself in the eye socket. Crumpling to the ground, its companions moved around the body. Sam's slingshot twanged, the bearing embedding in a brain with a wet crunch. Braiden took the opportunity while they reloaded and skewered one of the zombies through the temple with his screwdriver. Seconds later, the rest of the small group had been slain, clearing the way.

"All clear. Be careful out there," Denise whispered.

"You ready?" Braiden asked Ian and Anthony.

Their nerves had jumped a few notches at the sight of the open gate. Being on the other side of the massive stone walls had been fine in theory, even thrilling. Ten simple paces would see it become a reality.

"Fuck it, let's go," Ian raged, trying to psych himself. Remembering the lady stood close by, he apologised for the swear.

"No need, sweetie. Give 'em hell!"

Led by Sam and Braiden, they ran through the shadows and out into the light.

"No heroics. We're a diversion, nothing more," Braiden said.

"We've got your back, boys!" DB yelled from the ramparts.

Walking east towards the canal boat, the small group that Patricia had identified gave chase.

"We kill these and then we can pull the main horde away from the crane," Sam explained.

Anthony and Ian pushed a few arrows into the soil at their feet. Nocking their bows, they waited. Sam was more confident in his skill and picked a couple off as they approached. When the remaining six got within twenty yards, the archers drew their arrows and let fly at the fastest moving creatures. Ian's pierced through the forehead, but Anthony's was wide by a foot.

"Sorry, I'm just nervous."

Sam killed the zombie before it could become a threat. "It's no different to the corridors when we took the castle. Remember, just take your time, the next one's yours."

Ian had destroyed another and was already drawing the bowstring for his next shot. Anthony took a deep breath, drew, and loosed. The red flight fluttered as it found its mark, punching through the soft eye before bursting through the back of the creature's skull.

"I knew you could do it," Braiden said with a wink.

"Thanks."

A dull thud indicated the last cadaver had been slain, so the four boys jogged south towards the heavier concentration of undead. The adults and fellow students watched from above, nervous in spite of the high-powered assault rifles which watched over them.

Braiden let out a wolf whistle. "Grubs up! Come and get it!"

Sam, Anthony, and Ian commenced hollering and jeering the dead. Losing interest in the flesh on the wall, they obeyed their inhuman instinct and followed. Staying close, the boys danced and sang, ensuring they were the sole object of the milky eyed attention.

"It's all you now, buddy!" Sam called out and Winston saluted.

**

"Wait," Kurt whispered, holding the teen back.

The distraction team were working like a charm, luring the zombies away. Spreading out, the boys made sure to keep the attention of any stragglers at the back who may be tempted to return to the crane.

"Now!" Kurt hissed.

Sarah tossed the jerry can over the wall, playing out the rope until it touched down by the side of the machine. Winston took hold of the second rope, complete with knotted handholds down its entire length. A moment of vertigo took hold as his legs flailed in the open air, before wrapping firmly around the cord. Hand over hand, he dropped to the ground, scanning the area for lurking threats.

"Check the undercarriage," Jodi warned. "The bastards can get themselves wrapped around the axles."

"Thanks for the warning!"

Sure enough, the shredded remains of a couple of zombies reached fruitlessly. Their arms were gone, sharp protrusions of bone and tattered flesh replacing the missing limbs.

"Shall I try and kill them?"

"No, we'll take care of them when you get to safety."

"Ok," Winston replied.

Taking the can, he climbed up on the caterpillar tracks. Stepping gingerly across the lumps of gore snagged between the metal, he reached the tank. Tipping the fuel into the vehicle, the dark tube swallowed it gratefully. Capping the jerry can, he carefully lowered it to the ground and Sarah retrieved it. With a resounding clang, the metal bouncing against the stone.

"Shit! Sorry!"

Winston looked at the gurgling crowd, but they were too rapt on the tender young flesh on offer to respond to the noise. "It's ok. Here goes nothing!"

Staring at the ignition, he prayed for some luck. Twisting the key, the engine turned over weakly and failed to fire. *Shit, I can't believe I didn't flip the switch.*

"Try again, mate. It may need to draw some of the fuel into the injectors," Kurt called out.

Turning the ignition key, Winston watched the yellow glow plug light until it went out. Crossing the fingers on his left hand, he turned it all the way. The starter motor grumbled, energy fading. Just as he was about to give up, it coughed, the fuel finally igniting. Pressing the accelerator, the engine roared, black smoke spewing from the exhaust.

Winston leaned out of the cab. "Call the others back! I'm going to squash a few of the pus-filled bags of shit on my way in."

***

"He did it!" Braiden cheered, seeing the claw retract and the boom lower.

Gloria whistled, waving from the wall to fall back.

"Let's get inside. I'd say this was a job well done," Sam said, beaming.

As the four dodged around the swarm, they saw Winston veer away from the wall, heading straight for them.

"What's he doing?"

"I think he's planning on doing a little hit and run," Braiden replied.

Denise flung the huge gates open, taking up position outside with Patricia. DB and Jonesy were watching from above, rifles at the ready. The crane's horn blared, swiftly followed by the impact of steel on bone. Those that were lucky were brushed aside by the collision, the unlucky made disgusting popping sounds as their innards were expelled under the crushing weight. Applause and cheers rang out from the battlements at the destruction and Winston tooted the horn once in reply.

"Get ready, everyone," Kurt shouted, joining them at the gate. "There'll be some clingers accompanying our crazy guest."

"Will it fit under the archway?" Sarah asked, a tone of doubt entering her voice.

"It'll be tight, but the old girl will fit," said Kurt.

Peter moved clear to give the massive machine an unimpeded entry. The swinging arm and boom emerged from the gloom, closely followed by the tracks and heavy body with Winston whooping his enjoyment inside.

"Seal it up, mate!" Kurt yelled.

Driving under the arch, the light faded as the two portions of iron reinforced gate slammed shut. Denise dropped the bolts and stood to one side. Peter crept forward inch by inch until he felt the vehicle meet resistance. Pulling the handbrake, he turned off the engine and joined the others just as the dead reached the barricade. Their incessant hammering could not drown out the jubilation of a well fought mission.

CHAPTER 28

Hombre was moving cautiously through the dense underbrush, stepping on patches of bare earth to deaden the footfalls. The sounds of furtive movement were still drifting between the thick trunks as he forged deeper into the shadows. It lacked the uncoordinated bumbling quality of a zombie which could be identified from miles away as they thrashed between destinations. A huff and snort came from behind a sprawling briar patch. Sidling backwards slowly into a small nook of hedge, Hombre removed the ice axe and waited. A twig snapped and leaves rustled. Holding his breath, axe at the ready, he was awestruck when a small deer stepped into view. The creature was on guard, glancing around for any danger with big, brown eyes. That it had survived at all was nothing short of a miracle.

"Go on, get out of here!" Hombre said, revealing himself.

With a startled bleat, the doe jumped and bolted out of sight. The sounds of hasty retreat crashed through the woodland for a short while and Hombre paused, listening for anything that may have been drawn to it. No moans broke the still morning, so he rounded the prickly thicket and moved on. Craig would be eager to hear of the wild animals that still roamed the countryside. If they could hunt them, it would provide an excellent source of protein for the important prisoners. It would certainly be better than eating the other meat on offer. After the generator and fuel had been secured, he would borrow a rifle and see about bringing some juicy venison back.

The sounds of many clacking teeth brought him to a dead halt. They belonged to at least four distinct zombies if his hearing was still up to scratch. With axes at the ready, he tiptoed silently towards the disturbance. Dangling from a tree branch were four empty nooses. Their strangled victims all lay on the leaf covered ground, snapping heads separated from the bodies. After taking their own lives and reanimating, they had obviously thrashed in the air until the flesh and tendons of their compressed necks had decayed. Staring at the scene, he felt revulsion at their cowardice.

"Fucking pussies. Why not go out fighting?"

Lining up, he took a couple of steps backward and then ran at the first. Swinging his boot, the steel toe connected with the male head, sending it flying off into the distance with a sickly crunch. Wrapping the long, blonde hair of the second around his hand, he lifted the woman's head. Trying to crack it against a tree trunk, the scalp tore away mid swing and the hairless skull tumbled away. Sniffing at the locks, the scent of shampoo had long ago been replaced by the fetid stench of rot. *I wonder how I would look as a blonde?* he thought, lifting the gory hairpiece. Maggots writhed on the remaining scraps of meat, so he laughed and tossed it away before trying it on. The two remaining brains were mashed beneath his boot heel. After wiping the gore away on the soft foliage of the ground, he quickly checked the pockets of the decapitated bodies. Nothing of value presented itself.

In the next clearing, fresh rabbit droppings were scattered far and wide. Between the dense grass, burrow holes showed recent tracks of the animals hiding within. He added rabbit stew to the growing menu alongside the delicious venison steaks. If they could dry cure the meat, it would last even longer, reducing the pressure on the dwindling grocery store stocks. Over the tops of the trees, the first high rise apartment complex could be seen. According to the map, a few hundred feet further would take him out onto the grounds of a school.

Reaching the chain link, Hombre caught sight of the deer on the outskirts of the playing fields. The dead had trampled most of the fencing around the perimeter allowing the doe easy passage across the open ground. A loud crack from the side of the school building startled him. An inhuman shriek emanated from the stricken beast as blood flowed from the gunshot wound in its side. After taking a few unsteady steps, the animal fell to the ground, the air misting with its final breath.

"Fucking 'ave it!" yelled a man's voice. "I told you it would come back."

"Let's get it loaded and back to the others."

The men emerged from their hiding place, leading two blinkered horses. Quickly mounting up, they galloped over to the fallen creature. Expertly binding the front and back legs, they wrestled the carcass onto the biggest horse before securing it in place. Jumping back on their steeds, they pulled the reins and trotted north through a break in the treeline just as the first inquisitive zombies arrived.

"Fuck my luck!" Hombre hissed, blending back into the darkness.

Who the hell were those men? They looked hard, that much was clear. Their accent reminded him of the gypsies he had fought on the road. If any people were tough enough to survive, the nomadic travellers were at the top of the list. Born into a culture of isolation and fighting, they protected their own ferociously. At this current time, it was pointless to speculate. With their quarry gone, the monsters stopped, milling around in confusion. Ten became twenty. Twenty became fifty. The horde was growing by the second. Either he could backtrack and move around them using the forest as cover, or he could be bold and just run between the festering mass.

"I'm not hiding," he mumbled, picking up a heavy rock.

Leaving the safety of the trees, he started to jog across the field. The undead saw him and gurgled their excitement. Arms raised and legs shuffled as they gave chase. Darting between them, Hombre raised the stone, aiming for a classroom window. Roaring his rage, he threw it with all his might. The safety glass shattered into a thousand pieces just as he dove at the new opening. Rolling across the carpet and the small fragments, he jumped to his feet. The height of the sill was working in his favour. Outside, the zombies thrashed and moaned, the frame ending just below their chests and preventing their entry.

Looking around the dark room, he could not miss the spilled blood staining the cheap carpet. Chairs and tables had been tossed around in the chaos. The walls were coated with arterial spray, trails mixing with the innocent paintings of the dead students. Hearing the pattering of small feet, Hombre turned. Pintsized horrors streamed through the open classroom door, cutting him off. Grabbing a short table, he used it as a battering ram, barging into the zombie children. While they scrambled to stand, he dodged out into the corridor, slamming the door. Before the latch could engage, a stick thin arm pushed through, grasping the air.

"Fuck off, you little bastards!" he snarled, shouldering the straining barrier.

The arm broke with an audible crack, flopping against the frame, the blackened fingers still twitching. Bouncing his full weight against the door, it slowly sheared through the thin muscle until the limb fell to the floor. As the latch finally caught, a fresh procession of tiny monsters surged around the corner, accompanied by two of their teachers. Running to the left away from the wailing din, he kicked aside any solitary zombies which emerged from the shadows. The light increased around the next bend in the passageway, and he stumbled out into the hall. The cavernous room had served myriad purposes; assemblies, school performances, parent's evenings, lunch, and indoor sports. Climbing equipment was secured to the outer walls, with the ropes and wooden frames tidied away between physical education lessons. Tables and chairs had been laid out in preparation for the food that would never be served.

A fifteen-foot lunch counter was set back into the eastern wall, revealing the adjoining kitchen. Nearly every school across the country was similarly constructed to allow ease of service to the young patrons. The four entrances expelled a torrent of undead into the room, leaving him only one route of escape. Leaping over the counter, the metal trays went clattering, their vile, mouldy contents spilled over the red tiled kitchen floor. Two cooks bumbled forward, their uniforms streaked with dried blood and leaking grave fluids. Scooping up a kitchen knife, he buried the blade up to the hilt through the white hat of the nearest, pinning it to the skull. Moving to a stainless-steel freezer, Hombre pulled the handle and swung the door straight into the face of the slower creature, knocking it flat.

"Come here, you fat cunt!" Hombre growled.

Stepping forward, he dragged the thrashing body back to the cold storage. Lining up the head, he yanked the heavy door closed. The meaty legs and arms spasmed as the brain was crushed with a sickly crunch. Leaving the corpse, he returned to the serving counter. A hundred zombies had gathered, eager for a meal that bled and screamed.

"Dinner is most definitely not served, you festering bastards!"

Pulling the steel shutter down, there were too many arms trapped beneath to secure it, but at least it closed off the disgusting sight. If he had been blessed with time, Hombre would have searched the kitchen for food. The metallic pandemonium at the serving counter was already testing his last nerve, so he decided against it. A green safety sign indicated the position of a fire exit at the back of the room. Climbing on to the worktop, he peeked out of the high set window to check the way. The small courtyard was empty except for a line of commercial garbage bins, overflowing with black waste bags. Hopping down, he pressed the release bar and left the building.

As the door closed, he grumbled, "I really hate school."

CHAPTER 29

Looking out from the enclosed courtyard, Hombre could see through the school carpark to the main road. Most of the zombies in the vicinity had been drawn to the gunshot at the rear of the building. Only a couple of crawlers remained; one missing its lower body entirely, entrails stretching behind it, smearing a stream of gore on the concrete. Walking around them, he quickly checked the cars. Four had the keys in the ignition, but none of them would start. The engines were as dead as the monsters which slowly dragged themselves towards him. Leaving the metallic corpses to fall into their own inevitable decay, he hugged the fence and made his way out towards the road. A tangled mess of twisted metal blocked the entrance. During the outbreak, parents had been frantically trying to reach their children. They had crashed in their impassioned haste, airbags deploying explosively, the white fabric now covered in dried brown blood. How it must have felt being so close to their defenceless offspring, he could not imagine. Being surrounded and eaten by horrors that they knew in their agony stricken minds would be feasting on the children next.

"Poor bastards."

Some of the cars were alive with movement. The undead had pounced immediately, preventing them from even unlatching the seat belt. Trapped forever by the safety device, they grasped for Hombre as he ducked and moved carefully amongst the destruction. Removing the map, he checked the route he would be taking on the way back. If he had to divert around the crash, it would add another mile to the journey. There was no way of knowing if that route would be clear of obstacles either. With the high volume of undead in the area, the scouting parties had only cleared the roads up to the outskirts of town. *What to do?* There was a national coach repair facility on the periphery of the borough. The fifty seaters would make a good battering ram, but also pull every zombie for miles around at the first rending impact.

The generator and vehicle to tow it would need to be ready and waiting for the buses clamorous arrival. It would mean a lot of back and forth through the zombie infestation. Firstly, to the construction site to find a truck that worked, then back to the repair centre to secure a metal behemoth to clear the roads, then a final drive back through a swarm of the dead to retrieve the prize.

"Piece of cake," he whispered, grinning.

The thrashing of the trapped horrors had summoned a handful of their more mobile brethren. Seeing Hombre, their animation grew into a frenzy of clotted gurgles. Unconcerned, he rose to his feet and made for the nearest house. The front door was open, welcoming him into the abode.

Standing in the front door, he shouted, "Honey, I'm home!"

Nothing moved within. Turning to watch the zombies, he waited until they reached the porch before stepping back into the house. Passing through the dining room and into the kitchen, he pulled open the back door. Slamming it in the decomposing faces, the thwarted monsters beat against the glass. It would hold long enough for Hombre to traverse a few gardens. Looking over the shiplap fence, the next property was clear. Hoisting himself over, he dropped to the ground. Four more hops found him at the end of the row of houses. Peering over the boundary wall, a small side road snaked away south from the main thoroughfare. A smattering of zombies loitered on the tarmac.

Leaning through the gate, he clicked his fingers to get their attention. Shuffling towards him, they met their end at the razor-sharp point of his axe. Before breaking cover, he stacked the bodies in the garden and closed the gate. So far, the glass of the first home had held and the sounds of hammering died away as the zombies lost interest. It provided him a known course to backtrack through once the generator was hooked up. Keeping low and hugging the wall, he scurried to the corner and looked out on the main road. His earlier entourage spilled from the sealed home, wandering off in no particular direction. Half a mile awaited between the rear yard and the site itself. With the proximity to the centre of the town decreasing, the numbers of dead were increasing. If the same pattern repeated itself, there would be hundreds standing in his way, perhaps a thousand or more.

What now?

He could outrun them easily and reach the generator, but they would then mass in the area even if he managed to hide himself away. If he approached stealthily through the gardens, it would only take a single sighting to bring the rest down on his head. Neither option had much merit. Even if he secured the equipment, it would be hit or miss if the bus could punch through the crowd or grind to a halt in their midst, trapping him outside the complex. Fighting clear would be impossible. The long-haul coach would be his metal coffin.

I need to kill or trap them.

Soaring into the sky was the ten-storey apartment building which had been visible from the forest. It was the only place in the vicinity which would comfortably hold the sheer number of dead. To reach the tower would be a ten-minute jog, or a two-minute drive. Riding the horn would help to lure as many as possible towards the building. A short distance back up the road was a four by four with the boot wide open. Half packed belongings lay strewn across the pavement. He had spied the glint of keys contained within a leather handbag on the passenger seat. The reputation of the manufacturer for reliability was well known and he figured it was worth a try.

Sliding into the driver's seat, he tipped out the contents of the purse. Makeup, receipts, lip balm, cigarettes and other incidentals clattered onto the suede upholstery. Pushing the key into the ignition, he twisted and the engine started without issue.

"Proper British engineering," he said with pride.

Rolling to the corner, he stopped at the intersection. Seeing the dead turn at the grinding sound of the unused brakes, he gunned it, wheels spinning on the wet road. With one hand on the wheel and the other pressing down the horn, he veered between the abandoned cars. Zombies bounced off the hood, green blood splashing onto the windscreen. Pressing the power button on the stereo, he was rewarded with a burst of death metal from the speakers.

"Great taste!" Hombre yelled, headbanging to the dark rhythm.

The covering of gore grew too dense, so he sprayed the screen and set the wipers on full speed. Used to wrestling eighteen wheelers across the European landscape, the tiny vehicle was anticlimactic. The massive coach would be far more fun. Through the smears, the entrance to the apartments came into view. Skidding to a stop by the main doors, Hombre pulled the key and pocketed the cigarettes. As he climbed from the vehicle, the full force of the undead stench hit him. Retrieving the peppermint balm, he quickly wiped a liberal layer under his nose to banish the vile smell.

The gate to the building site was wide open; its fluorescent jacketed workers impossible to miss as they lumbered through. "Get back to work you lazy fuckers!"

Upset at the insult towards their lacklustre work ethic, they groaned in reply. Removing the pistol from his jacket, he switched the safety off and approached the building. Stealth was no longer a concern and the gun would guarantee a quick kill in the narrow halls and stairwells. One of the residents pressed a grey, sloughing face to the full-length glass door, spraying juices from the compressed pustules. A bullet punched through pane and skull both, sending the zombie crashing to the floor. Shards crunched underfoot as Hombre jumped through the newly formed opening. Four flats were open, with the others all locked up tight. The lift at the back of the passage was halfway open, bloody finger streaks covering the steel doors. Whoever had been trapped inside had fought back; the two dead zombies rotting on the floor were testament to the fact. The hunks of insect riddled meat and scattered limbs within the elevator cab told him of the fighter's ultimate end.

Switching on the torch, he lined it up with the pistol and kicked at the stairwell door. A wave of rancid odour washed out from the sealed shaft making his eyes water. Bodies were spread-eagled on the concrete floor, split open from the fall. They may have jumped, or even fallen in the chaos of the risen dead. It was irrelevant. The flesh had liquefied, spreading in a pool around the broken forms. A zombie rounded the corner of the next floor, face exploding from the bullet's impact before it could descend. The door was starting to close on a spring-loaded hinge which was no good. Reaching into the pile of putridity, he pulled a shattered bone free with a wet pop. Spinning back to the entrance hall, the sounds of disturbed glass announced the horde's arrival. Kicking the bone under the door, it proved adequate in holding it wide open for his new friends.

"Right this way, ladies and gents."

Racing up the first four flights of steps, he left the staircase well ahead of the zombies. On the landing, one of the apartments were open, but it was on the back of the building and not what Hombre was looking for. Kicking out at the opposite door, it smashed deeply into the plasterboard wall. An old woman in white nightie shambled from the living room. Loathe to waste a bullet on such a minimal threat, he backhanded the creature, sending it tumbling over its favourite armchair. Pushing the window wide open, he looked down at the swarm which was slowly entering the foyer in pursuit. The octogenarian monster was trying to reach him, fumbling haphazardly because of the gauzy shift which had ridden over her face. Everything was on display; her sagging, purple breasts and the grey thatch of pubic hair.

"Will you just fuck off, Gladys!"

Clutching her by the back of the neck, her cold, loose skin moved under his fingers. Taking her to the opening, he grabbed her by the drooping buttocks and heaved her out into the cold day. The material of her gown sighed as she fell before hitting the steel railing with a sickening crunch, her body tearing into two pieces. The crowd saw him and waved, so he gave them the finger and hurried back to his initial task. Emerging into the dark stairwell, the undead had made it to the floor below and the noise had grown to a guttural tumult. Waiting for a few moments, he swung a boot and punted the closest cadaver. The girls nose imploded, sending shards of bone up into the brain, killing her instantly. Now that he was doubly certain that the dead were hooked on his sexy bait, he jogged up the remaining stairs to the tenth floor.

"I've gotta... cut down on... the cigarettes," he gasped, chest blazing.

A final set of four steps led to the roof access with a red lettered sign stating *'No access to residents under any circumstances'*. As with a lot of social housing, the tenants had taken it as a challenge and the lock had been forced open long ago. Pressing against the surface, it opened a few inches then slammed shut as something brought its own weight to bear on the other side. Taking two steps back, he shoulder barged it and the zombie staggered backwards from the impact. Raising the pistol, the 9mm slug punched through the cheekbone and erupted from the back of its neck, effectively decapitating it. An illicit pigeon coop had been erected by one of the apartment dwellers. In place of the friendly cooing, was a gargled moan. Feathers festooned the chicken wire, torn from the birds as they tried to escape their owner's ravenous teeth. The keeper was desperate to feed and flung himself at the mesh. Pressing against the thin wire, his decomposing flesh sliced itself away in thin strips. Lacking the strength to break free of his pigeon shit coated prison, Hombre ignored him.

"Now I just need to get down," Hombre muttered, staring at the access door as it spewed out the zombies.

CHAPTER 30

"Right, boys. I think you need to spill the beans," Kurt said, waving them over.

Sam and Braiden looked sheepish and approached, bowing their heads.

"Winston, did you have anything to do with this?" Sarah called.

"I was an innocent bystander in their nefarious endeavours," he replied.

"But you *were* there? Come here!" Kurt ordered and he joined the procession of doomed souls.

"I told you this was a bad idea," Winston whispered fearfully. "Now I'm going to feel the pointy end of that war pick."

"Relax and let us do the talking," Sam muttered under his breath.

Kurt fed a few logs into the brazier and arranged the chairs in a circle around the crackling fire. Nodding at the cheap, plastic visitor's seats, he watched the boys timidly sit down. He had to hide the grin that was threatening to spread across his face.

"Good work out there, boys," he began. "All of you."

"You were all very brave," Sarah agreed.

"Now, what the hell have you lot been plotting behind my back?" Kurt got right to business.

"Please don't throw me from the tallest tower!" Winston blurted.

"I'm not cruel," Kurt said, shaking his head. "I'll just throw you over the wall right here."

Winston's eyes bugged until Sarah patted him on the leg and winked. "He's joking."

"Am I?"

"Yes," Sarah stated with a glare of warning. "Now, tell us what's been going on, please."

"We want to fight back and destroy those things," Braiden explained.

Kurt cocked his head in confusion. "Haven't we been doing that since the first day? How many is it now, fifty thousand, a hundred thousand?"

"We sure killed a few in Chichester with that explosion, Dad," said Sam.

"I feel a bit inadequate," Winston admitted. "I've only killed a few hundred."

"You really have been slacking," Kurt teased.

Sam leaned forward to warm his hands. "What my brother was trying to say, is that we need to kill a few million more."

"And the only way to do that is to train hard and face them whenever we can. That means we may have to go outside and fight," Braiden added.

"With all the people that we've lost, you want to put yourself at risk for no reason?" Kurt demanded, the earlier amusement turning to anger. "We're secure for the first time in weeks!"

"Hear them out, love," Sarah coaxed, trying to soothe him. "They're just trying to help."

"Dad, listen. We know how to fight them without putting ourselves in danger; you and Gramps taught us how. The other kids want to learn what we know so they can keep themselves safe, too."

"And please don't throw me from the wall, but the only way to learn is out there among them, sir," Winston said cautiously.

Kurt raised an eyebrow. "Sir now, is it? You kill zombies better than you kiss ass, that's for sure."

"Go on," Sarah urged.

"We have all the blades we need to arm ourselves," said Sam.

"What we need are more weapons to kill them at range," Braiden finished.

"You mean you need guns? I don't know if Jonesy and DB have enough to go around. Not if they want to remain armed themselves."

Sarah agreed with Kurt. "Besides, there are a lot fewer bullets than we'd like to admit. The fight for the castle took a large chunk of what we'd recovered from the hospital."

"I wasn't talking about guns specifically, Mum," Sam replied.

"The cracks of each shot are deafening which will only put us in more danger. We need a lot more bows and arrows to use."

"But you've already got bows and arrows!" Kurt objected, his frustration growing.

"They're cheap knock-offs, Dad," Braiden explained. "Miss Lunsford says they were only ever meant to be used for displays; the strings are already fraying and won't last much longer."

"And where on earth would you secure new ones?" Sarah asked, ignoring Kurt as he muttered and grumbled.

"There's a shop to the north. Holly saw it as they drove into town."

"Oh, she did, did she?" Kurt huffed.

"It's worth some thought at the very least, surely?" Sarah said.

Kurt closed his eyes and leaned back, the chill increasing as he moved his head away from the radiated heat. Every inch of ground they had bled for was meant to keep those he loved safe from the monsters. The boys were right, though. No matter how high the wall, the dead would still be waiting to strike. Humans too, as the prison proved.

Sam spoke up to break the lingering silence. "Sorry, Dad. It was a daft idea."

"Yes, it was," Kurt replied, "And if you keep secrets from me in the future, I'll kick all your asses, do you understand me?"

"Sorry," replied the boys, miserably.

"I've already explained why we need to keep the zombies at the walls, haven't I?"

They all nodded.

"But that's not to say there aren't ways you could get clear and take what you needed from the shop. Stephen has shown me the secret tunnels which emerge well away from the walls. I'll show you boys soon."

"Does that mean you're going to let us go out into the world?" Braiden wondered.

Kurt roared with hatred, startling the boys and his wife. "Yes! Fucking hell, yes, ok! But only in a limited way and I want to know the ins and outs of any excursion."

"I'm sorry you're angry with us, Mr Taylor," Winston stammered in fear.

"I'm not angry with you, boys. I'm angry with this whole fucked up world that means we even need to discuss this shit. You should be worried about school, girls, what TV shows you'll be watching, not how best to retrieve weapons to kill rotting corpses who won't stay fucking dead. I know that the stronger you get, the better your chance of surviving this hell. I just struggle to let go of your childhood and admit that you're all becoming men. The thought of not being there to protect you if you ever get in trouble terrifies me. I'd prefer fighting a hundred of those freaks with my bare hands to having you in harm's way."

"Oh, love," Sarah gasped, tears spilling down her cheeks. Reaching out, she took him in her arms as his own flowed unashamedly.

"We're growing into the men we are because of your bravery, Dad," Braiden said, the lump in his throat choking the words.

"Paige's and Gramps's too," Sam said, his own tears trickling.

"Come here!" Kurt husked, pulling his boys into the embrace.

Winston shuffled awkwardly. "I know you were going to throw me from the wall a minute ago, but can I get in on this hug?"

Sarah sobbed out a chuckle and beckoned him over. They split apart and pulled him into their world of family and love.

"Now listen, boys," Kurt said, breaking away and wiping at his face. "I don't want to hear of any more secret plans to take on the world. Here's what's going to happen, and I won't have any arguments about it, do you understand?"

"Yes, Dad."

"Yes, sir." Winston nodded.

"Cut that shit out, Winston! It's Kurt. Our first priority is to get enough food to last us through to the spring. We'll be planning a way to get the goods back inside the castle and I'd like you all to offer input. That'll need to happen before the week is out or we'll be eating the furniture."

"There's a nice leather couch I've got my eye on," Winston remarked.

"It's not the time," Sam whispered from the corner of his mouth.

"Sorry, I'm still buzzing from the hug."

Kurt continued. "Once the food's secure, we'll be making a move on the cathedral to see if the people inside need our help. Without knowing their own situation, I think it's best to do it as soon as possible after the raid on the supermarket."

"They could be starving," Braiden speculated.

"Couldn't we get to them first?" Sam suggested.

"No. My only concern at the moment is the castle and the survivors inside. I'm sorry, but it's got to be that way. Should the worst happen and we suffer a catastrophe, at least the people inside the walls will be well provisioned."

"If you're that worried, why bother?" Braiden asked. Seeing their looks, he clarified his point. "I want to rescue them too, but I could understand why it would be crazy to risk ourselves for strangers."

"I know what you meant, mate. But that's just who we are, at least I hope so. I don't want to become insular and say fuck everyone else, you're on your own," said Kurt.

"Purely from a numbers point of view it helps as well," Sarah added. "We are outnumbered by the prisoners by a factor of ten to one. Maybe less if you discount the ones who aren't psychotic and the hostages, but still shitty odds."

"They may also have important skills which we could use," Winston explained. "Maybe not the priests; they don't seem to have done us much good in the past few months. There may be some useful people trapped inside with them, though."

"Exactly. The one skill we are lacking for now is an expert in growing our own food. There are loads of books in the library on the topic which we can use if we need to. Textbooks are no substitute for experience, unfortunately. I would like to see this whole upper bailey section planted and growing by the summer. The quicker we can achieve self-sufficiency, the better."

Winston put a hand up meekly and Kurt frowned.

"This isn't a classroom. Spit it out."

"Well, it's just that there may be a slight problem with your plan," he confessed.

"And what might that be?"

"Erm… well. The plot of land within the walls won't be enough to feed the castle. It won't even be close," he said apologetically.

"What do you mean? There's at least three acres of ground to grow vegetables and fruit. Once we have a system in place it should provide us with plenty," Kurt replied.

"Begging your pardon, but it won't be enough. I did a project at school on the subject of people disappearing from civilization and living off grid. It takes two acres to produce enough food to last all year round for a family of four."

"What?" Kurt was dumbfounded.

"Two acres for four people and much more if any kind of animals are involved. I'm afraid we have quite a few more than that to feed."

"Fuck! That leaves us right in the shit!" Kurt held his head, shocked by the practicalities of surviving once the food laying unclaimed in the local shops ran out.

"If I may," Winston offered, urging them to join him at the wall. "The arrowhead of land which sits to the south east is large enough to provide for hundreds."

"Winston, it's outside. We can't exactly go planting in the field when the dead will be trying to eat us."

"Look at the shape." Winston pointed. "The River Arun curves around, enclosing it on the east, south and west. All we would need to do is seal off the northern edge and the river would do the rest for us. I'd guess it's about three hundred metres from water to water."

"That's three hundred metres of land which we can't even get to, let alone fortify and seal off," Kurt muttered.

"It was just a thought. Sorry I peed on your cornflakes."

"If what you say is true, people would be happy with piss soaked cornflakes when they start to starve," Kurt replied, dejectedly.

Sarah patted his leg. "It's a great plan, Winston. We'll give it some more thought on how we could secure it permanently after we've retrieved the food."

"They don't like the water. Why not use it?" Sam suggested.

"What do you mean?" Kurt asked.

"Dig a ditch, then flood it. Make the whole area an island, or as close as possible to one."

"Like a moat around a castle?" Kurt marvelled. "That may be crazy enough to work."

"I knew there was a reason I kept you guys around," Winston chuckled.

CHAPTER 31

Running around the perimeter of the apartment block's roof, there were only two routes down. An enclosed safety ladder dropped to a steel walkway, twenty feet below. It acted as an emergency exit from the building in event of the lift and stairs being cut off by fire. Or zombies, Hombre thought. The other option was to use the balconies, lowering himself carefully from the iron balusters to the platform below one by one until reaching terra-firma. *Maybe if you were young again. And pissed.* He had seen enough videos of the stunt going wrong to quickly dismiss the idea.

Dodging the rapidly increasing mass of undead, he climbed over the low parapet and descended the ladder. Movement from above caught his attention and he was just in time to see the zombie topple head first over the edge. Throwing up his arms to shield himself, the creature fell ten feet before its limbs became entangled in the protective metal cage. Blood trickled from the twisted, shattered bones, coating Hombre's upturned face.

Shouting his disgust, he hurried down the final length and moved out from under the disgusting drizzle. Another resounding clang came from above, caused by a second zombie falling down the chute. A third joined the writhing mass. The trapped limbs were stretching under the weight, joints separating as the skin and flesh tore.

"Time to go!"

Running down the first flight of steel steps, he watched in shock as a body sailed past him, still reaching as it fell out of sight. The body had already been weakened by decomposition and the addition of concrete and gravity was unforgiving. Splitting into unrecognisable chunks of meat, the outer wall was sprayed with blood during the explosive impact. Tremors shook through his hands which clutched at the railing for support. Above, more of the eager corpses were tossing themselves towards him, some hitting the steel frame while others missed completely. Their excited gurgles were cut off the instant they pancaked on the sidewalk below. Taking the steps two at a time, he raced for the bottom as the zombies fell like rain all around. Reaching the ground, the surrounding area was awash with dripping ichor and shuddering piles of rancid meat. Waiting for a few seconds, the lemming routine tapered off as the undead lost interest in their missing quarry.

The gate to the building site was a short distance away, but Hombre had another plan first. Taking the keys from his pocket, he hugged the wall and skirted back to the four by four. Jumping behind the wheel, he fired the engine and reversed away from the entrance, slamming into a parked Mercedes. Shifting into first, he floored the accelerator and aimed for the emerging cadavers. Bracing himself, the vehicle smashed through both the undead and door frame. The airbag triggered, inflating explosively as he came to rest in the dark foyer. Momentarily dazed, he shook his head and climbed through to the rear seats. Blasting through the rear windscreen, he kicked out at any loose shards and extricated himself from the wreckage. Looking back, the building had effectively been corked, sealing the dead inside for now. Any that chose to leap from the roof to reach him would be killed outright, or rendered immobile by the fall. It was just a shame the vehicle lacked a towing ball or it would have been perfect to pull the generator home.

"Oh well, come to papa!" he said, turning towards the construction site.

Pulling the gate closed, he looped the loose chain around the hasp a few times. The padlock was nowhere to be seen, so he slipped a discarded, rust covered screwdriver between the links to secure them. Two huge sand and cement silos sat side by side next to the site office. Someone had opened the valve and tonnes of yellow grains had poured out, covering the ground. A solitary hand flexed its fingers, the rest of the creature trapped beneath the crushing mound.

The partially erected steel frame of the high rise reminded him of their foe; skeletal and devoid of life. Three floors had been nearing completion with the bare concrete blocks giving it an austere, dystopian feel. A colossal tower crane stared down on the scene, the viewing windows sentient and watchful. It filled him with an uneasy foreboding, quite out of character for a bare knuckle fighting gun runner. For someone who valued personal solitude, it could be the knowledge that the survivors really were alone. Billions of souls frenetically living their hectic lives had been reduced to millions, perhaps fewer if everyone had been similarly caught off guard like the pathetic British government. Scratching from within the locked site office reminded him he was not alone, but he did not crave the company of filthy rotters.

"Where the hell is it?" he asked no one in particular.

Dozens of yellow cables ran into the building, trailing from beneath a heavy-duty cable cover. Following the protective ramp, it circled around to the rear of the site. The generator came into view, surrounded by the parked cars of the dead workforce.

"Marvellous," he sighed.

The muck and mire of the sodden, muddy ground would make it impossible to move them by hand, even if he had five strong men to help. The wheels had already sunk by a few inches from being stationary through the damp weather. Hoping against hope, he tried the doors but they were all locked tight. There was no doubt that the length of time between the outbreak and Hombre's arrival would mean most, if not all, of the batteries were too weak to start the engines anyway. Added to that was the difficulty in finding their owners, even in the high visibility jackets, killing them, and then praying they still had the keys in their pockets.

Leaning against a rusting Nissan Micra, he lit up a cigarette and tried to think of a solution. The blockade was arranged in such a way that if he could move just four of the cars, he could back up to the towing hitch and be away. The wheels were solid and, luckily, the generator had been set up on a concrete hardstand so the wet ground was inconsequential. Tossing the butt away, he approached the mobile unit.

May as well get it ready while I work out how the fuck to get it out.

Pulling the wires from the many adaptors, he coiled them on his arm and tidied them out of the way. The thick, armoured cable of the crane was directly connected into the main grid. The backup coupler was still in the box by the control unit which saved him the time of finding tools to disconnect it. Standing in the shadow of the gigantic, steel beast, a crazy idea formed in his mind. A batshit crazy idea from the town of utterly ridiculous ideas based in the country of what the fuck are you even contemplating this for. This was the kind of stuff that got people killed.

Let's try it.

Searching inside the storage containers, he found what he was looking for; large cylinders with heavy duty chain wrapped around them for the tower crane, and three oxy-acetylene torch kits from the frame erectors. Peeking back out into the light, he estimated the length between the cars impeding his ability to get at the generator, and the crane

251

itself. Unspooling the links, he made sure he had enough slack to cater for any mistakes on his guess work. Opening the valve on the acetylene, he sparked his lighter and the dirty yellow flame fluttered from the nozzle. Cranking the oxygen valve, the flame firmed up before turning bright blue as it oxidised. Lacking a visor, Hombre shuttered his eyes as much as possible and held the flame to the steel. After a few seconds, the metal started to glow, then soften and drip to the ground. Three more sections were cut and tossed out into the yard to cool down. Scanning the shelves, boxes of nuts, bolts and washers of varying sizes were laid out. Grabbing a handful of each, he pocketed them and moved outside to collect the chains.

"This is going to work," he declared, manhandling the lengths across to the cars.

Looping each section around the axle, he used three bolts to hold the links together, tightening them as much as his grip would allow. When all four cars had been secured, he carried the loose ends over to the steel frame of the crane. Pulling them taut, he climbed the ladder and looped them over the diagonal braces of the mast, before fastening them with the remaining bolts. Letting go of the rungs, he gingerly applied his weight to the dangling lengths. All four held fast. Satisfied, he descended and looked upon his work. The easy part was done. All he had to do now was topple the two-hundred-foot machine and it would drag the vehicles out of the way.

"This is actually a really shitty idea," he muttered.

If he used the coach to crash into the frame, it could buckle and topple towards the gate, crushing him and trapping the generator inside the compound. If he used the cutting equipment, he would need to get his ass clear pretty damned quick or he would be squashed as well. Few options led to a better outcome than being flattened like a bug.

Making his way back to the storage containers, he spied a Ford Ranger tucked behind the site offices. It was the pickup truck of choice of site managers across the country and the poor flower must have been afraid of it getting dusty which is why he had concealed it. Ignoring the crane dilemma for now, he tried the doors and was not surprised that they were locked tight. Given half a chance, the tradespeople under the manager's authority would prank him with glitter in the air vents or some other trick. Checking the rear of the truck, it had a shiny towing ball that had never even dragged a load.

The dull thuds and scraping were still emanating from the upper section of the temporary portacabin behind him. Removing the ice axe from his belt, Hombre climbed the steps and listened at the door. Several zombies were trapped inside, throwing themselves at the door after hearing the earlier commotion. If it was locked from the inside, the vehicle was lost; the converted shipping containers had no window and a solid metal door to deter thieves looking for computers and other equipment. Positioning himself at the top step, he leaned forward and slapped the handle down, withdrawing his hand in a flash. The door swung wide, crashing into the safety rail and the undead spilled out in a tangled heap. Hombre slashed down at the skulls, destroying all four brains before the things could even stand. Two suited cadavers were among the pile of dead flesh. Tossing the construction workers over the rail, he checked the pockets of the remaining men and found a key fob for the truck.

"Thanks," he whispered, patting the creature on its back.

Unsurprisingly, the keyless entry refused to work with the dead battery. Smashing the driver's window, he unlocked it and popped the hood. Beneath a plastic cover was the power source itself and all he had to do was find a way to jump start it. Running back across to the building, he followed the yellow cables inside. Damp concrete and wood were the predominant scents, but he could detect an undercurrent of decomposition on the draughts. Listening for a while, he could only make out the distant grumbling of the zombies in the apartment block. One by one he dismissed the wires when he found lights, bench saws and drills at their end. Shining a torch into a small room on the ground floor, he found what he was looking for. The charger packs for the cordless tools were all laid along a wall, their batteries either inserted or waiting for charge. He disregarded any that were still plugged in as the power would have leeched back into the grid over the past months.

"Fingers crossed," he said, checking those which sat to the side.

After checking six without luck, an eighteen-volt lithium ion battery showed two out of four bars of power on the indicator strip. *Yes!* If he could get enough of the juice into the truck, it would fire and he could leave it idling to recharge the battery fully while he took care of the other problems. Taking one of the corded drills and a bag of woodworking tools, he headed back to the Ford. At the gates, a few zombies had escaped confinement or arrived from elsewhere and pressed against the chain link. It would take a lot more weight to break through, so he ignored them and moved on. Ripping the plug off under his boot, he repeated the process with the drill itself, leaving the wires exposed. Using electrical tape, he joined two screws to the positive and negative terminals of the lithium battery and sat it inside the engine compartment. Wrapping the copper wire from the cable around each head, he then rifled through the bag and found two G clamps. Securing the other end of the cable to the clamps, he then carefully attached them to the red and black terminals on the battery. It wasn't ideal, but hopefully it would give enough power to turn over. All he had to do was wait.

Taking another break, he stared over at the crane. Now that he had the potential of a safer option by using the truck to tow them clear, he found the temptation to collapse the machine growing. *What the fuck is wrong with me?* he thought, already knowing the answer. *Bragging rights!* The story would see him showered with cigarettes and alcohol, as well as the adulation of his fellow inmates. As the inner dialogue went back and forth between insanity and sense, the power slowly transferred between the batteries. Opting to check the Ford first, he climbed behind the wheel and pressed the start button. The engine juddered and caught, causing the dash to light up and the fuel gauge indicator to swivel to three quarters full.

"Hell, you've got enough to tow every car out of the way, go on a tour of the south coast and still get back to the prison."

Still, he found himself looking at the acetylene equipment and the thick, steel columns of the mast.

CHAPTER 32

"How're your headaches now, sweetie?" Denise asked, joining Kurt and Sarah around the blazing fireplace.

"They come and go," he replied. "Your tablets were fantastic, though. Thank you."

"Not a problem. I notice you've had a wash since our last chat?" she teased.

"It was either that or I'd make him sleep in the dungeon," Sarah added with a grin.

"You're lucky I bothered. The water was bloody freezing!"

Sarah held her arms out in faux outrage. "You're the plumber! How about you figure out some way of heating the water for us so we can have a shower or bath in comfort."

"Fuck my life! If I'm not killing zombies, planning on how to keep us from starving to death or worrying about the imminent attack by the nutters of the prison, you now want me to get my tools back out and do manual labour."

"Men should know their place," remarked Gloria as she joined them.

"I agree," Sarah replied haughtily.

"Ever since you moved into the castle you bloody women want to be treated like royalty. Typical aristocrats making the lower class do all the work."

Denise fluttered a hand at her face. "Well you can't expect us to get our hands dirty, surely. We might break a nail."

"I can help!" called Bob from across the room.

"Good man," Gloria replied. "I expect it to be up and running by tomorrow night."

"Whoa, hold up. Tomorrow's Sunday. I don't work on the sabbath!" replied the handyman.

"Bob, it's Tuesday. And you're about as Christian as my left testicle!" Kurt fired back.

"Kurt!" Sarah was horrified. "Don't be so rude."

"I'm actually Jewish," Bob countered.

"Their sabbath's on a Friday evening to Saturday evening then," said Gloria.

"Shit! Ok, I'm in. Just let me know what you need."

"Thanks, mate."

"You owe me a bottle of whisky when you hit the supermarket!"

"Consider it done," Kurt confirmed and the maintenance man went back to his book, smiling from ear to ear.

"Where do you think you'll set it up?" Sarah asked.

"In here would be the easiest, but for privacy's sake I think one of the bathrooms. Most of them have their own fireplace and I can rig up some sort of moveable gravity system to heat it up directly from the flames. People will just have to be careful to monitor the temperature of the water before it gets too hot."

"My hero," Sarah gushed.

"Hardly. I'm going to charge everyone to use it."

"How much?" Denise asked.

"If you keep me supplied with drugs you're good to go."

"I have a few left. I'm sure we can come to some sort of arrangement." Denise winked.

257

"And what about me? I don't have any dope to supply you with."

Kurt grinned at his wife, raising his eyebrows suggestively.

"Pervert!" Sarah said. It was nice to see the way he looked at her, passion behind his eyes.

"I'm afraid my days of romantic liaisons are fading," Gloria sighed. "And I'm sure your wife would have something to say if I paid you in naughty cuddles."

"You can have him, the lecherous beast," Sarah replied, shrieking as Kurt tried to smother her in kisses.

"Come on now, daddy needs his sugar," Kurt growled lewdly as she tried to fight him off.

"You keep that up and all daddy will be getting is salt and a black eye," Sarah replied, pulling him into a tight embrace.

"Eugh. Get a room," Gloria muttered in her best moody teenager voice.

"No, let them do it here!" Bob chimed in. Half of the group laughed and the other half groaned their disgust. Holding up his hands in surrender, he squawked, "I was kidding. Jeez, get a sense of humour."

"Of course, you were!" Gloria replied to more laughter. Bob quickly retreated behind the book cover.

As the hall settled back into peace and quiet, Kurt snuggled up on the long chair behind Sarah. It felt surreal to be relaxed, even joking, with everything going on in the world, but Denise had been right. He was close to burning himself out and that would be no good for anyone. Hearing gentle sobs, they turned to see Denise dabbing at her eyes.

"What's up, love?" Kurt asked, sitting up.

"Nothing," she replied, trying to regain her composure.

"You can tell us," urged Sarah.

"It's just me being silly. I was thinking about my family back home and how I'll never see them again. Or whether I'd even want to see them knowing what they are now."

"I'm so sorry, Denise. Here's me acting like a complete fool when I should've been more considerate. I can't imagine what you're going through."

"It's ok, sweetie. I thought I'd cried my tears, but I was just so happy to see the fun you were having with your beautiful wife."

"I know it won't bring you any comfort, but I firmly believe that the American people are better prepared to fight back against this plague than anyone. If I may presume, your family is just as resilient and brave as yourself?" Gloria said, stroking her hand.

"They are," she confirmed.

"And they were well stocked with arms and ammunition?"

Denise nodded.

"Then if I were you, I'd dare to hope."

"It doesn't really matter as I'll never know," she replied, breath catching in her throat.

"Never say never," Kurt proclaimed. "If you'd told me when the world went dark that we'd still be alive all these weeks later, I'd have laughed. Not only are we alive, but we've made it to a fortress and made new friends. Who can say that when we get through the winter we can't find someone who can sail?"

"I can sail!" called Bob.

"We're not talking about floating a rubber dinghy with a beer holder in a swimming pool!" Kurt mocked.

"Seriously. I've done the journey twice with friends when I was a few years younger."

"Are you fucking with me?" Denise demanded.

"That's bang out of order if you are," Sarah cautioned.

"On my life, I've done it," he declared, hand on heart. "It took about three weeks each way and a shit load of money and preparation."

"Money isn't an issue any more, and we can take our pick of boats," Kurt mused.

"I know where my friend's family moor their boat. I'd be happy to show you."

"Bob, you're a true gent. Would you mind compiling a list of the provisions when you have a spare moment?" Kurt asked.

"It'd be my pleasure, mate. If we can ever get this Godawful mess sorted, I'll be happy to crew the vessel as well. We'd head south via Spain and the Canary Islands then west towards the Caribbean to pick up the trade winds."

Kurt was clueless. "You'll have to explain what that means to me at some point."

"Gladly."

"Thank you for giving a lady a dream, sweetheart," Denise choked through the tears.

"My pleasure, darling."

A glimmer of hope had been introduced into her life and she determined to fight with every ounce of her soul for the chance to make the journey. The chances her loved ones had survived were slim, but at least she could return home and find out for certain. If they had perished? She would cross that bridge when the time came, and put them down if necessary.

CHAPTER 33

The bright blue flame slowly chewed through the thick braces, runnels of molten steel trickling down and burning a path through the yellow paint. The creaks and pings of the crane shifting from the gentle breeze grew into a shrieking tumult as the centre of gravity was lost. Dropping the torch, he ran from the concrete base like a bat out of hell. Ducking behind a pallet of concrete blocks, he turned to watch the show. Considering the weight of the colossal structure, he was surprised at how slowly it toppled.

"Hurry up!"

The ballast block counterweights started to exert their influence, twisting the frame. As gravity and velocity took over, the boom swung skyward, lashing the dangling cable in an arc. The heavy hook whipped around, tearing through the roof of a house and bursting through the outside wall in a shower of masonry and timber. As the angle of the mast shifted, the cars were pulled aside like toys, clearing a path to the generator. With an ear-splitting roar, the weighted counter jib hit the ground, demolishing another two properties, sending debris flying in all directions. The one-hundred-and-fifty-foot main jib started its inexorable descent to earth, breaking the air with a hiss.

"Timber!"

The sound of the first impact was as nothing compared to the destructive force of the huge arm as it struck.

Buildings exploded and cars were crushed flat under the massive weight. The noise would carry for miles, drawing a new wave of zombies to the area. Time was of the essence, so he carefully approached the gnarled frame. Following the noise of the escaping acetylene through the settling dust, he turned the nozzle off to make it safe.

Returning to the truck, he drove it around the carnage and backed it up against the generator. Grunting with effort, he hoisted the tow hitch onto the ball. Leaving the engine running to ensure the battery had a chance to recharge, he looked over the shattered fence. Any zombies not trapped in the apartment building staggered into view, drawn to the commotion. When he was sure the crushed homes held more interest to the dead, he dropped down and crawled between the abandoned cars. Sighted by the roof dwellers, he stifled a chuckle as they launched themselves from the rim. The melodic accompaniment of bodies disintegrating on concrete followed him down the empty road.

***

Backtracking towards the coach facility, Hombre made mental notes of every bottleneck or blockage which would require removal. The heavy machine would be able to crash through most with ease and with the engine in the back, all he would need to be careful of was the front axle and tyres. The fallen crane had temporarily sated his appetite for destruction which went some way to ensuring he would not take silly risks on the return journey.

Reaching the school, the zombies who had been in close pursuit were excited to see him again. Moving between the cars, he funnelled them one by one into the blade of his axe. Zombies still thrashed and moaned from their metallic tombs as he passed. Looking back at the scene, it was clear the twist of crashed vehicles might be too much for the battering ram to push through. Approaching one of the twisted wrecks, the bloated, festering creatures strained at their harnesses.

"Hello, ladies."

Opening a switchblade, he lunged in and severed the polyester belt. Now unrestrained, the zombie toppled from the open door and Hombre stamped down hard, driving the face into the tarmac with a wet crack. Unable to get to the passenger door, he leaned in and stabbed at the buckle release with the point of his axe. After four attempts, he avoided the flailing arms and the red button clicked, sending the slime coated material back into the retractor. Flopping across the seats, the woman tried to grab at him. He waited, watching closely as she struggled to reach him. The gear stick pierced her decaying belly, tearing it open and sending rancid intestines and organs spilling into the foot wells. Unfazed, he hacked at the head, chunks of skull and brain joining the rest of the vile accumulation by the pedals. After cleaning his blade, he lifted the zombie from the impaling stick and dragged her through the open door. Tearing the denim skirt from the dead woman, he leaned in and used it to put the car in neutral before releasing the handbrake.

"Here goes nothing," he whispered, checking the coast was clear.

Bouncing on the hood, he tried to use the suspension to rock the chassis clear of the car it had driven into. The twisted carcass of each vehicle screeched and clunked, but held fast.

"Fuck it!"

The only other option was to bust through the school fence at the south end of the staff carpark and then circle around the building via the playing field. It was then only a thick hedgerow between him and the largely unclogged road to the construction site. Either end could result in a damaged tyre or debris working its way into the brake mechanisms or hydraulics. With any luck, the damage would be minimal and worth it to clear a path for the smaller truck and trailer which would be coming back. Realising he had no choice in the matter anyway, he left the mass of scrap metal behind.

The massive sign above the entrance read *Arun Travel.* Rows of coaches lined the yard, some were still fairly clean despite the apocalypse. Wherever they had been destined to go on that fateful day was now certainly infested with the dead. The uncollected passengers already at the end of the journey called life. Others were parked near the massive service bays at the rear of the complex awaiting repairs or maintenance. Staying low to the surrounding foliage, he performed a quick examination around the edge of the property. Dozens of zombies could be seen shuffling between the huge carriages and more were moving around inside the shadowy repair bays.

"Ninja Lee, time to do your stuff!"

Brandishing the axes, he slipped through the gate and ducked behind one of the buses. The noise of dragging feet caught his attention from the other side of the vehicle. Laying on the cold ground, he held the weapons above his head and rolled underneath. The zombie heard the noise but was unable to locate the source and turned in a full circle. Winding up his arm, Hombre slashed out at the legs. Crippled, the monster collapsed inches from his face. As its bloody mouth opened to snarl, the axe opened another hole in the top of its skull. Pulling the carcass into the shadows, another creature staggered into view. Waiting for it to pass, he stuck out a leg and kicked out at the heels of the heavy work boots. Slamming onto its back, the head impacted the concrete with a crunch. Brain oozed between the splits in the broken scalp.

"Oops, watch your step," he whispered, grinning as the milky eye twitched.

Leaving the dark underbelly, he made his way to the rear of the next vehicle. Peeking around the corner, four zombies milled around in the small passage. Moving into plain sight, he pulled the manual release on the coach's door and it hissed open.

"All aboard!"

Hopping inside, he waited in the shadows as the eager passengers started to climb.

"One for you!" he said, sticking the switchblade deep into the suppurating eye socket. "And you, sir?" he asked as another male cadaver pushed past the corpse of its friend. "If you insist." The blade sunk through the orb and into the brain.

Kicking the man in the chest, his truly dead body knocked the last two to the ground. Losing interest in the stealthy game, he jumped out and stamped the zombies to death, feeling immense satisfaction as the bone crumpled under his assault.

"Come on you fuckers, I haven't got all day!" he screamed, smashing windows up and down the buses.

Drawn by the bedlam, they moved down the narrow gap straight into his flashing blades. Within minutes, butchered corpses blocked both ends, stacked atop one another in a tangled heap. Streamers of blood and viscera ran from the black paintwork, pooling at Hombre's feet. Sucking in deep, shuddering breaths, he tried to calm his burning rage.

"Anyone else?" he roared.

The only sound was the bass thud of his heart and the racing blood in his veins. Moving forward, he tossed the bodies aside to clear himself a path. Emerging into the open yard, all was still. Threats could still lurk in the bays and offices, but his blood was up and he did not give a fuck. Marching over to the open shutters, he moved inside without hesitating. The aromas of grease, metal, and sweat brought back fond memories. His time on the wrench had been thoroughly enjoyable and it was only the winter cold which had forced him from the garage and into pulling eighteen wheelers laden with hidden guns. A dead mechanic thrashed in the pit to his right, lacking the cognition to turn around and climb the steps.

A rolling tool chest sat against the wall to his left. Stashing the axes on a workbench, he pulled it from its nook and pushed it towards the trench. Toppling in, the clatter of crashing metal and scattered tools was nearly deafening. Horribly crushed, the zombie struggled feebly against the weight.

"Fuck, sorry."

Spying an industrial trolley jack under the bench, he lifted it, grunting at the weight. Waddling back to the trapped creature, he lined it up carefully and dropped it. The corner smashed through the head, spraying blood which intermingled with the patches of oil.

Zombies emerged from the furthest corners of the building, tattered suits flapping in the breeze which carried through the open door. Feeling no kinship with these executive monsters, he lured them into the open holes. Once they had all fallen in, he left them crawling in the darkness, broken legs flopping uselessly.

Searching the building, he found the first thing he needed. The mobile response van was already open, boxes of spare parts half loaded for a job that was never completed. Rifling through the tools and equipment, he found the hidden treasure; a twenty-four volt, eight-hundred-amp rechargeable power bank. Pressing the button, the LED bulb burst into life, steady and bright. It was a good sign.

"My life would've been a lot easier if I'd had you a couple of hours ago," he told the battery.

Using the torch, he scanned the walls around the garage. Unable to locate his target, the administration was separated into two blocks. One section was for the mechanics, grimy and lived in. The other was for the managers and office staff, sterile and boring. Navigating through discarded boots and spilled paperwork, he found the key cabinet under the supervisor's desk. Scorch marks circled an overflowing ashtray. Resisting the urge to light up until he was safely trundling through the front gates, he saw a flash of metal under a folder. Tossing it aside, a gold Zippo lighter was revealed.

"Thank you very much..." He read the engraving. "Harold."

Pocketing it alongside a handful of numbered keys, he left the fragrant office. The dead had stayed dead this time and he reached the coach unmolested. Lifting a cover, he pulled the tray of batteries out and attached the cables to the terminals. Getting behind the wheel, he laid out the keys on the dash. Numbered one to twenty-five, Hombre picked up the first set and slipped it into the ignition. *Why didn't they just put the number plate on the fucking things?* It was probably to make any would be thieves life difficult if they ever got their hands on them. Set after set was tried and his anger grew with each discarded bunch.

"You wanker," Hombre hissed, tossing set number twenty-four out through the door.

Turning the last key, the engine turned over instantly. *Don't fuck with me. You don't want to be on my bad side,* he warned God, glaring up at the sky through the windscreen. Quickly removing the charger, he climbed back into the coach, eager to be on the move. Shifting into gear, he let off the parking brake and rolled out of the yard. Rounding the bend, the first blockage came into view. Downshifting and slowing to a crawl, he nudged against the bumper. Outmatched in weight, the car tyres shrieked as the rubber was pushed across the rough ground. Turning the steering wheel slightly, the vehicle twisted to the right and punched straight through a garden wall. Clear of the obstacle, he floored it.

"That wasn't too bad. Keep it up and we won't have a problem," he said to the sky.

The school building came into view and he slowed to a full stop, staring at the fence surrounding the carpark. Concrete posts held the wooden frames in place and it was those that would cause the biggest problem. *Fuck it,* he thought, accelerating straight forward. If the shit hit the fan and he destroyed the coach, he would just have to go back and get another. The thick tyres mounted the kerb, bouncing him in the seat. Covering his face, he hit the posts at thirty miles an hour with an almighty crack. The windscreen cobwebbed from the impact and he was forced to lean out of the window to safely steer around the remaining staff cars. Stopping briefly, he raced back to the destruction. The posts had snapped off cleanly instead of upending their massive foundation. Tossing them to one side, he boarded the bus and kicked out the shattered glass. Driving around the building, he came out onto the field and straight into the crowd of zombies who had been thwarted at the classroom window. Flooring the accelerator, the huge coach rolled straight through them, heads popping and bones crunching under the weight. Flecks of gore splashed through the empty window, hitting him in the face and chest.

"Dirty bastards," he grumbled, wiping the blood with the back of his arm.

Coming up to the dense hawthorn bush on the other side of the sprawling field, he gunned it once more. The shriek of broken branches dragging along the body of the coach was deafening until he reached the open road beyond. Greenery protruded from below the windscreen sill from the vegetation which had been ripped from the ground after embedding in the carbon fibre bumper. Not wanting to waste time pulling it loose, he drove on. The hiss of mud caked roots dragging across the tarmac was joined by a steady thudding of deflated rubber. Feeling the steering wheel pull to the right, he corrected it and ignored the flat tyre. *Nearly there!*

By the time the last obstacles had been cleared, Hombre was covered in twigs and leaves from the battered hedge which had blown through the opening. Thankfully, the entrance was clear; the zombies still enamoured with the scene of annihilation at the rear of the site. Abandoning the trusty carriage, he reached through the gap in the fence and pulled the screwdriver loose from the links. Tossing the chain to the ground and swinging the gate wide, he followed the purr of the truck. The previous owner had left the heater on and he sighed with contentment as the warm interior enveloped him, banishing the chill of the winter outside.

"This has been a good day," he gloated, lighting a smoke from his new gold Zippo.

`Rolling through the gates, he headed for home.

CHAPTER 34

The coach had done an excellent job of moving the cars and Hombre steered between the gaps with ease. The school boundary was similarly uneventful apart from a bit of bumping over the mess left behind. Passing the coach park, he came to a stop.

"How did I miss that?"

At the rear of the yard, past the repair bays were two petrol pumps. Common sense suggested the company would find it easier to fuel their fleet in house as opposed to driving the behemoths onto the notoriously small service station forecourts. It was handy to know that a sizeable fuel supply was only a few miles away from the prison. If the retrieval of a tanker proved impossible, they could utilise the submerged tanks of this facility.

Pulling away, he continued towards the main road. The peace and quiet reminded him of the time spent cruising the countryside of Europe. If Debbie survived and the prison became too volatile because of Mike's hatred of the woman, he would take her away. If he could secure an articulated lorry and get it back to the coach park, they had the materials to reinforce the engine bay and cab. They could be the next Bonnie and Clyde, surviving by pillaging and killing the dead fucks where necessary on the open road. There were plenty of remote areas of Europe, or even England, where it might be possible to settle down. The Ardennes were particularly beautiful, with lakes and rivers where food would be in abundance. Getting through the channel tunnel would be a bit of a challenge, though. Pressing the power button on the CD player, an eighties pop ballad burst from the speakers.

"Fucking trash!" he grumbled, ejecting the disc and tossing it from the window. *Why didn't I just take the music from the 4x4? Probably because the whole town was trying to eat you.*

The removal teams had done a fine job of clearing the roads and he made it to the small hamlet of Climping in less than ten minutes. Picturesque cottages lined the streets, their once award-winning gardens giving way to aggressive weeds and overgrown grass. A terrace of thatched homes had been burned out, the thick stone walls blackened and fangs of charred timber all that remained of the roofs. Bodies littered the ground, advanced decay leaving them as little more than skeletal husks. Their heads had been destroyed; devastating shotgun blasts laying the whole face and skull open. Scattered red shells littered the road among more corpses. These had the tell-tale craters of the more mundane blunt force injuries. Whoever had lived here had put up quite a fight and Hombre felt a modicum of respect for the villagers.

Turning the next corner, he felt the rage building inside. The road was still blocked by cars and a group of mouldering corpses.

"Those useless cunts, I'm going to peel them myself!"

Stopping the truck, he jumped out and withdrew the pair of axes at his belt. Frustrated beyond words, he hacked and slashed through the undead, rending them limb from limb. Kicking their scattered parts to the kerb, he listened for any other threat. Tucking the weapons away, he stomped over to the nearest car. Pulling the door open with enough force to risk damaging the hinges, he released the handbrake and started to drag it clear. The rear wheels bounced against the raised kerb and it stopped, leaving a gap wide enough for him to carry on the journey.

"Turn around. Slowly," said a voice, catching him off guard.

Reaching into his coat, he placed his hand on the pistol.

"I wouldn't do that if I were you," warned another. "I can pull this trigger faster than you can get to your axe."

"I know you," Hombre growled, leaving the gun and turning slowly. "You were at the field earlier."

"Indeed, we were."

Both men had long, greasy hair tied back in a ponytail. Their clothing was just as filthy and a waft of noxious air blew over him as the wind changed direction.

The hunting rifle was pointed directly at him, but Hombre just scowled. "What the fuck do you want? I've got somewhere to be."

"We wanted to have a word with you, that's all."

"So, it was you that blocked the road again! You nearly got someone flayed with this little trick, you wankers."

"Ooh, you're a cool customer for someone with a gun pointed at his face."

"It's not the first time. If you're going to kill me, hurry the fuck up. It's freezing out here."

"That wasn't the plan, but if you keep mouthing off I may put a bullet in your leg to teach you some respect."

Hombre stepped forward, eyes narrowing. "Put the gun down and teach me some respect the proper way."

"You want to fight us?" chuckled the taller man.

"It wouldn't go so well for you," warned the other.

"I'll take my chances." Hombre took another menacing step. "Or are you both fucking pussies?"

Sparks flew by his feet as the bullet ricocheted against the concrete.

"I won't miss the next time."

"Now drop your axes and cut the bullshit. This doesn't have to go bad for you."

Hombre scoffed. "You expect me to believe that? What the fuck do you want from me?"

"We watched the show at the building site. One man against all those rotters? It was quite impressive."

"If you wanted to suck my dick, why didn't you just ask?"

"Careful, now. We're having a polite conversation here."

"I'll show you how polite I can be when you put away that gun," goaded Hombre.

"You're in no position to threaten us, you cunt. This is your last chance!"

Making a show of it, Hombre pulled out the weapons and tossed them to the ground. Holding his breath, he waited for them to demand the same of his concealed gun.

"And the knife!" ordered the rifle wielding man.

Fishing the switchblade from his pocket, he threw that too.

"Good lad. Now we're going to go for a little ride."

"A little ride to where?" Hombre asked.

"We have a camp about half an hour away. You're going to come and see our mam and she'll decide what we do with you."

"And who's your 'mam'?"

"Claire Hampton," replied the man. From the look on Hombre's face, he could see her reputation was already well known. "You've heard of her then?"

"Everyone's heard of her. And if she's your mam, you must be her boys. Patrick and Frankie?"

"I'm Patrick," said the tall man.

"And I'm Frankie," said the one with the gun.

The Hampton gypsy clan were notorious across the whole country. Claire was the matriarch of the family and the only daughter of the famed bare-knuckle fighter Johnny

273

Hampton. He had passed away ten years ago and handed control of the criminal enterprise to the most capable child. Her six brothers were the muscle behind the drugs, prostitution, and illegal boxing. This was not going to end well if they managed to get him home.

Patrick put two fingers in his mouth and whistled. Their horses came trotting around the corner, the dead deer still firmly secured on the back.

"We're going that way. Move your ass!" Frankie ordered, waving the barrel to the east.

"We're going to walk the whole way?" Hombre asked as he moved past them.

"You are, we're not," they replied, slipping their feet through the stirrups, unaware he was still armed.

It was all the distraction he needed. Pulling the pistol out, he shot Frankie in the temple and turned to Patrick before his dead brother had even hit the ground. The horse reared up, blocking the shot. Pulling free of its ropes, the deer carcass flopped sideways, its hind legs hitting the gypsy full in the face. The startled horse's front hooves hit the ground and it bolted in terror.

"You killed my fucking brother. You're a dead man," hissed Patrick, holding his broken nose.

Shrugging, Hombre put two bullets into his abdomen. Standing over the man as he writhed in agony, he said, "And now I've killed you. Well, almost."

"Just finish it, you bastard," Patrick gasped, trying to stem the flow of blood from his ruptured gut.

"And ruin their fun?" Hombre asked, pointing at the approaching zombies. "They'll finish the job for me, don't worry."

"My family will come for you."

"They won't even know what happened to you. How the fuck will they come for me?" Hombre laughed and tossed the rifle strap over his shoulder.

Taking hold of the rope bindings, he pulled the deer back to the vehicle and humped it into the truck bed before retrieving his blades.

"I'll see you at the prison wall shortly, ok?"

Moving through the gap, he was expecting the gypsy to start screaming as the dead fell on him to feast. Not a peep came from the throng and Hombre had to give it to him. They really were tough bastards.

***

Reaching the designated stopping point, he turned off the engine and pocketed the keys. The massive generator would sit here until a plan could be formulated to get it inside the walls. That was an irrelevance compared to the delicious venison steaks he would be eating as soon as the meat had been carved. Mouth watering in anticipation, he wrestled the bloodied deer onto his shoulders. *It's like being at the gym,* he grinned to himself. Moving slowly through the buildings, he came to the tunnel entrance and kicked the ply cover out of the way. Tossing the meat into the hole, he climbed down the ladder and turned on the torch before resealing the passage. Caught up in the euphoria of the killings, the claustrophobia was forgotten. Calling out to the guard, he was nearly dancing with joy as he waited for the bolts to be removed.

"Good to see you back, boss. How'd it go?" asked the guard.

"Fucking marvellous! Piece of cake! Easy peasy lemon squeezy!" beamed Hombre.

Seeing him in the light for the first time, the guard's face dropped. "You're covered in blood. Wait here and I'll get the doc!"

"No need, mate, it's not mine. There's a present for Craig at the end of the tunnel. Get a couple of lads and see it gets to Bobby in the kitchen. Ok?"

Perplexed, the guard nodded. "Right away."

"Good man," Hombre replied.

"Is there anything else you need?"

"Not unless you want to join me in the shower to help scrub this blood off?"

He looked at him with uncertainty. "Erm…"

"I was joking, you melon. Get that thing shifted and then get a bottle of Scotch brought up to my room. I'm going to get rat arsed!"

CHAPTER 35

asmine held a hand to her mouth, stifling a belch. The plate of leftover food had grown cold while she had been reading the novel about illicit romance on a Mediterranean cruise. Only the escaping gas had brought her out of the story. The raunchy scenes had left her hot, and quite incapable of enjoying the flavourless meal so she tossed the remains into an overflowing bin. Her group had enough to last for the next few days, and then it was just a case of waiting until the others retrieved more. The elderly woman, Gloria if she remembered correctly, was all bluster. There was no way they would harm someone simply for taking food to survive. Light was fading as the flames of the fire faltered, so she stood, stretched, and placed a few logs on top of the glowing remains. Heat blackened the wood, crackling and spitting before the first tongues of fire licked at the fresh fuel.

Draining the last dregs of water from her glass, Jasmine went to refill it. Feeling the weight of the flask, she twirled it and realized it was nearly empty.

"Oh, for fuck's sake."

She lacked the young slaves of the bigger group. The students would always do as they were told, but not any longer for her group. Tomorrow, she would pick one of her members to be the water collector. They may complain, but it was either do as she said or they could beg to be let back into the *'chosen ones'* as she called them. That would include a lot of hard work and guard duty, so she had no doubt the weak men would acquiesce with a minimum of snivelling.

For the first time since escaping the sunny, cocktail laden fantasy, her swollen bladder made itself known. The build-up of pressure became almost intolerable and she picked up one of the fat candles on the mantel. Holding the wick to the hungry flames, drops of wax dripped into the fire, flaring and hissing. Holding the beacon aloft, she opened the bedroom door and reluctantly entered the freezing hallway. Some of the others had opted to have a makeshift toilet in their room, but Jasmine would not lower herself to that. Just thinking about the scent of stale urine and faeces permeating her chamber made her mildly nauseous.

Checking both ways, the flickering candle cast dancing shadows on the grey stone walls. This short trek was always the worst part of her self-imposed exile. In the Baron's Hall, everyone who needed to relieve themselves was accompanied by a guard out of the chamber. It seemed like such a waste of time that could be better spent relaxing and sleeping. Let them bugger around in their paranoia. The castle was clear of zombies, the gates were firmly sealed and the others were watching the walls. Jasmine certainly intended to make the most of the peace and quiet with reading and writing. On her desk was the first outline of an autobiography. She would embellish the tales of bravery of course, but when the world was back to normal, people would flock to sample her works.

Pushing into the bathroom, the darkness beat a hasty retreat. The bucket of water by the side of the toilet was dry and she sighed her frustration. Flushing would have to wait until morning.

"It's freezing," she complained, rubbing her hands together briskly.

The immaculate, luxuriously appointed room had a central fireplace as did most homes of the aristocracy of yesteryear. In future, she would ensure a fire was burning in both her bedroom and the bathroom. Sure, the others would probably have something to say about it, but it was only for a few more months until the temperature rose to bearable levels. Sitting down, Jasmine hissed her discomfort as the chill of the seat seeped into her buttocks. Before she was finished, the cold had started to hurt, further validating her decision. From its position on the basin vanity, the candle flame wavered as if disturbed by a draught from outside.

The bathroom door was always left open, partly due to an irrational fear of being trapped in the toilet. This anxiety came into being after a handle broke when she was a child, sealing her within the white tiled room for seven hours while her parents had been at work. The other reason was quite simple; the others all understood these rooms were hers, and God help anyone if they dared to trespass in the middle of the night.

Cleaning herself and pulling up her trousers, she called out, "Hello? Is anyone there?"

Was that a faint scuff of foot on stone she could hear, or merely an overactive imagination? The apocalypse had given birth to nightmares without end, so it was not unexpected when she heard ghosts and ghouls where none existed. Still, it was better to be safe than sorry and she retrieved the candle as well as the small knife hidden under the towels by the tub. Pausing at the doorway, she listened intently for any clue if the noise was in her waking realm, or that of fantasy. The candle was too weak to hold back the deeper gloom of the passageway. Straining her eyes, the effort only caused her vision to swim.

"Hello?"

Nothing.

"I swear if that's you, George, I'll kick you in the balls!"

Apart from the almost imperceptible sizzle of burning wax, silence.

"You've been warned, and I'm wearing my heavy boots."

Strutting towards her bedroom, she found her paces getting faster and faster until she was nearly running as she ducked inside. Slamming the door, she turned the key and leaned her forehead against the centuries aged wood. *You're spooking yourself,* she thought, bumping her head against the timber to try and knock some sense into herself.

A hand curled around her mouth, holding back the scream which rattled in her throat. The press of cold steel to her throat stilled any further protests.

"If you make a noise, I'll cut your tits off and gut you. Nod if you understand," whispered her assailant.

Jasmine nodded. Her mind raced, trying to identify the source of the voice; an intonation, a quirk in the words. No one sprang to mind.

"Step over to the bed, slowly."

The words sounded hollow, emotionless, as if uttered by a robot. If she was about to be raped, she would have expected the speech to be twisted with uncontrollable lust. There was nothing.

"Lay on the bed, face down, with arms by your sides."

Again, it was more comparable to a bored announcer reading out the offers at a local supermarket. Unsure whether to be more, or less, scared because of the detachment, Jasmine did as she was ordered. The duvet pressed against her cheek as she lowered herself, soaking up the tears which had started to flow.

"Arms."

She tucked them against her sides, sobs shaking her body.

"Please, don't rape me," she begged.

"I don't want to do… that," replied the man.

A note of disgust had entered the voice. It was the first sign of humanity, but it only served to confuse her even more. "What do you want from me then?"

He climbed on the bed, straddling her back and pinning her arms tightly to her body with his knees. "Only your life."

A layer of polythene pulled tight against her face, stretching her head back painfully. Terror gripped her as the room went opaque, her vision clouded by the covering. Trying to draw breath, the thin plastic sucked into her mouth by a fraction of an inch, starving her of the lifegiving oxygen. In desperation, she tried to bite down on the film, but her teeth could find no purchase. Her tongue probed futilely against the suffocating layer, smearing spittle on the smooth surface. She kicked and bucked beneath his weight, the soft mattress muffling the frantic blows. Unable to free her arms, her hands flexed spastically, clutching at the air which her lungs screamed for.

"Don't fight. It'll be over soon and I don't want you bruised," he said, the voice coming from far away.

The burning in her chest was a white-hot agony. As her brain started to shut down, lights blazed into life on the edges of her vision. She gulped convulsively, mouth gaping, striving for the air which would never again pass her lips. As her struggles weakened, the darkness descended, snuffing out the strobing flashes.

A whisper reached the last fragments of her dying mind as she finally succumbed to asphyxiation. "Now the fun begins."

***

George stirred in his bed. Sleep was always fitful these days, even more so since the strangers and their brutal leader Kurt had arrived. His demands to watch the walls and fight the undead were outrageous. Just because their group had made enemies on the road did not justify forcing the others to suffer. Let them deal with their own mess. If the prison attacked, so what? George and his group had done nothing to them to warrant ill treatment.

Coughing up a wad of phlegm, he spat it into the bedpan by his side. Spots of piss splashed out and soaked into the bedsheet. "Fuck it!" he grumbled. He was too tired to get up and change the sheets and decided to wait until morning, despite the worsening smell.

From the hallway outside came a noise. It sounded like shoes dragging across the stone floor. The room was only illuminated by the dying fire, providing barely enough light to see the hand in front of his face. Fear clasped his heart, a sign of his innate cowardice. The stealthy footsteps paused outside his door, before a gentle rapping and scraping commenced.

"Hello?" he asked, voice wavering in terror.

The knocking became more insistent. If it was one of the group, why did they not reply? A revelation bloomed in his mind. Could it be Jasmine? He had propositioned her during the first days, hoping to secure a companion to share the dark nights. She had shot him down with a derisive laugh, but since that day he had proved his loyalty repeatedly. She may be too proud to call out in case the others hear her. More thuds carried through the door.

"I'm coming, Jasmine," he whispered, loudly enough for her ears only.

Climbing out of his bed, the butterflies in his stomach were going crazy. What would he do if she wanted to spend the night? He would need to find an excuse to dispose of the soiled blankets before anything happened. He had never been with a woman before and, aside from watching copious amounts of porn, had no idea what to actually do. *Man up, you cry baby!* he berated himself, reaching for the door. Twisting the handle, the meagre light of the glowing embers revealed the beautiful woman waiting for him. His heart skipped a beat at her voluptuous figure and pretty face.

"What made you change your mind? Couldn't resist the goods on offer," he asked, wincing at how pathetic the words sounded.

Jasmine stepped forward, arms held out for their first embrace. George closed his eyes, puckered his lips and joined her, erection throbbing.

***

DB stared across the room at the sleeping doctor. Her blonde locks had fallen across her face and each breath sucked the loose strands into her mouth. After working flat out for sixteen hours, she was too tired to react to the annoyance. Carefully stepping between the slumbering bodies, he reached down and tucked the hair behind her ear, before gently stroking the warm cheek. Mumbling in her sleep, a hand reached up and caressed his own.

"We're lucky to have her," Kurt whispered from his chair by the fire.

"I know. I'd be crippled or dead if she hadn't been with us at the canal boat."

Kurt nodded to a chair. DB carefully placed her hand back under the blanket and joined him.

"You care for her?" Kurt asked.

"More every day."

"Does she know?"

"I think she does, but I can't betray my wife."

"I can't begin to imagine your pain, but I'm sure she would've wanted you to find happiness in this desolate world."

283

"You're probably right," DB sighed. "I just feel I'd be spitting on her memory if anything happened between Christina and myself."

"With all the horror, everyone deserves a little joy. I totally respect your principles, though."

"Principles don't hold you close in the night and tell you everything's going to be ok."

"No, they don't," Kurt replied.

"What would you do?" DB asked, his huge frame sinking into the chair. The growing feelings were tearing him up inside and each time he closed his eyes, the smiling face of his late wife waited.

"I can't speak for you, buddy. A man's words on his wedding day are sacred."

"That doesn't really answer the question."

"I want to see you happy, and Christina would make you happy. She's a remarkable woman. When we take this world back, we'll need children to secure the future for humanity."

"I don't know if I could take the pain of losing a child again. For days, I sat staring at my gun, yearning for the courage to end it all."

"I'm glad you didn't," Kurt said, reaching out and squeezing his shoulder.

A distant scream echoed down the corridors, tearing them from their conversation.

"Everybody up, now!" yelled Kurt, triggering a frenzy of terrified activity.

"What's going on? Is it Sam and Braiden?" Sarah shouted across the room, marshalling the older members.

"No, it came from the others," Kurt replied. "Denise, would you take Sarah and Patricia to collect the boys, just in case?"

"On it!"

Jonesy opened the door at the other end of the massive room, quickly scanning the hallway with his rifle raised.

"Do you want me to go with them?" he called out as the three women filed past.

"No, I want you and Gloria here to keep the group safe."

Jonesy and Gloria nodded in reply, taking up position at each end of the long chamber.

"Peter, Jodi, DB, follow me!"

Gloria snapped the shotgun closed before opening the opposing door. The scream came again, louder without the wooden obstacle. Torches guided their way as they raced for the location of the commotion. The source of the agonised wail reached a peak, then fell silent.

"Why did they have to stay so far from the hall?" Jodi snarled.

"Stupidity and arrogance make a dangerous combination," Peter replied, readying his morning star.

As they rounded the corner, Heidi staggered into Kurt's arms, covered in blood. Thrusting her away before she could bite, she fell against the wall, the gaping wound in her neck spraying crimson against the ancient portraits of long dead lords.

"Shit, they're inside the walls! Jodi, take Peter and go and tell the others to arm up!"

They rushed back towards the Baron's Hall, eyes searching for threats.

"Help me," gurgled Heidi, reaching out a hand which was missing three fingers.

"It's too late. Please forgive me," Kurt said, crushing her head with the war pick.

Leaving the body, they forged on down the hall. A door swung open to their left and one of the renegades came stumbling out, stinking of faeces. Apart from the voided bowels, he was unharmed and Kurt threw him down the hallway towards safety, ignoring the manic sobs as he passed the dead woman.

"Watch my back," DB whispered, hearing motion in the next room.

Kurt nodded and took up position as the huge soldier ducked out of sight. Inside the room, two shadowy forms were tearing at a third on the bed. DB aimed the torch beam and Jasmine looked up from her work directly into the light. The dead, white eyes reflecting the beam. Entrails hung from her bloody lips, swinging to and fro as she chewed. The second zombie sensed him and removed its head from the torn abdomen before turning. What remained of George's face hung in tatters from the bloody skull. The lips, tongue, nose and one eye had been consumed during the fateful embrace.

"You fucking idiots," DB growled, swinging his machete.

The top of George's head flew off and he crashed to the ground. Jasmine pushed herself from the bed and let the entrails fall from her mouth with a sickly splash. Taking a step back, DB narrowed his eyes in confusion. The woman bore no signs of any bite wounds. Dodging her clutching hands, he twirled her round in a pirouette, throwing her off balance. She fell to the floor, cracking her face on the stone. The blood saturating her body was all from her victims as far as he could tell. Before she could get up, he stuck the point of the blade straight through her vacant eye, scraping against the socket as it buried itself.

On the bed, the eviscerated man's mouth spoke a silent prayer. His steaming innards lay spread across the mattress, staining the sheets red. DB raised the bloodied machete and met the dying man's gaze. Blue lips mouthed the word *sorry*, before the glazed eyes closed forever. Hacking at the head, DB made a quick end of it.

"All clear, Kurt!"

"Ready to move up?" Kurt called back.

286

DB left the carnage and joined him back in the passage. A body lay at Kurt's feet, brain leaking across the stone.

"You ok?"

"All good."

They moved to the next open door and apart from the liberal smattering of blood and gore, it was empty.

"What's happening?"

Kurt and DB swung towards the source of the question. The last of Jasmine's band clung to one another, eyes wide with fear at the horrific noises they had heard coming from outside.

"Your friends are dead," Kurt seethed. "I told you not to do this, but you wouldn't listen. Get back in your fucking room!"

DB ignored them as they sealed themselves off and pushed against the door at the end of the hall. It was firmly shut, with no signs of blood, green or red, in the area. Opening the heavy exit, nothing lay in wait on the other side. Honey came running, tail tucked between her legs as she sniffed the damp air. Both men watched on as the heightened canine senses scanned for a threat. Slowly, her hackles lowered and her bushy tail commenced wagging as she relaxed.

"I didn't see any undead apart from the castle survivors," DB muttered.

"What the hell's going on?" Kurt replied, realising the soldier was right.

CHAPTER 36

"Come on, nearly home," said Billy, leading the horses and the stumbling, hooded figure.

Night had fallen an hour ago, but he knew the way well enough to use only the sparse moonlight to see by. The scarred Pitbull trotted by his side, sniffing the air for unfamiliar scents. Their companion was known to them, so the dog ignored him and spent most of the time cocking a leg to mark his territory. Unable to see through the fabric, the man fell occasionally and Billy had to carefully help him back to his feet. Knowing where the hidden traps were, he led the procession safely through the gauntlet and out the other side. Ahead, the faint glow of firelight could be seen past the empty buildings.

He came to a stop, and the dog stared up at him. "Don't give me that look. You're not the one that's going to get murdered."

The horses became restless, moving to the side of the road to graze on the tall grass. The hooded man swayed, waiting for the signal to move again. Beneath the hood was a gag, blindfold and a pair of headphones blaring into his ears. It was meant to keep him distracted until they made it back. Billy's heart raced. The knowledge of what may happen when he reached their destination played out in his mind on a loop. None of the scenarios was encouraging and, deep down, he knew if the procrastination continued he would turn around and try to disappear. Ultimately, loyalty to his family won out and he took a shaky pace forward.

"Will you miss me, boy?" he said to the dog who was more interested in the animal scents in the bushes.

All it would take was for someone to give him a bone and Billy would be forgotten.

"Fuck you then!"

The glow grew brighter and for the first time in an hour, he could see clearly. Nothing dead lurked in the shadows, they were all indisposed. He could hear the massed groans of thousands of them coming from nearby. Turning the corner, the sight before him always filled him with awe. A mound of compacted earth soared sixty feet into the air, stretching for a mile around the perimeter of the camp. Angled banks tapered down into the thirty-foot-deep ditch which surrounded the excavated earth. From the darkness came the growls and shuffling of the trapped zombies below. Standing by the indentation on the road, Billy could see the multitudes staring up at him.

"Who goes there?" came a shout from the makeshift wall.

Billy gave a final thought to bolting, but he had nowhere else to go and they would find him eventually. Sighing, he called out, "It's me."

"Billy? What the fuck happened?"

"Lower the bridge and I'll tell you."

"Lower it!" yelled the guard.

From inside the compound, two heavy machines grumbled to life. Chains clattered against the rickety metal frame as they moved forward, dropping the massive bridge into place across the void. The dog bolted, eager to be inside and warm. Pulling on the ropes, the horses and man followed obediently. Crossing the patchwork bridge, the guards covered him with their guns. The light gradually illuminated him and the men all gaped at the sight before them.

"Is that who I think it is?" asked one, pointing at the body draped across the horse.

"Yeah," Billy replied.

"Oh shit. And you came back?"

Billy shrugged, "What else was I supposed to do?

"I respect that, lad."

"With any luck, she'll make it quick," he said, stomach churning in fear.

"I hope so," said the man, "I truly do."

Emerging from the trailers were dozens of men, women, and children. No one spoke as he passed, they simply lowered their heads in pity. Engines roaring, the bridge was pulled back up, sealing them off again. The three-storey pub in the middle of the island had candles flickering in the windows, leading the way. His fate would be decided in the next few minutes, one way or another.

A man stepped from the shadows, holding out a hand. "Let me take the horses, boy. She's waiting for you."

"Can you bring him in for me?" Billy asked, nodding at the dead man.

"I can do that."

Keeping hold of the last rope, he led the stumbling man through the doors and into the bar area. Stony faced men and women stared at him and the trussed figure. Parting like the Red Sea for Moses, the empty passage marked his way. Lifting feet that felt like lead weights, he moved towards the private room and his fate.

"Bad?" asked one of the huge bouncers.

"Worse," Billy replied, tears beginning to flow.

Stepping aside, he opened the door and bowed his head. The woman waiting inside was leaning against the fireplace, staring at the grey ashes. The door closed, leaving them alone. The only sound was the shuffling of the hooded man who was unable to stay still. Billy's heart nearly stopped when the woman stood up straight, slowly turning. He started to tremble and urine flowed down his leg.

"I'm so sorry, Mrs Hampton. There was nothing I could do."

Staring at him, she turned to the man stood behind. "I saw it in the leaves," she whispered.

"I wish I could swap places with them," Billy sobbed, dropping to his knees.

"It couldn't be stopped. It was already written," she muttered, moving past him.

"Be careful. Please," he begged.

"He won't hurt his mam," she said, removing the hood.

Patrick's body was grotesque, dripping blood and vile fluids as he stood in the middle of the room. His face had fared no better, cheeks, lips, and parts of the scalp missing. The jaw clamped open and closed automatically on the wood strapped between his teeth, as if they knew what needed to be done even without the warm meat to chew.

A quiet rapping came from the door and, without waiting for an answer, the bouncer carried a body in. Gently laying it on the table, he bowed his head respectfully and walked out.

"My poor boys," she cooed, stroking the remaining hair before moving to Frankie.

The gunshot wound had destroyed the back of the ocular cavities. The eyes were staring in awkward directions, one protruding bulbously and close to falling out. The blood vessels had burst under the pressure of the expanding slug before it had erupted from the side of his head. Bits of brain and fluid were still trickling from the wound, coating the varnish on the old table.

"My poor, sweet boy."

"I'm so very sorry for your loss."

"Who did this thing to my children?" she snarled, face twisting into an insane mask of hatred.

"I don't know his name, but I followed him back to the prison. They have a tunnel that leads inside," Billy babbled, close to passing out.

"Tomorrow, you'll show their uncles where this hole is. Then we'll know what to do," she demanded, glowering down at him.

"Of course. Whatever you say, Mrs Hampton."

"Good."

"Are… are you not going to kill me?"

She smiled, and in her grief, it was a dreadful sight. "No. You brought my boys back to me, Billy. I'm thankful for that kindness. Go and get yourself a drink and a bite to eat, you'll need to keep your strength up."

Astonishment at making it through the meeting paralyzed him. Holding out a hand, she helped him to his feet and ushered him out.

"Lennie, can you come in please?"

The giant ducked under the door and joined her, tears streaming from the loss of his cousins.

"Tomorrow, Billy's going to show you the location of the prison and their tunnel."

"What do you want us to do?"

"Nothing yet," she replied, wiping at the shredded meat of her son's face with a hankie. "Find it and remember it. We'll sit down and plan how to kill those sons of whores afterwards."

"Good," he whispered, turning to leave.

"And Lennie?"

"Yes?"

"When you get back with Billy, take him to your little girl, the one who trained as a nurse."

"Kizzy? What for."

"My boy's going to be hungry," she muttered, dabbing at the stringy drool falling from the torn gums. "Tie him down and start with the meat on his legs. Tell her I want

Billy to last him right through the winter. If she needs specific medication, get me a list."

"I'll see it's done," Lennie said, closing the door on the macabre family reunion.

The End

AUTHOR BIOGRAPHY

Ricky Fleet has been a lifelong horror fan ever since he was (almost) old enough to watch the original Romero trilogy. Those shambling horrors gave birth to an insatiable appetite that has yet to be sated.

After spending years working in the plumbing trade, he then decided to start teaching, passing on his knowledge to the next generation of engineers.

Born and raised in the UK, cups of tea are a non-negotiable staple of the English life and serve as brain fuel for his first love - writing.

With the Hellspawn series receiving love from across the world, the growing saga has a dark edge that begins to explore the true horror of a world without rules.

Infernal – Emergence is the first in his new demon series. A tale of conspiracy, untapped powers and the vast armies of Hell who yearn to tear our world apart. Only one man stands in their way; he just doesn't know it yet.

Today he shares his time between his real life students, and the students of the zombie apocalypse in his first series: Hellspawn. At least the fictional students do as they're told. Most of the time anyway.

You can find me at the following places:
On Amazon: www.amazon.com/Ricky-Fleet/e/B072C2GX6X
On Facebook at my fan club:
www.facebook.com/groups/175304226349208/
On Facebook on my author page
https://www.facebook.com/Author-Ricky-Fleet-751475768315453/
And at my publisher:
http://optimusmaximuspublishing.com/

CHECK OUT THE OMP WEBSITE FOR
A COMPLETE LIST OF OUR TITLES

WWW.OPTIMUSMAXIMUSPUBLISHING.COM

BOOKS ARE AVAILABLE IN BOTH PRINT
AND ELECTRONIC FORMATS

Killing is the sole province of the religious fanatics, an axiom as true
today as it was some five hundred years ago; and no nation, region
or person is immune.

Europe had clawed its way out of the Middle Ages with the
dawning of the renaissance, only to be plunged once more into
darkness, as the dogs of war circled to destroy its resurgence during
the 16th century. The Islamic successor to the Roman Byzantines,
the Ottoman Caliphate, flexed its muscles to conquer much of
Western Asia, North Africa and South-Eastern Europe. Christian
Europe shuddered when the once invincible bastion of the Knight's
at Rhodes were defeated; and now trembled as the Ottoman army
rattled the very gates of Vienna. No Christian army, it seemed,
could withstand the ferocity of the Azabs, the Akıncı, the Sipahis,
the Janissaries, and ruthless Iayalar's of the all-conquering Islamic
hordes.

This then is the cauldron into which Gideon de Boyne is unwittingly
thrust with his small army of dedicated Christian warriors. On the
hostile island of Crete, at the doorstep of the Ottoman Empire,
Gideon must face not only the overwhelming force of Muslim
warriors but his own inner conflicts of the futility of war and his
very Christian beliefs.

Will he succeed and come out of it unscathed?

RICKY FLEET

HELLSPAWN

SERIES

10.35 AM, September 14th 2015. Portsmouth, England.

A global particle physics experiment releases a pulse of unknown energy with catastrophic results. The sanctity of the grave has been sundered and a million graveyards expel their tenants from eternal slumber.

The world is unaware of the impending apocalypse, Governments crumble and armies are scattered to the wind under the onslaught of the dead.

Kurt Taylor, a self-employed plumber, witnesses the start of the horrifying outbreak. Desperate to reach his family before they fall victim to the ever growing horde of shambling corruption, he flees the scene.

In a society with few guns, how can people hope to survive the endless waves of zombies that seek to consume every living thing? With ingenuity, planning and everyday materials, the group forge their way and strike back at the Hellspawn legions.

Rescues are mounted, but not all survivors are benevolent, the evil that is in all men has been given free rein in this new, dead world. With both the living and dead to contend with, the Taylor family's battle for survival is just beginning.

Book 1 in the Hellspawn series.

Kurt Taylor and his family have battled the living and the dead and now find themselves on the run, their home reduced to ashes. With unimaginable horror lying in wait around every corner, the onset of winter and the plunging temperatures only add more danger to their precarious existence. They decide to forge ahead and try to reach the protection of others who have hopefully survived the zombie apocalypse. If this fails, their only choice would be to try and reach an impregnable fortress, a sanctuary that has stood for a thousand years.

Standing between them and salvation are the villages and cities of the damned, a path that will test their spirit and resilience unlike anything they have faced before. More companions are rescued from the jaws of death and join them in their perilous journey. Mysterious attacks befall the group and it becomes clear the dead aren't the only things that lurk in the darkness.

Tempers fray and personalities clash. The group starts to fracture and Kurt is forced to commit acts that cause him to question his own morality. Can they survive the horror of their new existence? Will they want to?

The Hellspawn saga continues.

BALLYMOOR, IRELAND, 1891

Patrick Conroy, a young American student of medicine in Dublin, decides to take a break from the hustle and bustle of the big city and spend a month in the quietude of the wild and beautiful Glencree valley, County Wicklow. However, surrounded by local legends and myths, he is soon dragged into an ancient mystery that has haunted the village of Ballymoor for centuries. Set on the background of the tumultuous years preceding the War of Independence, and colored by Irish folklore, the Haunter of the Moor is a ghost story written in the style of Victorian Gothic novels.

To Fight Evil with Evil

England, 1392.
As the Black Death quickly spreads through the kingdom, the little hamlet of Blythe's Hollow suffers under the yoke of a sadistic Lord. Desperate, the villagers decide to seek out the magical help of a local witch, causing the wrath of the Church. Torture and murder befall on those accused of being in league with the Devil, adding more sorrow to the beset folk of Blythe's Hollow. Yet, one man will rise against the tyranny; a man willing to learn Black Magick to fight back.

A modern dark urban fantasy, telling of two powerful families who uphold a secret duty to protect humanity from a threat it doesn't know exists.

Though sharing a common enemy, the two families form a long-standing rivalry due to their methods and ultimate goals.

Forces are coalescing in a prominent Central European city criminal sex-trafficking, a serial murderer with a savage bent, and other, less tangible influences.

Within a prestigious, private university, Lilja, a young librarian charged with protecting a very special book, finds herself suddenly ensconced in this dark, strange world. Originally from Finland, she has her own reason for why she left her home, but she finds the city to be anything but a haven from dangers and secrets.

Book One in a planned series.

Meet Mason Ezekiel Barnes, former NFL tackle turned successful author of the naughty ninja adventure series Mia Killjoy. Mason is obsessed with winning a Pulitzer and is thwarted by his fellow author and nemesis, the twerpy little gnome Conrad Bancroft.

Perk Noir is full of comedic relief, pop culture, NFL, jazz, a little touch of romance, and flashbacks of Lightning and his family during both the first half of the 20th century and later during the Civil Rights movement. Mason and Shelly and their adventures is a fun filled thrill ride that will appeal to all readers, there is something for everyone at the Perk.

Two hunters pursue the same prey.

Fate has forged the slayer, Trey Thomas and the Sandrian vampire, Adalius, two natural enemies, into an uneasy alliance against an evil more powerful than either have ever faced. Only together do they stand a chance of defeating Anna; if they don't destroy each other first.

As they pursue Anna, the apprehensive Lycan watch as a confrontation looms on the horizon between vampires, the New Bloods and the Old Guard, which threatens to plunge the vampire world into civil war and trigger an all-out supernatural conflict which in the end could destroy them all.

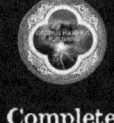

Collected tales of Madness and Terror

Maximus SHOCK

An OMP Magazine

Complete
Collection

0

16 Mind-Shocking Tales!

RICKY FLEET   JEFFREY KOSH   EMIR SKALONJA

KEITH MONTGOMERY   SCOTT CARRUBA   CHRIS GARSON

LORRAINE VERSINI   MAURA ATKINSON BUTLER   MATT HAY

LEON BROWN   WK POMEROY

EDITED BY
CHRISTINA HARGIS SMITH

www.ingramcontent.com/pod-product-compliance
Lightning Source LLC
Chambersburg PA
CBHW060533180626
46817CB00002B/545

* 9 7 8 1 9 4 4 7 3 2 3 5 6 *